FOR AN EYE

A Detective Loxley Nottinghamshire Crime Thriller

By
A L Fraine

The book is Copyright © to Andrew Dobell, Creative Edge Studios Ltd, 2023.
No part of this book may be reproduced without prior permission of the copyright holder.

All locations, events, and characters within this book are either fictitious or have been fictionalised for the purposes of this book.

Book List

www.alfraineauthor.co.uk/books

Acknowledgements

Thank you to Crystal Wren for your amazing editing and support.
Thanks to Kath Middleton for her incredible work.
A big thank you to the Admins and members of the
UK Crime Book Club for their support, both to me and the wider author community. They're awesome.

A big thank you to Meg Jolly and Tom Reid for allowing me to use their names in this novel. I really appreciate it.
Thank you also to the Authors I've been lucky enough to call friends. You know who you are, and you're all wonderful people.

Thank you to my family, especially my parents, children, and lovely wife Louise for their unending love and support.

Table of Contents

Book List 2
Acknowledgements 2
Table of Contents 3
1 5
2 17
3 28
4 40
5 46
6 52
7 65
8 75
9 81
10 93
11 99
12 116
13 122
14 130
15 138
16 148
17 152
18 166
19 177
20 186
21 195
22 201
23 207
24 216
25 225
26 238
27 242
28 249
29 262
30 265
31 272
32 280

33	288
34	297
35	306
36	312
37	319
38	327
39	334
40	343
41	350
42	363
43	365
44	370
45	374
Author Note	380
Book List	380

1

Wary of the shadows and darkness all around him, Gavin walked home with his hands stuffed deep in his pockets and his collar up high. He hated being out this late, walking along the edge of Nottingham's Forest Fields estate, making his way home along Sherwood Rise before bearing left into Mapperley Park.

But tonight he had an errand to run.

He thought back to the message his mum had sent him, asking him to pick up a few things. He'd said yes, but he regretted agreeing to it now.

At the next junction, he paused as he looked right, glaring up the street into Forest Fields with its line of terrace houses. When he closed his eyes, he got flashes of that night a year ago, and the only clue he had to where they'd taken him. Was it here, or one of the countless other urban spaces that looked just like this?

A few hundred metres up the street, he could see the corner shop, sitting there, waiting for him. Outside, a small group of people were standing and talking. The sight of them sent a chill down his spine.

As he watched, they moved off and rounded the corner, disappearing behind the shop.

Setting off up the side street, Gavin adjusted the tight grip he had on the item he kept in his pocket. Its presence made him feel safe and secure, confident that if anything bad should happen, there was a chance he could get himself out of it.

Christ. If his dad only knew, he'd go crazy.

But he'd not seen his dad in days, not since the weekend. He'd been spending most of his time at his mum's. She fussed around him as usual, constantly annoying him and asking him to cheer up.

She didn't know, but that was for the best. She didn't need to know.

Gavin shook his head to banish the dark thoughts from his mind. It had been a year since the incident, since he'd seen a new side to his father. It really was time to let it go. There was no need to wallow in it, not now he was getting along so well with his dad and Justine. Things seemed to finally be returning to normal. Better than normal, actually. He'd never got on so well with his dad's girlfriend as he was now. She was kinda fun, actually.

As he walked along the path, the glow from the shop spilt across the street up ahead, announcing its presence, reminding him where he was. He hoped it was empty. He hoped the kids he'd seen moments earlier had disappeared.

Gavin gripped the item in his pocket and chewed on his lip, his eyes scanning the street, peering into the shadows, scouring for anyone he needed to avoid.

He would never be a victim again, not like that. No way. He'd fight like a demon to make sure it never happened again.

The events of that fateful night a year ago were affecting his mood. His mother had noticed, but there was little he could do about it. Hell, it would be weird if his temperament hadn't been affected.

No one should have to go through that... ever.

He sighed as he gazed up the street. It would only be a quick stop, and then he could head back the way he'd come and make for greener pastures.

Fishing his phone out of his pocket, Gavin woke it with a deft tap against the fingerprint reader on the back and opened WhatsApp.

His mother's message sat at the bottom of the screen, asking him to pick up milk, bread, cereal and something for himself on his way home.

He ran through the list again, committing it to memory, and started to ponder which bar of chocolate he fancied.

Reaching the shop, he pushed the door open and stepped inside. Behind the nearby counter to his left, a radio played.

He could hear voices deeper in, but he paid them no mind and focused on his task.

In and out.

Just grab what his mum wanted and set off home. Easy.

Wandering up one aisle, he heard the voices erupt in laughter. They seemed to be enjoying themselves, but he found little humour in it. Instead, the tone sounded mocking, and for a brief moment, he was back in that room, surrounded by shadows laughing at his pain.

He banished that image and browsed the bread, picking a 'best of both' loaf and pulling it from the shelf. One down, he thought to himself. He needed to find the cereal, but that aisle was further in, closer to the voices.

A ripple of anxious fear fell over him.

He took a steadying breath and pushed deeper and closer to the voices. Rounding a corner, he looked up a long aisle. Towards the back, close to the fridges, a group of four teens laughed and talked as they picked items off a shelf.

Gavin wasn't really interested in what they had to say and instead noted with worry that the cereal was up there. He didn't like the idea of putting himself in their field of view, but there was no other option.

Between him and the youths, a woman in her thirties or forties was doing her shopping while trying to ignore the small gang...

Gang.

The word trigged those unwanted memories and set his mind racing.

They wouldn't be... Would they?

They couldn't be part of that same gang? Surely not.

No, that was silly. He was letting his mind run away with him and seeing ghosts where there were none. He needed to get a grip.

Ahead, the woman looked up as he rounded the corner. Their eyes met, and she gave him a brief smile. He saw so much in that short expression. He saw the concern she had about the group further up and their antics. He saw the surprise and worry that he, a young man, had appeared on her other side. At first, she looked pleased that someone had joined her, but that look had lasted barely a moment before it was replaced by concern.

He smiled back at her, wanting to ease her concerns, trying to let her know that he wasn't a part of that group. But he wasn't sure she got it.

Looking past the woman at the laughing hyenas further along, he pushed his hand into this jacket pocket and fingered the item he concealed there.

His last line of defence.

After a brief moment of hesitation, he walked towards the cereal, between the shelving that hemmed them in on either side.

The woman looked up again, saw him coming, saw his hand in his jacket pocket, and looked away. She picked up the packet she'd been pondering and strode towards the youths with her head down.

Was she that worried about him? Did he scare her that much?

Gavin stopped at the cereal, only briefly looking at the gaudy boxes before sneaking a glance at the retreating woman.

She approached the group, aiming to slip by.

"Alright, love? Fancy a nice meaty sausage? I've got a lovely girthy one for yeh 'ere." He waved a Pepperoni at her.

The woman ignored their comments with barely a glance as the other three laughed. Surprisingly, the group was half female, and the girls seemed to enjoy the woman's discomfort as much as the guys did.

Their callous disregard for her feelings concerned him, and try as he might, he could not focus on the products before him. The contents of those shelves swam in his vision. He couldn't focus on anything. What was he looking for? Cereal? Cornflakes?

It was no use. No matter what he did, all he could think about was what was going on just a few short metres away.

But as he watched, the woman slipped by the group while the mouthy one continued to vocalise what he'd like to do to her. It was disgusting, and he felt sorry for her. Why should she have to put up with that shit when she only wanted to pick up a few things from the shop. She probably had a husband and kids waiting for her at home.

How would they feel, knowing she'd been treated like this?

As he watched, one of the girls turned, and for a terrifying moment, she locked eyes with him as she laughed.

Filled with sudden mind-numbing panic, he looked away.

Don't see me. Don't notice me.

He prayed to a god he didn't believe in for her to ignore him as he furiously browsed the shelves, trying to find the cereal he liked.

It wasn't here. He couldn't see it.

Don't notice me.

He looked back. She was still looking at him, and she wasn't laughing anymore. They locked eyes again, and it took him far too long to look away.

What the fuck are you doing? Don't look at her. Don't attract her attention!

"What you lookin' at, twat-face?" Her voice was a little deeper than he'd expected? Was she putting it on, trying to make herself sound powerful?

Gavin stared at the suddenly intensely interesting products on the shelf without really registering what he was looking at. He felt paralysed.

"Oi, fucker, I'm talking to you."

She came stalking toward him. He could see her out of the corner of his eye as she approached, her gait full of swagger and self-confidence. He stuffed his hand in his pocket and gripped the item.

No, he mustn't.

He withdrew his hand again.

"You listening to me?" she asked, closing the last couple of metres.

Clearly not.

"I said, are you listening to me?" She was right beside him now, leaning in, her hands on her hips, her feet planted wide. Behind her, the other three closed in.

There was no avoiding this. "Um, no. Sorry. I didn't mean…"

"Didn't mean what? Eh? Didn't mean what?"

"I'm sorry, I think there's been a misunderstanding," Gavin said and moved to turn and walk away, but the mouthy one stepped in his way. Beyond him, he noticed the woman had rushed to the counter to pay for her stuff.

At least she was getting out of here.

"She asked you a question, idiot," the mouthy guy said.

"Look, I don't want any trouble." He should have walked away. He should have got out of there as quick as he could, and he should definitely not have looked at them.

Why did he look at them? Why on earth did he do that?

His mind raced as he desperately searched for any way out of this. What were they trying to do? What was their goal and what were they trying to achieve? Was it purely out of boredom? Did they get some kind of perverse enjoyment out of this?

He knew better than most how some people seemed to revel in this kind of mental torture, but here, in a shop?

"What if we do want some trouble, aye?" the girl asked. "Maybe you're the kind of trouble we're looking for? What about that?"

He needed to get out of here. This was already threatening to spiral well out of control, and...

"We've got some friends who'd love to meet you," the mouthy guy said, cutting him off and snapping Gavin's attention to him.

Were they part of that same group? Was it not over?

No. No, he couldn't do this again.

He couldn't.

With his mind in a feverish cycle of terror, Gavin tried to push past and get away.

He didn't get there. Someone grabbed him from behind, and suddenly he was on the street a year ago, being dragged into that van.

Stuffing his hand into his pocket, he withdrew the handle, and pressed the button on it as he turned, seeing nothing but the dark interior of that van, and the pain that followed.

Except this time, he could do something about it.

Someone screamed.

He was back in the shop. The girl's face was a picture of shock, with her mouth and eyes open wide. Something warm and wet covered his hand as the girl dropped. She fell to her knees as he watched. For a moment, he couldn't hear anything. It was just him and the girl as she stared up at him, her mouth a great O on her face.

"You fuckin' stabbed her," one of the others cried.

"You bastard!"

"Do something."

"Call an ambulance!"

"I ain't calling no fuckin' ambo. I don't want the pigs 'ere."

"Do it, she'll die."

"It's this fuckers fault. I'm gonna fucking kill 'im."

The words came quick in a babble of scared voices. Pain exploded on the side of his head, and he fell, landing on the shelves as a flurry of kicks and punches rained in.

Gavin yelled and screamed. He heard shouting nearby as the two guys hit him again and again. Pain filled his world as their attacks hit home, and he was back in that room again, a year ago, wondering if this would be the end for him.

He still clutched the flick knife, unable to drop it but equally unable to use it.

Had he actually stabbed her? Had that been him?

The punches and kicks stopped as a new voice joined the fray. A glance up from the floor rewarded him with a view of the shopkeeper chasing the two guys away with a cricket bat.

Not really its intended use, but a good one nonetheless.

Gavin curled into the foetal position and squeezed his eyes shut against the pain. He'd be bruised where they'd kicked him, but he didn't think anything was broken.

Maybe he'd be okay? He'd survived and hadn't been dragged into another van. For a giddy moment, he was happy.

The girl beside him groaned.

"You bastard, you fucking bastard. What have you done to her? Oh my god, Kelly. It's okay. We'll get you help, I promise. You'll be fine, just hang in there."

Gavin turned and pushed himself up. Beside him on the floor, the girl who'd confronted him lay on her side, her hands pressed against her belly as she stared into nothingness.

There was blood everywhere.

For a brief, mad second, he considered running. If he ran now, he could maybe escape. They didn't know him. This wasn't somewhere he visited regularly. He was only here because his friend wanted to meet at a pub on Nottingham Road.

Now he wished he'd pressed to meet elsewhere, closer to home, and never come here.

But that was wishful thinking. He heard the shopkeeper on the phone, calling for help, and he could hear the stabbed girl's friend switching between comforting her and insulting him.

But all Gavin could focus on was the blood.

There was just so much of it.

2

"It's the waiting I hate," DI Rob Loxley remarked, sitting in the passenger seat of the van. "I hope this isn't a great big waste of our time."

"We'll know soon enough, guv," Phil said.

Rob turned to the Detective Sergeant in a seat behind him. Phil was balding with buzzcut hair around the sides of his head and a stoic, serious expression on his face as he stared out the front window of the vehicle.

He glanced at Rob and nodded. "You'll see."

"Are they in there now?" DC Guy Gibson asked from the driver's seat.

"Yeah," Phil replied, referring to the undercover officer he was the handler of. "They said they were verifying the gear that had been stored there for their boss before it got moved on. They'll call me when they're clear."

Rob noted the careful use of language, and how Phil was always careful not to give anything away about his charge. He never used gendered words, never said their name, nothing. He was good at this. "And that'll be our alert to move in and catch them red-handed," Rob remarked as Guy nodded, staring across the junction.

They were parked on Overend Road in Worksop facing west, looking across at the block of flats at the end of Sandy Lane beside the roundabout. The three-story high, wide grey edifice looked drab and ominous. A hive of scum and villainy, he thought to himself with a shake of his head. Criminals and their victims mixed with good, innocent people scraping through their lives in squalid conditions. The building had seen better days, and places like this were a mecca for the low-level street gangs made up of teens, moving drugs about for those higher up the chain. Rob felt sorry for the less fortunate families that were trying to live their lives surrounded by this kind of criminality. What chance did their children have when they were confronted with the harsh reality that they could earn more in a day than their mum or dad could in a week by running a few packages across town on their bikes?

The answer was simple, they had no chance. No chance at all. It was a vast, spiralling vacuum, sucking in the poor and vulnerable and dragging them down to the very bottom, where they usually ended up in a cycle of violence, criminality, or drug abuse that rarely ended well.

He was under no illusion that this raid, if it was successful, would barely dent the business of the powerful firms that ran these street gangs, but it might just give the residents of this block a few months of relief from the hell they were living in.

A moment later, Phil's phone rang. "Here we go," he said and climbed out to take the call. He slammed the door shut behind him and walked away from the vehicle.

"Their boss?" DC Scarlett Stutely asked from the row behind Rob and Guy. Sitting forward on the edge of her seat, she appeared to be filled with nervous energy and kept checking her watch. "Did Phil mean the undercover officer's boss or the Manton Massiv's boss?"

"At a guess," DS Nick Miller replied. "He was probably referring to the Mason Firm rather than the undercover officer's superior in the police. Besides, he's their handler, so they'll report exclusively to him."

"Makes sense," Scarlett replied. "So, this Mason Firm. They run this gang, the Manton Massiv?"

"They do," Nick replied. "They're Rob's favourite people, the Masons."

Rob grunted, feeling his stomach churn at the mention of their name.

"What?" Scarlett asked, looking confused. "I think I missed that briefing."

Nick looked confused for a moment before he seemed to realise something. "Oh, he's not told you, has he."

"Told me what?"

"His real name," Nick stated. "Rob's surname isn't Loxley. It's Mason."

"Actually, legally, it is Loxley," Rob remarked.

"I know," Nick confirmed before turning back to Scarlett "But it was originally Mason. He changed it when he ran away from his family."

Rob chewed on his lip as he listened to Nick explain this particular part of his sordid history to a rapt Scarlett, who gave Rob a shocked glance, her mouth open in surprise. It was something he rarely spoke about, but Scarlett had been on the team long enough by now that she should really know this small detail.

"Oh. I see. So... Shit. I had no idea. I've seen these Masons in the local newspapers, sponsoring charity events and stuff. So that's your family?"

Rob gave her a solemn nod. "My estranged family, yes."

"I take it these community initiatives they're involved in, it's all about whitewashing their name, right?"

"Appearances can be deceiving, and the Masons are good at hiding what they do. What might be a somewhat open secret on the underworld grapevine, can be tough to prove in court," Nick explained.

"Is that right?" Scarlett asked Rob.

"Something like that," Rob confirmed, preferring not to think about his estranged family and the stories about who they really were. Not right now, at least.

"He doesn't like to talk about it," Nick mock whispered.

"No, I get that. I wouldn't either if I were in his position," Scarlett agreed. "So, Loxley? Nice name. I take it you chose that because…"

"Of the Robin Hood thing, yeah," Rob admitted. "I saw it in a film. I liked the name, and I'd just moved to Nottingham, so…"

"I like it," Scarlett said, brushing a lock of her blonde hair behind her ear while shooting Rob a warm smile.

Rob shrugged. "Thanks."

"And you both were already aware of this?" Scarlett glanced between Guy and Nick."

"I was," Nick answered.

"I'd heard the rumours," Guy added. "People talk, so I was aware before I joined the unit."

"And I'm guessing the force knows, too, right?" Scarlett asked.

"Absolutely." Rob explained, "I didn't hide anything during my vetting procedures. It would only bite me on the arse later if I hid it. Everyone knew. It's probably one of the reasons Bill's got such a hard-on for taking me down."

Nick smirked.

"Everyone knew? Well, screw me then, I guess," Scarlett remarked with a snort of mirth.

"It's nothing personal," Rob said as he noticed her smile. She was having him on. "It's me."

"A classic excuse there, Rob," Nick said. "It's not you. It's me. Like it."

Guy smirked. "Aye up, looks like Phil's back."

The side door rumbled open as Phil got back into the van. "Our officer is clear. Time to go."

Rob nodded and lifted his radio. "All units, this is Alpha team, code green. Go, go, go."

"Let's do this." Guy slammed the van into gear, and it lurched forward as he revved the engine. Pulling into traffic, they sped across the roundabout towards the block of flats. Around them, Rob spotted the other police vans they were using in this sting, some of them marked, others not, but all filled with officers ready to storm the building. Guy drove across the front of the block, along Sandy Lane. Turning, he bumped up the kerb, between parked cars, onto the grass to the right of the building.

Rob's door was open before the van stopped. He jumped out and ran. "Scarlett, Nick, take the front, Guy, you're with me. We'll go round back."

"Aye," Guy called as he jumped from the van and followed, hot on Rob's heels. He sprinted to join the group of uniformed officers storming the rear door, feeling the weight of the stab vest he and his colleagues in the East Midlands Special Operations Unit, or EMSOU, were wearing over their shirts.

As he ran, Rob scanned the estate. The other blocks seemed quiet, with just a handful of people standing and watching. As his eyes passed over the nearby parked cars, he saw someone walking away from the building and squinted to get a better look. It was a woman, and as he eyed her, she glanced back, looking right at him and his colleagues, before she turned and went on her way.

Was that the undercover officer? Was it a woman? Or was he looking at some random person and drawing unfounded conclusions? He dismissed the thought and returned his focus to the job at hand.

The leading officers got the back door to the block open and rushed inside. Their voices echoed up the main stairwell that fed the upper flats as they joined the team running in the front. At the third-floor landing, the team rushed out of the door onto the balcony that ran along the front of the building, feeding the flats. The metal beneath their feet rang out as they stomped along it until the lead officers reached the target door and flanked it.

Rob stopped as an officer carrying the large red battering ram fed himself through the crowd. He hefted the ram, which they liked to call their Big Red Key, and slammed it into the front door.

Unlike the reinforced doors on your average crack house, this one had seen better days, and it was off its hinges in two hits. The officer with the ram stepped back as the others slipped past and charged into the flat, shouting 'Police' at the top of their lungs.

Rob glanced across the strip of grass in front of the block. Uniformed officers were standing watching, looking for anyone escaping, and there'd be more at the back. They were already being joined by Joe Public in ever greater numbers who stopped to watch the spectacle.

Seconds later, Rob rushed into the flat too and spotted two officers holding a man down while a young woman attacked one of them, having jumped on their back.

"Scarlett," Rob barked.

She rushed forward and grabbed the woman, hauling her off the poor officer she'd been attacking, and threw her to the floor. Two other uniforms, both female, rushed to her aid and between them, they got the suspect cuffed.

The place was small, little more than a few rooms, including a tiny kitchen and bathroom. In the front room in the corner, another young woman wearing a dirty grey tracksuit sat in the corner, her arms wrapped around her legs and head.

Elsewhere in the room, chaos was erupting. Four officers were fighting a huge man, well over six foot tall, who was proving difficult to restrain.

But a shout from Rob's right drew his attention to a scuffle that was now being lost by one of the uniforms.

"Aaaagh, help!"

A smaller young man dressed in the typical baggy hoodie, tracksuit bottoms and pristine white trainers had somehow managed to get the upper hand in a fight with one of the officers.

The gang banger was on top and throwing vicious punches at him, roaring as he went. Rob rushed forward and tackled the young man to the ground. He grabbed onto Rob and bit him on the head.

Rob yelled, threw his head back and sent the young man to the floor. When Rob jumped back onto him again, he was joined by Guy and another officer who forced him down and got him under control.

Elsewhere, the large man had also been detained by the efforts of Nick and several other officers.

"Good job, guys."

Nearby, Rob heard sobbing. He glanced across at the woman in the corner who was now being comforted by a female officer. She was upset, but she wasn't the one sobbing loudly. Instead, it was the young man Rob had seen being arrested first while the officer was being attacked by the woman.

The kid lay on his front, defeated and utterly upset. Tears flowed down his dark cheeks.

"Shut it," the vicious one snapped. "Stop being a fucking baby."

"Did you hear him, Rice?" the girl demanded. "Did you? Are you listening? Because you'd better fuckin' be."

"But," the upset kid who the girl had referred to as Rice answered. "I ain't ever been... You know."

"I don't give a fuck," the vicious kid snapped. "You know what to do."

"Shut it, you," one of the officers barked.

Rice sniffed. "I know. Shit. My mum's gonna kill me."

Rob smiled as he listened to the exchange, making note that the one they called Rice seemed to be a weak link. Maybe he could use that?

Looking over the room, he noted the blankets on the sofa, the plates and food cartons, and the discarded clothes. It looked like someone was living in this one room.

"Guv?"

Rob looked up and moved towards a nearby stretch of corridor. At the end, Nick was talking to a uniformed officer. When he saw Rob, he waved him down.

Rob joined him beside another door, except this one had been sealed shut with three big padlocks.

"Thought you might want to see this." He pointed to the hefty locks. "What do you make of that?"

"Well, if I take it that the woman curled up in the corner is the tenant, I'd guess she's been cuckooed by these idiots. She's been forced to live without a bedroom, and whatever they're storing is in there. So I want in," Rob replied.

"I thought you might." Nick nodded and summoned the battering ram. It took a few hits, but the door was soon open, revealing a double bed that was devoid of sheets. Instead, half of it was covered in stacks of money, and half with plastic bags and clingfilm-wrapped packages.

Nick stepped forward, pulled out his pen knife and opened one of the plastic packages. He stepped back after a quick investigation.

"Drugs," Nick confirmed.

Robs smiled. "Jackpot."

3

Across the room, on the other side of the table that was fastened to the floor, two very different people were sitting, waiting for them as they entered the interview room.

On the left, a young man slouched into his chair with his hood down, revealing his mid-brown skin and faded buzzcut with patterns cut into the sides. He watched them with a sullen look of utter contempt as Scarlett closed the door behind them.

If looks could kill, he'd be eviscerated and long dead by now.

On the right, sitting beside the youth, was a petite woman with mousey brown hair and fair skin, wearing a skirt suit and holding a leather binder and pen. Her upright, straight-backed pose was the polar opposite of the young man. She held herself with poise and grace, compared to his casual indifference.

This was Matilda, and she met Rob's gaze with a familiar warm smile, and for a moment, they weren't in a room with a hardened criminal.

Rob couldn't help but smile back. "Miss Greenwood."

"Inspector Loxley," she replied with a bob of her head. "Constable Stutely."

"Evening," Scarlett said as she kicked the back of his heel, reminding Rob of the job at hand.

Rob coughed and approached the two vacant chairs. "Mister Dodson—"

"Fuck off," the young man spat. "It's Dodders, 'aight"

"Cedric Dodson," Rob ploughed on, taking pleasure in annoying the youth. "You've gone and got yourself into a bit of a pickle."

"What you talkin' about?" Dodders replied.

"Heh," Rob stammered. He sighed.

He knew where this was going already. He'd been in plenty of interviews with young men of this kind, and they always went the same way, with only perhaps a handful of exceptions. He didn't think this would be one of those, but he might as well try anyway. This was the job, after all.

"Let me lay it out for you," Scarlett said, cutting in. "We found you, Cleveland Levine, Ambrose Gordon and Carmela Kerr in Tia Dunn's flat. This is a property that she rents and lives in, as I'm sure you're aware. You and your friends do not and never have lived there. Tia's brother, Tyrone, was a friend of yours until he was tragically shot a year ago."

"So, there is a link," Rob chimed in. "We're aware of that, and it could be that you were just paying her a visit, right? You were being friendly and kind, and given that she's on the Spectrum, that would certainly be a lovely thing to do, for sure. But, you see, we're just not sure about that, are we?" He directed his question to Scarlett.

"I'm not buying it," she agreed. "Not with that massive elephant in the room."

"The big white powdery elephant, you mean? The one in the bedroom?"

"That's the one," Scarlett confirmed. "I mean, it just doesn't make a lot of sense to me unless you weren't there as friends because I get the impression that she doesn't like you much."

"So let's talk about that, shall we?" Rob said. "This is Tia's flat, and the one bedroom in it has been locked up tight with three separate padlocks. Three big, chunky, strong padlocks that little Tia would never be able to break through. And where do we find the keys to these locks? Hmm?"

Rob waited to see if Dodders would answer, but he said nothing. Instead, he remained slumped in his chair, his arms crossed, staring at them with hate-filled eyes.

Rob turned to Scarlett. "Remind us, where did we find those keys?"

"In Cedric's pocket," she replied, gesturing across the table.

"Well, fancy that," Rob remarked in mock surprise. "In your pockets? Now, why would we find them in your pockets?"

Dodders shrugged. "I was just lookin' after 'em, won' I. Not my keys."

"Let me guess, those weren't your drugs in there, either, were they?"

"I din' 'ave no clue about dem drugs, man. Nuthin' to do wi' me."

"Cedric, Cedric. Come now. Do you really think that's going to float with a jury? Really? With your record? Scarlett, would you do the honours?"

"Ahem." Scarlett cleared her throat. "GBH, ABH, Handling illegal substances with intent to supply, dealing, aggravated robbery... I could go on, but I think he gets the point."

"And let me remind you about Tia, shall we? She has no criminal record, at all. And I'm willing to bet that once we offer to protect her, maybe change her identity and move her away from the area, she might choose to talk to us. What do you think? And then there are your friends, too. Cleveland and Carmela we've had the pleasure of meeting before. They're familiar with these walls, aren't they? But Ambrose isn't, is he? This is all new to him, and I have to tell you, he isn't dealing with it very well."

"He's a little upset and scared," Scarlett added. "But don't worry, because I think we might be able to help him."

"And who's to say the other two won't grass you up, either? That was an awful lot of drugs we found you with,

Dodders." Rob made sure to lace that last word with as much contempt as he could put into his voice. "Do you think they want to go down for this, when they could just pin it on you? And we know you're the ring leader here."

"But here's the thing," Scarlett said. "We know you're not at the top of the food chain. We know you answer to people, people who distribute those drugs to you and take most of the profits, leaving you with the dregs."

"That's right," Rob agreed. "Because, in all honesty, while it's good to get you off the streets, you're not who we're really after. So if you wanted to maybe help us out and give us some information that we can act on, who knows what we could do for you? This might not be something you need to go down forever for. You could come out of this smelling of roses."

"Or a more manly scent," Scarlett added with glee in her voice.

"Oh, absolutely," Rob agreed.

"No, fucking, way," Dodders answered in a flat, serious tone.

"Don't throw this away," Rob pressed. "This is your life we're talking about here. We know your gang is affiliated with the Masons. We know this is who you're dealing with."

"They don't care about you," Scarlett said. "They have a hundred more guys like you all through this county and beyond. They don't care if you go down, because they'll just move on to the next poor sap and use them instead, leaving you to be fed to the wolves. They don't care, Cedric."

"She's right," Rob agreed. "They don't. You're nothing to them. You're not important. You're a useful street thug, and that's it. A tool. Nothing more. Are you really willing to go to prison for them, to do hard time when they have zero loyalty to you?"

"No comment," Dodders answered, his arms still crossed and his jaw set.

Rob stared at him for a moment, but his expression was resolute, and at least for now, there was no getting to him.

"Fine," Rob said and stood up. "You stay in here for a bit and think about it. Meanwhile, I think we'll see about chatting to your mates and see what they have to say." Rob glanced over at Matilda, who'd remained silent throughout this exchange, taking notes. She met his gaze and gave him a conciliatory smile and a quick shrug.

Rob clenched his jaw and ground his teeth, before stepping out with Scarlett following him.

"Well, that was pointless," Scarlett said once the door had closed behind them.

"Maybe. Maybe not," he answered. They were in the Nottingham Custody Suite, not too far from Nottingham Central Station, Rob's old stomping ground.

Outside, in the corridor, there were a handful of people standing and talking or going about their business.

As he looked up, he locked eyes with a man a short distance away. He had a shock of dark hair, wore a suit and coat, and was speaking with a woman. Like the man she was talking with, she too had the look of a detective.

A second after meeting the man's gaze, he seemed to recognise Rob and motioned for the woman to follow.

"Loxley, isn't it?" the man said as he approached.

"Aye," Rob answered and glanced at the man's ID card hanging around his neck. He was a detective.

"Sorry, I'm Karl. This is Amelia. We're just here interviewing a suspect. But when I saw you, I just wanted to come and say hi."

Rob looked askance at the detective who was probably a similar age, and wondered if this was some kind of joke. Within the CID he was perhaps a little infamous within certain circles for his family connections, and the rumours had a habit of spreading. But this seemed different.

"Okay. Hi."

"Sorry. I didn't mean to freak you out. I just know who you are. I used to be part of the EMSOU before it imploded, and I've been keeping abreast of it since."

"Oh, I see," Rob replied, suddenly curious. "You were part of the unit when it got shut down? When it was run by Superintendent Garrett?"

"Oh, you know him? Yeah. It was a right mess." Karl sighed, a melancholy falling over him. "I take it you're aware of what happened?"

"Only the broad strokes," Rob answered. "It was a drug sting against an OCG that went bad, right?"

"That's right," Karl confirmed. "The gang knew we were coming and laid a trap. People were killed."

"I'm sorry to hear that," Rob said.

"Yeah, sorry," Scarlett added.

"It's okay." He seemed sad but resigned to it. "So you know DCI Garrett?"

"I've seen him around," Rob replied.

"Well, we were—" Karl began as Amelia stepped closer to him.

"Eh, Karl. I'm not sure that's a good idea," Amelia interrupted him before she looked over at Rob. "Sorry."

"No, that's okay. It's none of my business."

"Well, at least you're still with us," Scarlett said, changing the subject.

He snorted. "Barely. Anyway, after the DCI Orleton case, I saw you were part of the new EMSOU, and then you were part of that prostitute killer case over in Clipstone, right?"

"That's right," Rob confirmed.

"Making a name for yourself."

"Just doing my job." Rob shuffled on the spot, uncomfortably shifting his weight from foot to foot as he looked down at the floor. He certainly didn't see himself as any kind of celebrity.

"Well, enjoy it. The EMSOU I mean. I loved being a part of it, dealing with those cases. It doesn't get any bigger or better than that. I miss it."

"You seem busy enough." Rob nodded up the corridor, guessing they'd been in one of the other interview rooms.

"Yeah, we are." He glanced at his partner.

"I keep him busy, that's for sure," Amelia said. She offered her hand. "I've heard of you too… Probably from Karl but…"

"I was about to say," Karl added. "I've probably spoken about my time in the EMSOU."

"I'm guessing you weren't in the EMSOU?" Scarlett asked Amelia.

"No. I was assigned to Karl after he was moved. But he doesn't shut up about his adventures in your unit."

"Told you," Karl added as Amelia smiled. He addressed Rob, "Sorry, I've taken up far too much of your time. We've got some phone calls to make, and then I need to get home. My girlfriend will be wondering where I am. It was supposed to be date night."

"Don't keep her waiting," Scarlett remarked.

"I know. I'm playing with fire there," Karl agreed.

Behind them, a door slammed open, and a man Rob recognised stormed out. He glanced up the corridor at them before marching off the other way.

Amelia pointed at him. "Wasn't he watching our interview?"

"Yeah..." Karl said with a frown. "No doubt because of who his dad is."

"And what he said about him," Amelia added in a low voice.

Karl sighed. "Shit. This might blow up."

"Blow up?" Rob asked, curious. "That was Chief Superintendent Tanner. How big is this?"

Amelia gave him a look before turning back to Karl. "I don't think..."

"It's fine, Amelia," Karl retorted. "Rob's part of the EMSOU and took down a corrupt DCI. I think we're okay."

Amelia sighed.

"Sorry," Rob said. "I didn't mean to pry."

"No, you're good. You'll probably find out about this anyway. We were just interviewing this nineteen-year-old kid, Gavin. He stabbed a girl over in Forest Fields in an off-licence, and then he hung around trying to help. Anyway, we bring him in, and it turns out he's Gavin Garrett. The son of Lee Garrett."

"Superintendent Garrett?" Rob asked, shocked.

"The very same. He was my boss in the EMSOU when it went boom."

"Crap," Scarlett exclaimed. "That's messed up."

"Bloody hell, he'll never live that down," Rob added.

"That's not the worst of it," Karl added.

"Karl," Amelia said, the word laced with warning.

Karl went to speak, but then relented. "Yeah, you're right," he said to Amelia. "No need to go spreading rumours."

"That's probably wise," Rob agreed. "This is your case, not ours."

"Right, anyway. We'd best go and make these phone calls to Gavin's family."

"And get home to your lady friend," Scarlett added with a knowing smile.

"Aye," Karl agreed.

"Good luck," Rob and Scarlett offered before Karl and Amelia stalked off up the corridor. Rob watched them go before he felt Scarlett's eyes on him. He looked down to see her incredulous face staring back at him.

"Holy shit. That's crazy."

"You're not kidding," Rob agreed. "If I had a son... Or daughter I guess, as a serving police officer, I would not want to get a call like that."

"Me neither," Scarlett agreed. "That would suck."

As Rob nodded in agreement, he saw Nick and Guy step out of the room they'd been interviewing one of their other suspects in and walk over.

"Any luck?" Rob asked.

"Nope, sorry, guv," Nick answered. Cleveland won't talk. It's just a string of 'No comments'. Not very helpful."

"We know they're linked to the Masons," Guy added. "They probably know something that could be useful. If we could just prise it out of one of them."

"Aye," Rob agreed. "Getting that shit we found in the bedroom off the street is great, but stopping it coming in entirely would be better."

"Agreed," Nick said. "Let's keep going, keep the pressure on, shall we?"

Rob agreed and made his way back towards the interview room.

4

Lee drove north along the A614, Blyth Road, past New Ollerton towards Perlthorpe, Thoresby, and eventually, the A1. But he'd be turning off before then and making his way into Clumber Park.

But his mind wasn't on the drive or the meeting he was going to. It was stuck thinking about Justine and her current moods.

They'd been getting on so well recently, better than they had done, possibly ever. Certainly as good as they had in those early weeks around a year ago when they'd first met.

Christ, it had been something of a whirlwind romance that had come out of nowhere. He'd not been looking for it, not after Shelley had left him because he was, according to her, so obsessed with work.

That in itself was crazy. What was he supposed to do, tell the criminals not to commit crimes outside of office hours so he could go home on time? Or maybe she thought they could somehow, between them, convince the government to up the police budget so they could recruit more officers and reduce the amount of overtime he needed to do?

He shook his head. Honestly, he had no idea what she was thinking. She was only thinking about herself, as far as he was concerned, and she certainly wasn't thinking about their son and how their separation would affect him.

And it most certainly *had* affected him.

But that was the whole problem with Justine now, too, wasn't it?

Mood? She was in a foul mood for some god-forsaken reason that he couldn't possibly fathom.

Shit. And they'd been getting on so well recently too. Last weekend had been amazing! The day out with her and Gavin had been incredible, and it was one of the few times in recent memory that they had actually felt like a family.

And then it all went to shit.

Gavin went to stay with his mother, and within days, Justine's mood changed. It seemed to flip like a lightbulb, but he had no idea why.

And now he'd been pulled away to this meeting, which pissed him off too. This was supposed to be his time to heal and sort his head out after everything that had happened with the EMSOU and the fallout from that monumental fuck up.

He had some pretty major regrets from that, too, such as everything that had happened to Gemma. Although, he couldn't see a way around that. The shit had to fall on someone, and it just so happened that she was in the firing line.

Christ, it was a mess, and it seemed to be infecting everything around it, even his family life.

Changes needed to be made, he concluded. It could not continue like this anymore, and he had a much clearer idea of the way he wanted to go with it.

Maybe, just maybe, this meeting could be the start of that.

He shrugged to himself as he passed the massive wooded area on his left. Whatever will be, will be, he thought. Get through this meeting and see where he stood.

Maybe him getting out of the house and giving her some space was exactly what Justine needed?

As he approached the entrance to Clumber Park, his phone started ringing.

He saw Justine's name on the screen, and for a moment, he considered answering it until he saw a police car approaching on the opposite side of the road. Grunting, he dismissed the call and dropped the phone in the passenger seat. She could wait. He didn't really fancy getting another earful of bile from her right now, anyway.

Reaching the grand, ornate stone entrance to Clumber Park, Lee turned left and drove through the central arch onto Lime Tree Avenue. Ahead, in the dark, the road stretched across the long clearing hemmed in on either side by trees. Even in the dark, the scene was calming and a balm for his racing mind, allowing the fears and worries to fall away, if only for a moment.

He crossed the clearing and reached the treeline, where the road was suddenly boxed in by a double avenue of lime trees on either side, each with its distinctive protective dark ring painted around the truck. He wasn't sure what that dark ring did, exactly, but it was probably something to do with keeping the trees healthy.

The park was quiet at this time of night, and the facilities, run by the National Trust, would be closed, but you could still drive in after dark and explore some of the woodlands while dodging a Park Warden.

It made for a perfect meeting place.

Turned to full beam, his headlights lit up the trunks and canopy on either side and above as they slid by the car. It was hypnotising to watch the shadows dance as the car moved by.

Eventually, the road angled slightly left, and the low wooden bollards ended. They lined the sides of the road up to this point, preventing cars from parking amongst the precious trees. Lee slowed and turned right, manoeuvring the car between the trees before coming to a stop and turning the engine off.

His surroundings fell into darkness, and he couldn't see much for a moment until his eyes started to adjust.

Hopefully, he wouldn't need to wait too long. He was a long way from home and wanted to get back before it got too late.

Lost in thought, Lee's mind drifted through the possibilities of what this meeting might be about. He wasn't sure how long he'd been sitting there when headlights appeared on the road from the direction he'd come.

Was this them? Or would this just be a car of bored horny teenagers looking to get laid in the woods?

When the car slowed and then turned off the road towards him, he knew this was his contact.

His phone rang.

"Shit." Grabbing it, it noted it was Justine again.

The car pulled up a short distance away, a dark figure in the driver's seat. Lee flicked on his car's interior light, as they always did. But the other figure didn't do the same. Instead, with his blindingly bright lights still on, he got out.

Lee answered the call.

"Lee!" Justine said, she sounded upset.

"Justine, I can't talk right now." Wondering what the hell was going on, Lee opened his door. It was probably some new guy they'd sent to pass on a message or something who didn't know the routine. He climbed out.

"You need to listen to me," Justine cried.

"No, you need to listen to me," Lee interrupted her as he walked around his car. The figure was approaching but still behind the glare of the headlights. He couldn't see anything beyond a vaguely human shape of a head and shoulders. "I don't know what's going on with you or why you're upset at me, but I'm sure we can work it out. Anyway, I have to go."

"Lee, please. I'm not calling about that. It's about Gavin..."

"Gavin? What about him?"

"He's been arrested."

"Arrested? Why? What's he done?" Lee looked up at the approaching figure as they stepped into the light.

"He stabbed someone, a girl."

"Wha..." Lee saw the figure, recognised them, and then registered the gun levelled at him.

The figure gestured with the weapon to end the call.

"I have to go." He ended the call as Justine shouted his name. "So, it's you. Don't do this, please."

5

Sonia gave the handbrake a yank, causing it to emit that satisfying clicking sound as it anchored the Land Rover to the spot. She'd made her evening rounds of the park, checking the usual places where unruly teenagers would occasionally hang out to cause trouble or just drink themselves into oblivion.

But tonight, there were none, and it looked as though she'd have a qu...

She stopped herself before she finished the Q word, knowing full well that to utter it was to tempt fate and jinx the whole night. Well, no, sir. She was not going to fall into that trap tonight.

No chance. She wanted to have a nice, quiet evening of trundling around the park in the darkness, listening to music and enjoying her time away from the chaos of home.

She loved her family and spending time with people in general, but she also loved some peace and quiet and some time to herself, so she could think about... well, whatever she wanted to think about.

But right now, she had only one thing on her mind. Something that had been sitting in her bag in the passenger footwell, quietly tempting her to stop and enjoy it. But she'd remained strong for several hours while she'd made her rounds, promising herself that she'd have it once her work was finished and not before.

It was a reward for a job well done and not to be touched before that.

Well, her first round of commitments had been fulfilled, and she could finally afford to take a break, which meant she could hopefully now enjoy that tasty treat.

Reaching for her bag, she lifted it onto the passenger seat and fished around inside.

For a heart-stopping moment, she thought she'd lost it somewhere, dropped it on her travels, meaning she'd need to forgo the deliciousness of chocolate for several more hours until she headed home. But, two seconds after that terrible fear had gripped her, she wrapped her fingers around the crinkly wrapper and breathed a sigh of relief.

She pulled out the bar of chocolate and admired it.

A Yorkie Bar.

She loved these things with their chunky segments of delectable chocolate. It's how a bar of chocolate should be, she thought. She didn't want small, delicate bites. She wanted solid mouthfuls with each bite!

Their old advertising campaign, when they used to say this bar wasn't for girls, amused her. How to shoot yourself in the foot, she thought. Which idiot thought it was a good idea to alienate half the buying public?

Well, screw that!

Unable to wait another moment, Sonia ripped it open and took her first bite. It was utter heaven, and as she relaxed into her seat and closed her eyes, she could imagine herself sitting somewhere far away without a care in the world, just enjoying herself.

After her third bite, the silence of the park was momentarily broken by a loud snap in the distance that echoed over the trees.

Sonia's eyes shot open as she took another bite. She frowned and peered into the darkness. She couldn't see anything, but she'd been around Clumber Park and hung out with the game keeper long enough to recognise that sound.

That was a gun shot.

Was Greg here tonight? No, of course, he wasn't. Then who...

This needed investigating. Stuffing the second to last chunk into her mouth and holding it between her teeth, she slammed the Land Rover into gear, released the handbrake, and accelerated at speed. If she had to guess, she'd say the bang came from somewhere close to Lime Tree Avenue. She was moments from the scene and gunned the engine to get there quicker.

Bombing along the road, she ripped the wrapper off the final two chunks of chocolate and stuffed them both in her mouth, cursing whoever it was who was ruining her brief moment of joy. Was someone hunting rabbits? It wouldn't be the first time.

Sonia turned onto Lime Tree Avenue and accelerated. Moments later, she saw lights up ahead. She pushed the 4x4 harder and soon had a clear view of a car reversing back onto the road and then accelerating away. They weren't hanging around either. As she got closer, she saw a second car parked on the grass between the double row of trees on the left.

The fleeing car was easily faster than hers, so even if she did give chase, there was no way for her to catch it. And besides, once the car was out of the park, there was little she could do. She wasn't a police officer, after all.

Choosing to investigate the second car, she slowed her vehicle and turned left, onto the grass, bringing her headlights to bare and illuminating the scene before her.

Sonia slammed on the brakes and gasped. "Oh my, god."

Blood was everywhere, all up the side of the car, and on the floor, a man, also covered in blood, lay utterly still on his back.

For what felt like an eternity, all she could do was sit and stare at the horrifying scene, unsure what to do. It felt like an age before she finally tore her eyes away and took a breath.

She needed to think about this logically and professionally. If that man was dead, certain things needed to happen, and even if he wasn't, he'd need help.

She took another look and concluded that whoever it was, he was almost certainly dead with that kind of blood loss.

Taking another moment to steady her nerves, Sonia fished out her torch and climbed out of the car, alert for any movement or sounds nearby. But apart from the rustle of the trees, and the occasional hoot of a nearby owl, everything was quiet. The local fauna had probably been startled into hiding by the gunshot and the roaring engines that followed.

Steeling her nerves, Sonia stalked towards the body. It was a man. He looked fit and was dressed in jeans and a shirt. He lay on his back with his arms wide and his head back, so she couldn't really see his face.

Frowning in frustration that she'd need to get closer, she pressed on. Her headlights threw the man's thrown-back face into shadow, hiding whatever rictus grin he might have.

Bringing her torch to bear, she shined the light into the man's face. His mouth and eyes were open and frozen in place, staring out at nothing. She'd usually consider such a man to be quite attractive, under normal circumstances, if it wasn't for the ink black hole in his forehead that was still oozing blood.

With a shiver, she turned away and returned to her vehicle, impressed with herself. Somehow, she'd managed to do all that and keep her Yorkie Bar down. Thank God for small mercies.

It did, however, look like she wasn't going to get that quiet night after all. Resigned to the circus about to descend upon the park and no doubt close it to the general public, she grabbed her phone and punched in 999.

6

"We need to talk to the other two now," Rob said to Scarlett, Nick and Guy in the corridor outside the interview rooms. "See what we can get out of them. I'm hoping for at least one weak link."

"You and me, both," Nick agreed as the door to their right opened, and Duty Solicitor Matilda Greenwood stepped out. She jumped when she spotted them standing right outside the door.

"Oh, sorry. Didn't see you there," she said, as a custody officer walked in to escort Dodders back to his cell.

"Hi," Rob said, smiling.

"Hey," Matilda answered before she pulled her eyes away from him and addressed Scarlett and the others. "Evening."

They each greeted her in turn before a sudden and awkward silence fell over the group as Dodders was walked out and off down the corridor by the officer, his head hung low.

They were unable to keep talking about the case with the suspect's Duty Solicitor here. But Matilda, like many of the other regulars, was well known to them and basically a work colleague, and she didn't look like she wanted to walk away.

Rob met Matilda's gaze once more, and they shared a smile.

"Nick, Guy, come with me," Scarlett said and gently guided them away. "We'll be over here."

"Oh, sorry, Rob, cramping your style," Nick muttered before Scarlett managed to walk him away.

Rob smiled at Scarlett as she retreated before looking back at Matilda. "Everything okay? How is he? Ready to talk yet?"

"I, err. No, I don't think so."

"Okay." A second silence grew between them for what felt like an age. Rob wanted to fill it with some kind of conversation, but words failed him.

"How've you been?" she asked finally.

"I'm okay, thanks. Yeah, I'm good."

"You've been a part of the East Midlands Special Operations Unit for a few weeks now, and from what I hear, you've been quite busy."

"You mean the Clipstone case? Yeah. That was intense. But it's good to have a team around me that I can trust and a boss who doesn't hate me."

"That's DCI Nailer, right?"

"That's him. He's been a good friend of mine for a while now." Which was putting it mildly. Nailer had been a mentor and a father figure who'd guided and helped him get into the police force and turn his life around. He couldn't ever say thank you enough for what Nailer had done for him.

"That's great."

"What about you?" Rob asked.

"I'm good." She smiled. "Busy with casework and being on call to come here. It never seems to end, does it?"

"No, never," Rob agreed.

"It's good to see you again." Tilting her head, she moved half a step closer and with a gleam in her eye, added. "We should catch up sometime."

"Okay, sounds good," Rob agreed.

"Guv?" Scarlett strode up to them with her phone to her ear. "We've got a scene to attend. We're going to have to leave this with Nick and Guy for the time being."

"Oh, where?"

"Clumber Park."

"The other end of the county? Bollocks. Alright, I guess we'd better get going."

Scarlett nodded and stepped away to finish her phone call.

Rob turned back to Matilda. "Sorry about that. Looks like duty calls."

"Doesn't it always?" She gave him a resigned smile. "I'll catch up with you some other time."

"Count on it."

"Until then, then."

"Guv," Scarlett said, attracting his attention. "We'd better go."

They made it out into the car park in no time. Within moments they were out on the roads and heading north through the city in Rob's Black, 1985 Mark Three Ford Capri. The GT Coupe, 2.8 injection V6 ate up the road in a way that Rob thoroughly enjoyed, and at this time of night, the streets were mercifully quiet. Rob kept his distance from the centre of town and the throngs of revellers out on Friday night and threaded through the city using its main arteries. Before long, they were blasting north along the A614 and making good time.

Beside him, Scarlett sighed. "You know she likes you, right?"

"What?" Rob said, momentarily confused by the sudden comment stated without context.

"Matilda. She likes you. You see that, don't you?"

"Oh, okay." Rob blushed. "Where's this come from?"

She snorted. "I'll tell you where it's come from. It's come from me watching you two dance around each other these past few months without either of you actually doing anything about it. It's maddening, and I just can't watch it anymore without saying anything."

"I see," Rob replied and sighed to himself. "She could just be being friendly."

"No, no. Believe me, it's more than that. She's flirting with you every chance she gets. It's blatant."

"To you, maybe. But you could be wrong, and I don't want to ruin our friendship."

"But, you are interested… in women, I mean?"

"Yeeeaaah," he answered, drawing the word out. "Sorry if that wasn't clear."

"No, it was. I was just checking."

"Also," Rob added, "she's a duty solicitor. She represents the criminals. She's working for them."

"So what. She's just doing her job and is working on behalf of the law, not the criminals who break it."

"Depends how you look at it," Rob replied. Scarlett was right, from a certain point of view. Matilda might well be sitting on the other side of the table with the suspect, but everyone was innocent until proven guilty. They deserved a fair trial and representation by someone who knows the law. But that shouldn't mean that she and the other Duty Solicitors were his enemies. They were just parts of the system like he and his team were.

However, he could see it being a sticking point between them if anything were ever to develop.

He smiled to himself. Did he want something to develop between him and Matilda? He liked her, he had to admit. She was attractive and friendly, and he always remembered that night he'd spent with her at the bar. They'd had a great time, and it was there that they'd struck up this friendship.

Was Scarlett right? Did Matilda want there to be something more between them?

A frown creased Rob's brow as he thought it through.

What Matilda wanted wasn't really his issue, though. It was him and what it would mean for Matilda should he get involved with her.

To say he came with baggage was something of an understatement.

"Depends how you look at it?" Scarlett scoffed. "Rob. Life's too short. If you keep pushing people away, you'll be old and alone and filled with regrets before you know it. You need to find happiness wherever you can and grab it. So few people truly find that kind of happiness. What if this is your chance?"

Rob blinked in shock. "Jesus, Scarlett? What are you on? That was deep."

"Sorry, I'm just a little frustrated over this."

"Clearly. Look, I do like her. I do. But I just have a history of bad choices, and… well, that taints things. Also, she'd be taking on a lot with someone like me."

"Don't you think that's her choice to make?"

Rob sighed. "Maybe."

"Think about it. But honestly, I think you should take the risk."

"I promise to think about it." She had a point, and she was far more likely to understand Matilda's point of view than he was.

But finding the time to think about it could be a problem now they had another case on their hands.

"Good. Sorry, I needed to say something before I took the weekend off. It's been on my mind."

"Oh, crap. That's this weekend?" Rob asked, surprised.

"Yep," she replied with a smile. "I can't wait. I've got all my bridesmaids coming to stay."

"This is the weekend of shopping, right? Finding the bridesmaid's dresses? Is that it?"

"You got it. It'll be a really girly weekend with friends from uni and school. Chris's sister too. I can't wait."

Rob nodded, but could think of a thousand things he'd much rather do than that. But then, that was why he was working all weekend. "Well, I'm sure you'll have a great time. We'll miss you."

"No you won't."

"We will," Rob insisted. "And I'm sure you'll miss us too."

"Oh, yeah, sure. I'll be crying into my merlot, wishing I was at work."

Rob grinned. "See, I knew you'd miss us."

By the time they reached the scene, the entrance to the park had been taped off. A patrol car partially blocked the road with a cold-looking officer standing guard, who let them through.

Nearly a mile down Lime Tree Avenue, they found the scene of the crime and the familiar gaggle of police and forensics vehicles and their flashing blue lights.

The inner and outer cordons had been set up, officers were on guard, and the Scene of Crime guys were working the scene.

Rob parked up and wandered in through the cordons with Scarlett at his side.

"Will you be out with your mates Saturday night then?" Rob asked.

"Of course, tearing up the town," she confirmed. "Nottingham won't know what's hit it."

Rob smirked. "Are you sure it won't be the other way around? These nice cosmopolitan Surrey girls coming up to rough and ready Nottingham? I think they'll be the ones who won't know what's hit them."

Scarlett shrugged. "We're tougher than you think."

"Guv?" A uniformed officer Rob recognised as Sergeant Alex Soto, one of the EMSOU assigned guys, approached.

"How's it going?" Rob asked.

"The area's secure, and the police surgeon has already been and gone. We're getting photos of the scene, and SOCO are starting their investigation."

"Excellent, and what have we got?"

"One body. Male, perhaps in his fifties. He's been shot in the forehead at close range. It looks like he was executed. There was no messing about with this."

"Not a passion killing then," Rob said as they approached the scene.

"Doesn't look like it, but you're the brains of this operation."

"It reminds me of that other assassination, recently. Radek, from the Clipstone case. We found him shot in the head."

"We did. We found a calling card at the scene too, remember?"

"White with a red hourglass on one side," Scarlett agreed.

"We haven't found a calling card here," Alex said. "But, it is dark, so..."

"I doubt it's related, but, it's something we can keep in mind. What else do you have?"

"We have the park warden who found the body here, too." Alex waved towards a stocky woman in a green uniform sitting sideways in the driver's seat of her Land Rover.

Rob strode over with Scarlett and Alex in tow. "Good evening. I'm Detective Inspector Rob Loxley."

"Hi." She took Rob's offered hand. "Sonia Jennings."

"I understand you work here, right?"

"I'm one of the wardens. I'm on the night shift."

"I see," Rob said. "And you were the one to discover the body?"

She nodded. "Yeah."

"Would you mind running us through what happened?"

Sonia agreed and outlined what she'd heard and seen in the run-up to the gruesome discovery. Rob listened and made notes as she spoke.

"Thank you. So, this car you saw leaving. Did you get a number place?"

"No, sorry. It was dark and too far away. I couldn't see what kind of car it was either, other than a saloon or something like that. Sorry I can't be more help."

"What about cameras?"

"There's none on this stretch of the avenue or on the entrance. We only have them further in."

"You might want to look into that," Rob said, cursing inside at the lack of security. "And the park is open all the time?"

"Twenty-four hours a day, yes. Most of it's just woodland, and it would be impossible to close off such a huge area every night. It's just not practical. That's what I understand, anyway. I don't make those decisions."

"Alright, thank you." Rob turned to the uniformed officer who'd been talking to Sonia. "Have you taken a statement?"

"We have, sir."

"Great, thanks." He turned to Alex. "Right then, let's have a look at it then."

Alex nodded and led them deeper into the cordon. "You can put your suits on here." Alex motioned to the back of a nearby van.

Several minutes later, they'd pulled on their forensic coveralls, complete with shoe coverings and masks, to match the SOCO team. Alex showed them towards the tent that obscured the body but stopped a short distance from it.

"This is as close as I go without one of those cute little suits."

Rob and Scarlett pressed on and slipped inside the tent. One of the white-clad SOCOs stood up.

"Rob, Scarlett," Alicia said in greeting. "Good to see you. You might want to come around here and take a closer look. See if you recognise him."

The body lay on his back, spread-eagled with his head thrown back and blood splatters on his top. Work lights illuminated the scene, throwing the body into sharp relief. Rob walked around until he could see the face and then gasped.

"What, who is it?" Scarlett asked, curious.

"It's Superintendent Lee Garrett," Rob announced.

"Correct," Alicia said. "The ID in his pocket confirmed it for us too."

"Holy crap," Scarlett exclaimed. "And his son's in custody over in Nottingham for stabbing some girl."

"What, really?" Alicia asked. "You're kidding?"

"I wish she was," Rob muttered.

"Could they be linked?" Scarlett asked.

"The stabbing and this?" Rob frowned. "I don't know. Maybe? It is a coincidence that these two things happen so close to each other. There could be something in it. I don't know what, though."

"Or it might be to do with the botched operation he presided over that got the EMSOU shut down three months ago."

"That's just speculation at this point," Rob replied. "We need to focus on the facts and see where they lead us. Alicia?"

"Sir," she replied.

"What do we know? Have you found much?"

"Tyre tracks, footprints, but not much else. We need to wait until dawn when we can see more. The bullet passed right through his skull, so with any luck, we'll find that and maybe the casing too. Talk to me again tomorrow, and I might have something for you. Right now, I'm just trying to preserve the scene."

"Fair enough. Keep at it."

After a good hunt round, with Rob making notes as he went, they soon walked away from the tent and removed their coveralls.

"Damnit, looks like this could be a really juicy one," Scarlett complained.

"See. I knew you'd miss us," Rob remarked.

7

Scarlett pulled into the drive of her Park estate home in the centre of Nottingham and took a moment to herself. Sitting in her purple VW Polo, she tried to relax and let the stresses of the day drain away before she walked through her front door.

No doubt her friend Ninette would be here by now, and Chris would be waiting for her so he could head round to his mates for what would probably be a boozy weekend of fun.

As long as he kept out of her hair for the weekend, she didn't mind what he did. She just wanted some proper girly time with her mates, preparing for their wedding.

Running her hands through her hair, she massaged her scalp and closed her eyes, thinking over the events of the day and the case she was leaving with Rob and the rest of the team. The murder of a Superintendent was huge, and she felt guilty swanning off for the weekend and leaving that great steaming pile of shit for Rob to sort out without her. He'd insisted it was okay and reminded her that she'd had this booked in for weeks now. She agreed, but it didn't really assuage her guilt.

Still, even if Rob did find the killer over the weekend, there would be plenty of mopping up to do come Monday, so she'd be involved in it one way or another anyway. In the meantime, she needed to somehow separate that part of her brain and shut it away for the next two days. She wanted to enjoy this break and forget about work. Murders, stabbings and drug gangs could be a real mood killer.

Christ, she thought. It was a hell of a job!

Sometimes, in moments of weakness, she questioned her choice of career. But those were fleeting feelings and not really how she felt about her work.

After a quick check in the mirror to make sure she didn't look too frazzled, she made her way into their house to find Chris and Ninette talking in the entrance hall, both standing beside packed suitcases.

"Babe," Chris said and pulled her in for a quick hug and a kiss. "Another late one."

"Sorry. I know you needed to get off, but we had a scene to attend up in Clumber Park and, well, you know how these things go." She shrugged. "Sorry."

"That's okay. I've been chatting to Ninette."

"I hope he's not been boring you," Scarlett said, addressing her friend.

"No, not at all. It's been good to spend a little time with him, given he's going to be your husband soon." Ninette gave her a knowing smile. "Scarlett Williams. It's got a nice ring to it."

Feeling herself flush, Scarlett turned to Chris. "So, are you off then?"

"Yep," Chris confirmed. "I spoke to Lucy. She'll be up first thing tomorrow. She's looking forward to meeting your friends."

"Great."

"Is that your sister?" Ninette asked.

"Yeah," Chris confirmed.

"You'll like her. She's about five years younger than us and full of energy."

"Oh, good. We'll need some youth and vitality after a full day of shopping tomorrow," Ninette said.

"Well, have fun with that," Chris commented and pulled Scarlett in for a longer hug. He took the opportunity to give her arse a squeeze, too. "I'll miss you, babe," he whispered in her ear.

"I'll miss you too," she replied and kissed him, letting it linger for a couple of seconds, but pulled away before it got too awkward with her friend close by. "Behave yourself."

Chris laughed. "You too."

"Never. Where's the fun in that?"

She saw Chris out the door and closed it behind him before turning to her friend.

"Well, you two are well and truly loved up," Ninette remarked.

"Sorry. I'm just gonna miss him."

"No, it's okay. It's cute. I'm pleased for you."

"Thanks. Right then, let's show you where you'll be sleeping so you can dump your bag. And then, how about we have a drink?"

"A drink would be great."

Kicking off her shoes, Scarlett led her upstairs and asked about her train ride up. She showed Ninette to the room she would be sharing with Autumn, her other university friend, before disappearing off to her room to remove her constricting bra, loosen the neck of her shirt, and put some comfortable slippers on. She breathed a sigh of relief, scratched an itch, and after a quick bathroom break, went hunting for her friend.

Moments later, they made their way back downstairs and into the kitchen, where Scarlett set about making drinks.

"Fancy a gin?"

"Oooh, yeah, I'd love one. Thanks."

Scarlett pulled out two bulbous gin glasses and poured them a double pink gin each. She topped them up with tonic water before handing one to Ninette.

"So, I'm sharing with Autumn?" Ninette asked, lifting her drink. She seemed a little shaky and steadied herself against the island in the kitchen.

Scarlett frowned at the stumble and sensed a hint of annoyance in her friend's words, but chose to ignore it. "Yeah, hope that's okay."

"It's fine." It sounded anything but fine, by her tone of voice.

"So, how about you?" Scarlett said, choosing to change the subject. "Is there a man on the scene?"

"No. I'm sworn off them for a bit," Ninette answered. "Can't be dealing with the hassle."

"Really?"

"I don't need a man to define me, Scarlett." She'd answered quickly, almost snapping at her.

Scarlett raised a hand in surrender, a little taken aback by her friend's prickliness. "Sorry, I didn't mean anything by it."

"I... Sorry. I know you didn't." She sighed. "Tell me about you. This weekend is about you anyway. How are things going up here? How's the job?"

"It's good, actually. I wasn't sure when I first moved up. It's a long way from home, you know? Family and friends. But Chris had such a good opportunity offered to him by his work that he just couldn't pass it up. He's onto a really good thing, you know."

"I can see that," Ninette replied, waving at the house around her. Again, there was that underlying tone. She sounded annoyed, or, jealous maybe? "You've landed on your feet, that's for sure."

"It's not bad," she replied humbly, aiming to minimise the issue. "It keeps the rain off our heads."

"And the job? Is it much different to the Surrey Police force?"

"It is different, sure." Scarlett was glad of the subject change. "Different city and county means different issues. But I'm still chasing after some very naughty people. I got assigned to a Detective Sergeant who recently got promoted to Inspector. We had a doozy of a first case, and from there, we got shifted over to the local Special Operations Unit, dealing with organised crime, murders, that kind of thing."

"Sounds like you did okay."

"I guess so." She laughed as she thought back to that first case and the end result.

"What's funny?"

"Just the circumstances of that first case. We ended up discovering that our boss, the DCI, was corrupt and on the payroll of a local gang."

"What? So, you ended up arresting your own boss?"

Scarlett nodded as she thought back to that incredibly surreal moment that happened within days of starting her job. "Yep. It was insane. We have a better DCI on the Special Ops Unit now, though. I don't think we'll be arresting him."

"Are you sure about that?" Ninette teased and then took another sip of her drink. Scarlett noticed the slight shakiness of her hand, something she'd spotted earlier, mixed with the occasional spikey comment.

"Pretty sure." Scarlett sipped her drink. "Tell me about you, though. Are you okay? If you don't mind me saying, you seem a little shaky?"

Ninette smiled, but it seemed forced. "No, I'm fine. I just…" She took a breath. "It's the old… problem… again."

"Oh, no. Really? Still? You need to let it go, Anni. You can't let that idiot ruin your life. It's years ago now."

"I know but…"

"But what? What's happened?"

"Look, I've been meaning to tell you for ages, and I didn't really want to get into it this weekend, but something happened, and…" Ninette's voice caught in her throat, and a tear fell down her cheek. She wiped it away as if trying to hide it. "Look, I'm sorry. You don't need this now. I shouldn't have said anything."

Scarlett got up and walked around to pull her in for a hug. "Don't be silly. If something's upset you, and I can help, then I want to know. Even if I can't practically help, just talking about it and sharing the burden can do wonders. It's only dress shopping. I can do that, have fun, and deal with this. I was there for you at uni, and I want to be there for you now. So please, tell me about it. I want to help."

"Are you sure?"

"One hundred percent."

Ninette sighed. "Okay. Yes, it's him again, Sebastian. That... creep."

"He's a bit worse than a creep," Scarlett replied. "He's a stuck-up, narcissistic, misogynistic rapist. He's scum. That's what he is."

"I know."

"Good. So, what's happened?"

"He's messaged me again."

"What? What do you mean, again? How long has this been going on? I didn't know..."

"I know. I didn't tell you."

"Why?"

"I just... Look, it started after we left uni. He'd send me texts and messages online. They were just streams of consciousness and abuse. He blames me for ruining his life. That's the crux of it. He hates me because of what I did to him."

"We did, what *we* did to him," Scarlett corrected her.

"Maybe, but he blames me."

"And yet, he's the one who raped you. What did he expect you to do? Not report him? Bloody idiot."

"I guess, yeah, that's what he expected. He comes from a rich, well-connected family, so..."

"Yeah, I know." Scarlett thought back to the fallout from that whole incident and how Sebastian Cunningham thought that his money and connections could prevent them from going public and trying to get him convicted for what he did to Ninette. But he soon found out he was dead wrong. "So, even though he's rich and wasn't convicted of rape, he's still moaning and feeling aggrieved by us trying to get him sent to prison for this? Right?"

"That's about right, yeah. He's been stalking me online, sending me messages from all these different profiles to get around the blocks I put on him. He doesn't message every day or anything. It's just once every so often."

"It doesn't matter that it isn't often, Anni; it's still stalking and abuse. I take it you have records of these messages?"

"Yeah, I screenshot them and keep them. I... I try not to read them."

"Good. Don't. In fact, tell you what, why don't you send them to me, and I'll keep them. That way, you can delete them off your phone."

"Um yeah, I could do that."

"You can do that."

"Anyway, he messaged me today, and it just gets to me. That's all."

"Understandably so. You shouldn't have to put up with this. You should have gone to the police."

"Like last time? Last time he raped me, and he got away scot-free. These are just words, so I can't see the authorities taking this any more seriously. I've not seen him or met him again. I don't even know where he lives anymore. The police won't do anything because he's not really done anything to harm me."

"I'd beg to differ because they should, but, I understand your frustration, and look, you can always talk to me about it, okay? I want to help."

"I know," Ninette replied. "Thank you."

8

Justine stared across the lounge at the far wall. Sitting on the sofa, she had her feet up and her arms wrapped around her legs with a cup of tea in her hand that had long since gone cold.

She might have been *looking* at the wall, but she wasn't really *seeing* it. Instead, her mind was lost in a chaotic mess of dark thoughts, and questions with no answers... Or no good answers, anyway.

The news of her boyfriend's murder the night before had kept her awake all night.

She'd taken herself to bed not long after the policewoman had left the previous night and tried to sleep, but she just couldn't. She'd tossed and turned, unable to calm her mind. All she could think about was, what if she'd done something differently?

Maybe Lee would still be alive and not lying dead on the grass in Clumber Park.

They'd argued in recent days, although she'd never really explained why she was upset with him. She'd been unsure about saying something, and now, she'd never be able to. She'd left it too late, and he was gone.

But the worst of it was that they'd been getting on so well recently. Up until a few days ago, things were going so smoothly, with days out at the weekend and meals at the kitchen table filled with laughter and happiness.

But now the house was silent.

For several hours late last night, it had been utter chaos, with the police asking countless questions and their Family Liaison Officer walking her through the procedure.

She knew how most of it worked anyway. You didn't date a policeman for all this time and not pick up on the general procedure around things like this.

In the end, when things had calmed down, she'd refused their offer of leaving someone here to protect her and demanded that they let her rest.

They'd be back again today, probably with a detective or two, asking more questions that she didn't have answers to or answers she couldn't give.

Things had been going so well for them. But now things were different. They'd also told her about Gavin and how he'd been picked up after stabbing some girl on his way home. It explained his lateness and why he wasn't answering his phone, but she couldn't help but wonder if the two incidents were related to each other. Had Gavin heard about the murder somehow and vented his rage? Or, was it the other way around, and the stabbing triggered the murder?

She wasn't clear on the timeline, and it was leaving her confused, with more questions than answers.

There was a sudden loud knocking at the front door.

The noise shocked her, and she spilt some of her tea over her feet, sofa and carpet.

"Shit, shit, shit."

Jumping up, she panicked for a moment. She needed to put something on that to soak it up. The police were here earlier than she'd anticipated, but they'd need to wait a moment.

"Hold on," she shouted at the dark shape on the other side of the door as she ran to the kitchen and grabbed a handful of kitchen paper towels. Returning to the lounge, she pressed it into the carpet and sofa. Standing up, she eyed the wet patches. "Crap," she muttered to herself and left the room. "Coming," she called out and unlocked the door.

It slammed open, hitting her hand and foot as the man behind it barged through.

"Aarrgh," she yelled, and the man grabbed her arm and then her throat.

"Scream or try to escape, and Jonas here will decorate the walls with your brains."

The man's face was inches from hers, and she recognised Carter Bird immediately. His was a face she wasn't about to forget anytime soon. Slowly, she looked to her left and saw one of Carter's thugs pointing a gun at her head. The darkness inside the gun barrel gaped wide, threatening instant death should she disobey.

She nodded.

"Say you understand," Carter demanded, briefly tightening his grip on her throat.

"I understand," she croaked through his grip.

"Good."

"The pigs were round here yesterday," Carter said.

Justine couldn't suppress the brief look of surprise that crossed her face before she nodded, confirming his statement.

"Yeah, we know. And we know they'll be back again today, asking questions. Right?"

She nodded again. "That's right."

Carter inched his face closer to hers. She could feel his warm breath on her face and smell his cologne. Keeping his left hand on her throat, he let go of her arm with his right and pressed his finger to her lips as he stared into her eyes.

"You keep this pretty mouth of yours shut, missy." Running his finger over her and around her lips. "You don't say a word about us or our arrangement. Otherwise..." Carter used a finger to part her mouth, pressing her lower lip down, and then pushed his finger into her mouth and pressed it onto her tongue. "Otherwise, I will rip out this lovely tongue of yours and let you bleed to death, choking on your own blood." He took the end of her now dry tongue between his fingers and pulled it out. "You wouldn't want to lose this now, would you?"

She tried to say no but was unable to form the word without the use of her mouth and tongue. She added a slight shake of her head to make sure he knew what she was saying.

"Good." He let go of her tongue. Loosening his grip on her throat, he ran his hand down, off her neck and over her chest to her right breast. For a moment, he cupped it in his hand, making her shiver in disgust. He gripped her nipple through her pyjama top between his finger and thumb and twisted, hard.

Justine whimpered, clamping a hand over her mouth to keep herself from screaming out while glancing at the gun still aimed at her head.

"You'd better not be lying," he warned.

Justine shook her head insistently. "No, never."

"Good. Because if you are, I'll be seeing you soon."

"I wouldn't lie to you. I won't say a word."

"Good girl," he said patronisingly.

She hated him. She hated everything about him and the way he'd just manhandled her. She hated herself too for letting him, but what could she do? She glanced at the gun and the grinning thug pointing it at her. He seemed to be enjoying the show a little too much.

"Come on, let's go," Carter said, and seconds later, they were gone, their car's engine retreating back from where they'd come.

Justine locked the door behind them and sank to the floor in floods of tears.

She just wanted Lee back. But he was gone, and now everything was turning to shit.

9

"Morning Guv," Ellen said, greeting him as he walked into the EMSOU office that morning. She was crossing the room as Rob walked in, and smiled as she drew near. "I heard it was a late one for you last night."

"Yeah, part way through the interviews, we got called out to a scene up in Clumber Park. One of our own was murdered."

"I heard. Nailer's here. I'll let him know you're in. The briefing will probably be in a few minutes."

"Excellent. Did you wrap up that domestic case you and Tucker were on?"

"Near enough. The hard work's done, so we'll be with you on this new one."

"Perfect. We'll need all hands on deck with Scarlett off."

"We'll manage," Ellen said, full of confidence.

"I'm sure," Rob agreed and walked to his desk, where he set about pulling together the notes he'd been working on last night after he got home from attending the Clumber scene.

They were dealing with a cop killer, which meant the top brass would be watching. There was no room for screwing this one up.

He was soon ready, and it wasn't long before he spotted Nailer and the others making their way to the incident room. Rob gathered his things and joined them.

"Guv," Rob said in greeting to Nailer as he walked in.

"Rob," Nailer replied with a curt nod. He was all business this morning, but given that the previous head of the EMSOU had just been murdered, that wasn't terribly surprising. It brought home how tenuous their position was and how easily things could be brought crashing down around their ears.

It was always the same whenever an officer was injured or killed in the line of duty. It reminded him of the nature of their job and what they were doing, day in, and day out. They were putting their lives on the line for the general public every single day, and for some of them, it might very well lead to a brutal end.

"Right then, settle down," Nailer called from the head of the table. "It was a busy night with our sting against the Worksop Gang, known as the Manton Massiv, yesterday. Rob, would you like to run us through what happened and the results of that sting for the benefit of those who weren't there?"

"Of course, sir. The sting was successful following information from an undercover source that the gang had cuckooed a flat on Sandy Lane. They were taking advantage of the sister of a now-dead gang member. This Tia Dunn has learning difficulties and is a perfect target for the gang. They barred off one room, locking it up with padlocks, then storing drugs and money in there as they processed them. It became something of a hub for the gang, a convenient place to keep their gear as it came and went. We arrested four members of the gang who were in attendance. Cedric Dodson, otherwise known as Dodders, and the leader of the gang. Cleveland Levine, known as Lev to his mates and Dodson's right-hand man. Ambrose Gordon, AKA Rice, and Carmela Kerr, who prefers to be known as just K. We secured the scene and caught up with our suspects at the Custody Suite. Scarlett and I only got to interview Dodson before we were called out to the scene at Clumber, but Dodson wasn't talking at all. Nick, did you get anything else out of them before you called it a night?"

"Not much," Nick replied. "However, we think that Ambrose Gordon could be a weak link. Our initial interviews didn't give us much, but I think if we apply just the right amount of pressure, we might get something out of him."

"This gang," Nailer said. "They're affiliated with the Masons, right?"

"That's right," Rob confirmed.

Nailer turned to Nick. "Don't try to get this Ambrose to leave the gang. He'll be more useful as an informant. Can you convince him to send over any useful information he comes across?"

"I don't know," Nick replied. "Maybe?"

"Offer him our usual rate for actionable intel and the chance to walk out of here without charge. See if he goes for it."

Nick glanced at Guy, who nodded in return.

"We could do that," Guy agreed. "I think we can get him to see the error of his ways and do what we can to protect him in the meantime."

"Yeah. We'll see if he'll go for it," Nick accepted and nodded to Nailer.

"Excellent. You can pin the drugs and cash on Dodson, the leader, and maybe one other easily enough. So let the other two go so as not to draw too much attention to Ambrose."

"Sounds good," Nick replied.

"Excellent. Right then, onto other business. I'm sure you're all aware by now that Detective Superintendent Lee Garrett was murdered last night in Clumber Park. He was fatally shot at close range and almost certainly died instantly. Rob, and Scarlett, who's sadly absent this weekend, attended the scene. SOCO has been there all night and will be there all day today as well, now they have daylight. Lee's immediate family have been notified of the situation. That's Shelley Garrett, his wife, who he's been separated from for a year now, and his current girlfriend, Justine Palmer. We sent FLOs around to both last night, and they'll be returning again this morning. Lee's body has been taken to the mortuary, and there'll be a post-mortem today.

"Now, I'm sure I don't need to tell you that I have Landon on my back about this, and I'm sure she has her boss pushing her too. We need to find out who killed Lee, and we need to do it fast."

"Of course, sir," Rob confirmed.

"Then let's go through it. Lee Garrett was the previous Superintendent of this unit, before it all went wrong. They were working on Operation Major Oak, which was the culmination of a long surveillance and undercover operation to try and bring down part, or maybe all of, the Mason Firm."

Rob caught the glance from Nailer at the mention of his family, and he wasn't the only one who looked, either.

Nailer continued, "What they didn't know, going into the sting operation to capture the leaders of the gang with a major haul of drugs, was that the gang apparently knew they were coming and laid a trap. It seems they wanted to teach us a lesson. When the sting was launched, things went bad quickly and in the resulting shootout, four detectives out of the eight on the EMSOU team that were there, were killed, as well as several support officers brought in from other departments. Superintendent Garrett did not attend the sting. The four dead were DS Katie Glover, DS Rowan Childs, DC Toby Graves, and DC Isobel Dickerson. That left DC Wally McKay, DC Rebeka Bowman, DI Karl Rothwell and DCI Gemma Flint, who survived the ordeal.

"Also, DCs Wally McKay and Rebeka Bowman only survived the operation because of the selfless and heroic actions of DC Isobel Dickerson. Actions that got her killed. Following the operation, an investigation was launched to find out what happened. Allegations of corruption were thrown around, and no one looked good. In the end, the team was disbanded until new officers could take over. And as you know, our Superintendent Landon was given that job."

"What happened to these officers?" Tucker asked. "The ones who survived, I mean?"

"Superintendent Garrett maintained his innocence through the investigation but seemed to suffer mentally," Nailer explained. "He went into therapy and had actually been on extended sick leave based on his therapist's recommendation."

"So, he wasn't even working when he was killed?" Rob asked.

"No, he wasn't," Nailer said. "But he was due to come back in about a week. Meanwhile, DCI Gemma Flint took the brunt of the fallout. She was the senior officer on the scene on the day of the raid, and it was due primarily to the testimony of Lee Garrett that Gemma got blamed for much of it. This was all kept internal, and she ended up taking a deal and resigning to save face. Although, I personally think she was scapegoated and pushed to leave. DI Karl Rothwell was reassigned and kept his rank. DC Wally McKay was reassigned and also remained a DC. DC Rebeka Bowman, however, decided that CID wasn't for her and returned to uniform. All of them, including Lee Garrett, are or were still under investigation by the PSU for possible corruption, so it might be that we have a Professional Standards Unit officer working with us on this who will be reporting back."

"Anti-corruption?" Rob asked.

"That's right." Nailer gave him a solemn grimace. "So play nice."

Rob rolled his eyes. Knowing his luck, it would be DI Bill Rainault, the 'Sheriff of Nottingham'. Wonderful. He sighed at this revelation, but there was little he could do.

"On top of all this," Nailer continued, we have another wrinkle. Last night, Lee Garrett's nineteen-year-old son, Gavin, was arrested for stabbing a girl in a shop over in Forest Fields. From what we can gather, we think this happened before his father was killed. We're still trying to work out if the two events are connected somehow and, if so, in what way."

"How's the girl?" Ellen asked.

"She'll survive, meaning Gavin has dodged a murder or manslaughter charge, but he won't get off scot-free. He's likely to be charged with GBH, but with the circumstances surrounding his father's murder, who knows if he'll serve any of that. But that's up to the courts to decide."

"How did this happen?" Ellen asked. "Why did he stab her?"

"Gavin claims they were harassing him, and he was convinced they were about to attack him. This is probably true based on eye witness reports, but it's not much of a defence. Also, he admits that he had been carrying a knife around for his own protection."

"Protection from what?"

"That, I don't know," Nailer answered her.

"We saw the two officers that arrested Gavin, last night at the Custody Suite," Rob said. "One of them was Karl Rothwell, one of the surviving officers from Operation Major Oak. He's working with…" Rob checked his notes. "DC Amelia Brady."

"I know Amelia," Ellen said. "And Michelle, Karl's girlfriend. I've met them at police parties before and hung out with them."

"Are they close friends of yours?" Rob asked, turning to Ellen.

"No, I wouldn't say so," Ellen answered matter of factly.

"Okay, good." If they had been, it might have been better for her to sit this one out, but he didn't see the need for that in this case. He glanced at Nailer, who nodded in acceptance. Rob looked back at Ellen. "Thanks for being honest."

"Pleasure," Ellen answered.

"Of course, that would be enough of a wrinkle on its own," Nailer continued, "but I have one more curve ball to throw at you. It seems that during Gavin's interview last night, before he knew of this father's murder, Gavin worked himself up into something of a frenzy and ended up saying that his dad was a corrupt police officer. He said he was on the take from the gangs, and he needed to get it out of his system."

"Jesus's holy farts," Tucker exclaimed.

"Does he know about his father now?" Rob asked, curious.

"I believe so," Nailer answered.

"Right, let's go through this. We have Gavin stabbing a girl in Forest Fields, and, during questioning later, he says his dad, a Superintendent, is corrupt. Then later in the night, his father turns up dead, murdered with a single gunshot wound to the head." Rob frowned. "I can't believe these aren't linked, somehow. It's too much of a coincidence."

"My thoughts, too," Nailer agreed. "Although, we have no proof that they are linked. It *could* just be a coincidence."

"I guess, but I doubt it," Rob replied as he thought it through. "Following Gavin's accusation about his dad, who knew he'd said this? Who knew Gavin had accused his dad of corruption?"

"The Duty Solicitor assigned to him. The interviewing officers and their superiors watching in the observation room, and then whoever they told. I also found out last night, before Lee was discovered," Nailer said. "The news spread quickly."

"Of course it did. Probably because of Garrett's history with the EMSOU that blew up on his watch. He was already under suspicion and off work on sick leave for mental issues. I'm not surprised this news spread so quickly." Rob thought back to the night before and the conversation with the interviewing officers. "While we were talking with Karl and Amelia last night, we saw one of the observers march out of the observation room. It was Chief Superintendent Tanner."

"The man who told me," Nailer remarked.

"This could also be related to Operation Major Oak," Nick said. "A gunshot to the head sounds like a gang-style execution to me."

"I agree," Nailer said. "During my research into the Masons, I've found multiple hits that were carried out like this, by enforcers within the firm. There's a high chance this was a gang hit."

"There was that assassination of the Polish Gang leader, Radek, recently," Rob said. "He was shot through the head, too. But there was also a calling card."

"Do you think it's linked?" Nailer asked.

"Word on the street," Tucker cut in, "is that the Masons have denied being involved with that. They're distancing themselves from it."

"That's not surprising," Nick added.

"No, it's not, but they don't usually go to lengths to distance themselves from these things if they did them. Also, the calling card with the hourglass on it, suggests a new player."

"I'm not sure it's linked," Nailer said. "Let's work on the hypothesis that they're separate issues until we know otherwise. If a calling card appears, then we'll take it from there, but right now, we treat this case as its own thing, okay?"

"So, a gang hit?" Nick asked.

"But if that's the case, how does Gavin stabbing someone fit into this?" Guy asked.

"Maybe he found out about his dad?" Rob suggested. "If he knew his dad was working for a dangerous gang, it might cause him to walk around carrying a knife."

"For protection," Ellen added.

"That fits," Nick agreed.

"That still doesn't tell us who killed Lee, though," Nailer said. "We need to find the killer. So, Rob, I want you to head over to the Custody Suite and speak to Gavin. See what he says. We might need to take this stabbing case off of the guys at Central, but we'll see. Ellen, you go with him."

"We need to head there too," Nick said. "We need to continue our interviews with the gang members while we still have them."

"Agreed," Nailer replied. "You and Guy do that. Tucker, I need you to attend the post-mortem of Mr Garrett and start to go through the evidence that's already coming in."

"Sir," Tucker replied.

"Also, Rob, we have Gavin's mum and Lee's wife, Shelley Garrett coming in later this morning," Nailer added. "You can talk to her when you're back."

"Looking forward to it," Rob stated.

10

Running her finger over the porcelain mug, still warm with the half-drunk coffee in it, Scarlett thought about the horrific situation that Ninette found herself in, with this sicko sending her messages.

She'd been over it a thousand times already as she put herself in Ninette's place, and tried to think about the best way for her to deal with it. A yawn gripped her, making her whole body shake. The preoccupation she had with Ninette's nightmare had kept her awake for what felt like ages, tossing and turning, sleeping in fits and starts and never really getting the kind of night's rest that she needed.

She found it bizarre that she'd dealt with some terrible crimes during her time on the force, and while some had certainly given her pause for thought, she'd never had a night like last night. She knew she'd slept a bit, and maybe caught a few hours, she must have, but it honestly felt like she'd had about five minutes of actual proper sleep, and spent the rest of the night feeling annoyed and frustrated and powerless. She felt so angry too and wanted desperately to find this creep and make him feel how he was making her feel.

But that kind of thing was not exactly becoming of an officer of the law. Still, surely there was something she could do. She was a detective, after all. Could she not maybe try and find this guy, hunt him down and…

And what?

What would she do then?

She might have the power of arrest, but there were laws and rules about it, and it must not be abused. If she accessed the Police National Computer to find this Sebastian, and she was found out, her career would be over. She'd be breaking the law, and at the very least, she'd be sacked and maybe reprimanded.

It was one of the few times in her career that she felt utterly helpless and unable to use the powers she had at her fingertips to do what was right and just.

She ran over it again and again, trying to figure out what the best course of action for Ninette was. Obviously, it was to report it, to register the complaint and make sure the authorities knew about it. There was a clear history and there were steps that could be taken.

But she felt like Ninette didn't want to do that. She'd kept it a secret for years and it seemed like she'd only recently decided she wanted to ask for help. Would she want to go to the police and file a report?

She had no idea, apart from a lingering fear that Ninette would say no.

And then what?

She could maybe make a report on Ninette's behalf, but, it would always come back to Ninette herself in the end, and if she just didn't want to engage with the police then, what could she do?

Annoyingly, she found she could sympathise with her friend and the desire she had not to go to the police. The authorities had failed her last time and her rapist had gone free, leaving her high and dry. What promise did she have that it wouldn't happen again, and she'd be made to feel like she was over reacting or being a 'hysterical woman'?

Scarlett sighed. The answer was simple. She had none.

There were no guarantees, no promises, and even in this age of liberation and empowerment for women, there was still so far they had to go.

Scarlett glanced at her watch. They'd be in by now, and maybe have even had their morning briefing. Rob would be off, hunting down leads on this case, trying to find out who killed this Superintendent and bring them to justice.

Part of her felt useless sitting here, doing nothing.

"Good morning," Ninette said as she walked into the kitchen, pulling a hoodie on. "Sleep okay?"

Scarlett went to say yes, that she'd slept fine, and then pulled herself up on it. Why? What would that achieve? She had a moment here, before her friends started to arrive when she could talk to Ninette about it, alone.

"Um, no. Not really."

"Oh? Why? Were you excited about today?"

"No. I um... I was thinking about what you told me about last night, about *him*. About his messages."

"Oh, Scarlett. I should never have told you. I knew you'd get like this. Don't worry about it. You just need to forget it. I will deal with it, okay? He's just a small, scared man, railing at the injustice of the world, that he can't shag any woman he likes and get away with it. Screw him."

"Look, if I'm careful, maybe I can look into him for you? Maybe find out where he is or see what I can find out? I might find something useful."

Ninette stared at her for a long moment, before she sighed deeply, and relented. "Okay, fine. If that makes you happy, then sure. Feel free, and let me know what you find. But please, not this weekend. I just want us all to forget about our troubles and just enjoy ourselves. You especially. This is your special day we're planning, and you've been up all night worrying."

"I know, I just, I couldn't get it out of my head, that's all."

Ninette shook her head. "You're very sweet, Scarlett, but you really need to forget about it for now. Okay? Can you promise me that? Can you try to enjoy this weekend?"

"Yes, yes, sure," Scarlett said, feeling both relieved that she had Ninette's blessing to look into it, but also guilty for letting it ruin her night's rest. She pulled a face at herself. Nothing that endless coffee couldn't sort out!

She'd have preferred a tea, but needs must on a day like today.

"Good, and thank you for thinking of me," Ninette said.

"You're a friend, of course I'm thinking about you. Anyway, thanks, and I promise to try and enjoy myself, okay?"

"Deal."

"Good. So, what would you like to eat or drink?"

They busied themselves about the kitchen, getting their breakfast and catching up on old times and speculating about their friends and what they were up to in their lives until the doorbell finally sounded.

Scarlett rushed to the front door and opened it to find Chris's sister, Lucy, beaming at her.

"Scarlett! Aww, it's great to see you. Come here," she exclaimed and pulled her in for a hug. "How are you? You look tired. Are they working you too hard over at that station?"

"Something like that," she lied. "Come in, come in." She turned to find Ninette in the hall, watching while holding her warm mug of tea in both hands. "Oh, Lucy, this is my university friend, Ninette."

"Call me Anni," Ninette said, and walked forward to shake Lucy's hand. Lucy gave her hand a look, before plunging in for a hug.

"A hand shake? No way," Lucy said.

She pulled away from Ninette, all smiles and boundless energy. "Right then, who's up for a drink? Shall we crack open a bottle of white or something?"

"Don't you think it's a little early?" Scarlett suggested.

"What? No! Not at all. Come on, let's get this party going, shall we?" She issued a woot and danced through to the kitchen.

"Do you remember being like that?" Ninette asked once she was close enough to whisper.

"If I was, I think I need to apologise to a few people."

11

"You're lumbered with me then, for the time being," Ellen said as they neared the Nottingham Custody Suit.

"I know. I'll just have to make do." Rob smiled. "You're no Scarlett, after all."

Ellen laughed. "I know. I'm twice the woman she is."

"How'd you figure that?"

"Common sense." She smirked before returning to a more serious tone. "I bet she was gutted to miss this after going to the crime scene."

"That was the impression I got, but she'd had this planned for a while, with her friend coming to visit. She couldn't exactly postpone it. Not easily, anyway."

"I'm sure we'll be neck deep in it still by Monday."

"Probably. Any thoughts on all this so far?" He shot Ellen an expectant look.

"Um, well, it's all a bit of a coincidence, so I'm leaning towards Gavin's incident or interview being linked to his dad's murder if I'm honest. I have a bad feeling that word got to another corrupt officer somewhere along the chain, who then passed the word onto the gang, who then ordered Lee killed."

"Because Lee was a liability at that point, so they might as well cut ties."

"Exactly," Ellen agreed.

"What about Gavin? Is he a liability now, too?"

Ellen shrugged. "I'm guessing it depends on what he knows. If he doesn't know much, then maybe he'll be fine, and his father's murder will help to keep his mouth shut?"

"Plausible. I guess we'll have to speak to Gavin and see what his deal is."

"I guess so," Ellen agreed. She sighed.

"What's up," Rob asked.

"If this is a gang thing, do you think there's any chance of us finding and arresting Lee's killer?"

"There's always a chance," Rob replied, doing his best to remain confident. He knew what she was getting at, though. Some of these gang members, the leaders especially, seemed almost untouchable, and it was often difficult to even find them, let alone arrest and convict them. Certainly, those higher up the chain were often ghosts, living the high life and keeping the violence at arm's length.

They might give the orders, but they rarely got involved in the dirty work themselves. And when you did finally catch them, their wealth usually afforded them some of the best lawyers money could buy, and that wasn't even touching the corruption angle.

With a grimace, Rob put that particular line of thought to bed. There was no need to get all worked up over this when they didn't know the details yet.

They soon made it to the Custody Suite off Radford Road and parked up inside the security fence. Nick and Guy parked nearby and joined them in walking inside.

"Keep me updated on how you go with these guys," Rob said. "I want to know of any developments."

"Will do," Nick replied. "You know, there is an angle on this we haven't considered. We did just raid and capture a whole load of drugs and guns from a gang that owes allegiance to the Masons. Any one of them could potentially know something that could cause the firm some serious headaches."

"Yeah, I know," Rob agreed. "That occurred to me. Which means Lee's murder could be the gang's retaliation against the police, and Gavin's stabbing and outburst are unrelated."

"Or it's both?" Ellen suggested.

"Yeah, maybe. I think we need to keep an open mind for the time being, though. We've not spoken to any of the old EMSOU team yet or the families of those involved. There could be whole angles to this that we're unaware of. Remember the Clipstone case? That ended up being about anything but the whole gang angle."

"Fair point," Nick conceded as he opened the reception door. "We'll keep you up to date."

"Thanks," Rob said as he made to follow Nick in, only for his teammate to stop just inside the door.

Nick looked back over his shoulder. "Um, good luck, Guv. I think you're going to need it."

"What?" Rob asked as he followed Nick through the tinted glass door to find a detective he recognised standing in reception, smiling.

"Bill," Rob stated, resisting the urge to add an insult to the end. Nailer had warned him that the Professional Standards Unit, the PSU, would be involved, and at the time, Rob had wondered if Bill might show up.

It seemed his powers of precognition were on point today.

"Robert," Bill replied with a somewhat smug grin on his face.

"I'll see you later," Nick said, making his way towards the reception with Guy before heading inside.

Rob watched him go before turning back to Bill. He sighed. "Let me guess, you're going to be working on this too?"

"Congratulations," Bill remarked, his tone laced with sarcasm. "Give the man a prize."

Rob raised an eyebrow at the ridiculous man.

Bill's tone hardened. "The previous members of the East Midlands Special Operations Unit are under active investigation for corruption and malfeasance in the line of duty, and following Gavin's outburst last night, it was deemed necessary that we become an active part of this investigation. The murder inquiry is all yours, of course, but we need to maintain some open channels between our departments for any developments."

"Okay, fine," Rob relented. "But. You'd better not get in my way."

Bill smiled. "Don't worry, I won't. I'll mainly be watching and only step in when I have a question to ask."

Rob wasn't sure he believed that, but he was willing to give Bill the benefit of the doubt and see how this all came together. "Okay, fine."

Bill nodded, and still, he wore that smug, self-righteous smile. "Good. I'm going to enjoy observing you, Rob. Keeping a close eye on you. I think this could be very enlightening."

"Oh, it will," Ellen cut in. "Because finally, you might realise that you're wasting your time harassing Rob."

Bill made a conceding gesture. "Or, it might finally give me the missing piece of the puzzle."

"And that missing piece," Ellen spat, "is that you're a bloody idiot."

"Ellen!" Rob barked. "That's enough."

"Fine." She threw her hands up in the air. "Whatever."

"Good morning, Rob." He turned to see Matilda Greenwood walking through the reception door.

"Oh, morning. Back here again?"

"I'm something of a regular," she said with a smile. "It's good to see you again. Scarlett not with you?"

"No. She's off for the weekend, so I've got Ellen with me today." Rob ignored Bill.

"Pleasure." Matilda shook Ellen's hand.

"Pleasure's all mine," Ellen said, smiling warmly.

Bill groaned. "Shall we head inside?"

He sounded impatient, so Rob let him take the lead and sign in first.

"So, Scarlett's off, is she? Not ill, I hope?"

"No. She's having a weekend with her friends, going bridesmaids dress shopping."

"Bridesmaids dress shopping? Really? You mean…"

"Scarlett's engaged."

"Aaah, I didn't know," Matilda replied. "Well, lucky her. I hope she has a great weekend."

"I'm sure she will," Rob confirmed and smiled back at Matilda, who was shooting him friendly looks and grins. As they moved through reception, they found themselves away from the others for a moment, and Rob had the idea of asking her out for a drink.

Combinations of words flitted through his head as he wondered how to phrase the question, followed by thoughts and fears about what he'd do should she say no.

But then Bill and Ellen walked over, and the moment had gone before he'd had a chance to make his move. He cursed himself and his hesitancy as they walked inside.

The building was new, custom built just a few years before to replace an older site well past its prime. This new building was state-of-the-art and filled with the various innovations and developments that the police had made when it came to detaining suspects and criminals. The ethos of the site was all about breaking the cycle of crime and trying to show those who came here, that there were other options. There were nurses, mental health specialists, as well as drugs and alcohol teams all working around the clock to help everyone who came here.

It was admirable, but some detainees were more amenable to these services than others.

"I'll see you around," Matilda said once they were in, and she set off up the corridor to whatever appointment she had. Rob watched her go, admiring her from afar until he realised that Bill was watching him.

He wasn't lying when he said he'd be observing him, clearly. Rob turned away from the retreating solicitor as a custody officer directed them to a side room where they found DI Karl Rothwell and his partner DC Amelia Brady.

Karl stood, ending the conversation he'd been having with Amelia. "Rob, good to see you. We were told you wanted to speak to Gavin about his dad. Is that right?"

"It is," Rob said. "Thanks for coming to meet us."

"No worries," Karl replied.

"Amelia," Ellen said as she walked into the room. "Good to see you. How's things?"

"Great, thanks," Amelia replied and gave Ellen a quick hug. "And you? How's Chrissy?"

"She's good. Still obsessed with cats."

Amelia laughed. "When are you gonna make an honest woman of her?"

"When I'm good and ready, and not before." Ellen looked over at Karl. "Morning, Karl. Good to see you. Give my regards to Michelle, won't you? I've not seen her in a while."

"Of course," Karl answered. "She's very well. I'm sure she'd like to see you again soon."

"We should arrange something."

"You'll have to fit it in between their date nights," Rob remarked, remembering Karl's comment from the night before. "Did you have a good night?"

"Well, kinda. Until I heard about Lee's murder, anyway. That ruined the night for me."

"I can imagine," Ellen agreed. "Sorry for your loss."

Karl shrugged. "We were friendly, but we weren't that close. He was my boss for a while, but we didn't hang out much."

"Still, it can't have been nice to hear that he'd been murdered," Ellen said.

"Of course not. No one deserves that. I hope you catch whoever did it, and if there's anything I can do to help, please, let me know. It would be good to work with the EMSOU again."

"Me too," Amelia agreed. "Happy to help."

"Well, you can start by updating me on Gavin," Rob replied. "I hear that he's been told about his dad."

"That's right," Karl confirmed. "He was told last night by the custody officers. I think someone passed down the message that he needed to be told. Anyway, we came in this morning to chat, see how he is, and ask him about his allegation of corruption. Which he now denies, saying he was just angry. He says he doesn't want to talk about anything to do with his father anymore. So he's changed his tune completely."

"What about the stabbing?"

"That's cut and dried. Gavin still admits to it. We have good video evidence from the shop's CCTV, and we have several witnesses who all independently corroborate Gavin's story. I'm not sure if the victim will press charges, but we have enough to move forward regardless, so once you've spoken to him, we can charge him."

"And release him?"

"That's what he wants. We've spoken to his mother, and she's keen to have him back."

Rob sighed. "There's a chance, if Lee's murder is linked to Gavin, that he could be in danger."

"Oh?"

"We think the murder was gang-related, and we wonder if it might have something to do with Gavin's outburst."

"Do you have any proof of that?"

"Nothing solid."

"Well..." Karl started.

Rob raised his hands. "I know. We're coming up on our twenty-four hours. We need to charge and release him on bail or apply for an extension."

"Which we're not guaranteed to get," Karl reminded him.

"True. Well, we'll talk to him. I want to get a sense of how he feels about all this. But, at the very least, keep him here for the full twenty-four hours, okay?"

"Alright. We can do that," Karl confirmed. "I'll hold fire for now."

"Thanks. Right then, we'd better go and see him," Rob said.

Leaving Karl and Amelia behind, they were shown through to an interview room, where Rob took one of the two seats. He turned to offer the other to Ellen, only for Bill to cut in and take it.

"No, no, you have it," Ellen remarked. "I didn't want to sit down, anyway."

"Good," Bill said. Behind him, Ellen rolled her eyes and gave him the finger.

Rob smirked, but hid it from Bill.

"What do we do if Gavin's going back on what he said about his dad's corruption?" Ellen asked. "I mean, it makes sense that he'd be angry and upset after stabbing the girl. People do say silly things when they're stressed."

Rob shrugged. "Bill, any thoughts?"

Bill gave Rob side-eye and then sighed in exasperation. "I'll reserve judgement until…"

"That'll be a first," Ellen muttered. Rob pressed his lips together, trying to stifle the smile that threatened to break out on his face.

Bill pulled a face. "As I was saying, I need to speak to him and get a sense of who he is. But, there were questions about Superintendent Garrett and his possible corruption following Operation Major Oak. It is possible that Gavin found out something and blurted it out while under pressure from DI Rothwell's questions."

"And DC Brady's questions," Ellen added.

"Indeed," Bill agreed, reluctantly, it seemed.

"That would be my first guess too," Rob agreed, "but it's still early days, and we have a lot of people to talk to, so we need to take this with a pinch of salt."

The door opened, and an officer walked Gavin in, followed by a duty solicitor that Rob didn't know. Shame it wasn't Matilda, he mused to himself as the officer stepped out.

Gavin eyed them as he walked around the table, looking nervous. The nineteen-year-old appeared ill as he stared at them with bloodshot eyes, sporting dark rings beneath them.

He'd found out his dad had been murdered, so he probably didn't get much sleep last night, and it showed. But there was more to it than that. He seemed hesitant and perhaps unsure of what was going on as his eyes flicked back and forth. Was he scared?

At his solicitor's urging, Gavin took a seat opposite and fixed his gaze on the table.

"Gavin Garrett," Rob began. "I'm Inspector Loxley. This is Inspector Rainault and Constable Dale. I know you've been through a lot over the last few hours, so I won't keep you long. I just have a few questions."

Rob paused to see if Gavin would react, but he said nothing and just stared at the table.

Rob continued, "I know you've been made aware of the tragic murder of your father last night. So, let me begin by offering my condolences. I'm sorry for your loss and that it happened while you were in here. But circumstances can't be helped, and all we can do now is to get this resolved nice and quick, so you can go home to your family."

Rob paused again and waited to see if Gavin would react. After a moment, he gave a quick nod but nothing else.

"Okay, then I mainly want to ask about the statement you made last night. You claimed that your dad, Superintendent Lee Garrett, was working for a criminal gang while he was a police officer. You said he was corrupt and that we needed to know. Do you still stand by that claim?"

"No," he answered quickly.

"Why not?"

"Because it's not true," he answered, still staring at the table. "I was lying."

"Why? Why were you lying?"

"Because I was…upset. I wanted to get him into trouble."

Well, you certainly did that.

"That's not it," Bill jumped in. "What you said last night wasn't a lie. You were telling the truth. But *this*, now, *this* is a lie. You're lying to us, Gavin. You're wasting police time. Do you know that? Do you understand what that means? It means you're in trouble. Deep trouble."

"I'm sorry. I'm telling the truth now. I mean it. I'm not lying."

"How do we know? Huh? How?"

"I... I don't know."

Rob raised his hand as Bill went to launch into another tirade. He stopped himself, but Rob could see the boiling rage inside him. "Gavin. My colleague is right that wasting police time is not a good idea, but we also understand and sympathise with you that this is a difficult time. So I think we can forgo any kind of formal charge for wasting time." Rob gave Bill a scowl as he spoke, and Bill backed down, sitting back in his chair. "Tell me about the girl you stabbed."

"Huh? Oh. Yeah. I didn't mean to. I was just scared. They scared me, and I thought they were going to attack me or something. I had to defend myself."

"With a knife?" Rob pressed.

"The streets are dangerous. I need to be able to protect myself. That's why I had a knife."

"And that's also why you're in here," Rob said, making sure to sound pedantic.

"I know, and I'm sorry. I've confessed. I know what I did was wrong, and I'm happy to face the consequences. I also know it's wrong to lie to you, but that's what I did when I said my dad was...doing those things. It was wrong, and I'm sorry."

"No," Bill snapped. "What's wrong is that you're lying to us now. That's what—"

"Bill, stop," Rob hissed. "I think that's enough. We're done here. Thank you, Gavin."

Bill collapsed angrily into this chair, his arms folded, while Gavin was escorted from the room by an officer. Once he was gone, Bill jumped up.

"He's lying," Bill bellowed. "Can't you see it? It's blatant. The little shit."

"You don't know that, and the fact that he's happily owning up to the stabbing and accepting responsibility will stand him in good stead."

"So you think he's telling the truth now?"

"I didn't say that, and honestly, I'm not sure. It's odd. It's such a specific thing to say and then retract..."

"Unless he's telling the truth," Ellen said. "Could he have told those lies because he's angry with his dad over something? But once he found out his dad had been killed, he realised what he'd done and felt guilty, so he retracted it?"

"So, he was worried that this might stain his dad's reputation?" Rob asked her.

"That's bullshit," Bill spat. "But then, you're quite familiar with that."

Rob held his tongue.

"Yeah," Ellen continued, ignoring Bill's comment. "It fits."

"So, what about his dad?" Rob asked.

"I don't know. Because if he was lying, then maybe he didn't know if his dad was corrupt or not. Maybe he was, and he stumbled onto this, accidentally setting off a sequence of events he had no control over. Maybe this really is just a coincidence?"

"Hmm," Rob mused as he thought through what they knew and the conclusions they'd come to so far. "We still don't know enough to make these leaps or connections."

"That's crap," Bill snarled. "I don't believe it. He knew his dad was up to no good, and he was speaking the truth that first time. Now he's in deep, and he's trying to save his own skin."

"Everyone's entitled to their opinion," Rob said and stood up.

"Unfortunately, yes, they are, even when they're wrong." Bill led them out of the room and down the corridor. "I'll be looking into this allegation of corruption, and you can expect to see me in the EMSOU offices soon." Bill grinned, but it was the smile of a predator taunting his prey. "I'm going to enjoy working closely with you and your team, Rob. Maybe I can take down two bent coppers in one go."

"Feel free to try," Rob remarked, staying close to Ellen and letting Bill march off ahead.

Bill grunted and strode off, leaving them behind. Rob watched him go, getting the distinct feeling he'd be seeing Bill again today. He took a moment to take a breath before refocusing on the case at hand.

"I'm going to ignore Bill for the time being," Rob remarked.

"If only we could ignore him entirely," Ellen added.

"Chance would be a fine thing. Anyway, I don't know if you noticed, but Gavin looked dead tired to me, and nervous."

"I noticed," Ellen said.

"Something's changed for Gavin. Outside of his father being killed, I mean."

"But what?"

12

Bill strode into Sherwood Lodge, the Nottinghamshire Police Headquarters, feeling good about himself and the day ahead, and made his way to the PSU office.

His first interaction with Rob on this new case had gone well. Or as well as could be expected, anyway. They made the usual pithy comments, Rob and his partner Ellen. He frowned. Wasn't Rob usually paired up with that other blonde woman, Scarlett? He should probably find out where she was. He wondered if there'd been some kind of falling out or something, meaning there might be some kind of leverage there.

He'd need to look into it.

But their silly comments didn't bother him. He knew he was fighting the good fight, working to keep the force clean and corruption free. If only people would sit up and notice the one oversight they'd made! Rob bloody Loxley, who came from a family of criminals!

Was he the only one to see the obvious issues with having him be part of the police? They needed to be beyond reproach and trusted by the population they served, otherwise, the whole system would fall apart.

But if he had to do this alone, without any backup, then so be it. He'd prove everyone wrong if it was the last thing he did.

Suddenly aware of how worked up he was, Bill took a moment to clear his head and focus on his breathing. He needed a clear head if he was going to talk to his boss.

As he continued his walk towards the PSU office, he thought back to the interview with Gavin Garrett, and how things had taken a turn. He'd been hopeful that the boy might provide them with some valuable info that could break open the Operation Major Oak investigation and shed some light on what happened. But it seemed as though Gavin, in his infinite wisdom, had chosen to clam up and claim he was spouting nonsense.

But he knew better than to believe Gavin's obvious lies. The boy wasn't coming down off of some rage-induced fantasy to smear his father, he wasn't making stuff up in the heat of the moment. He'd been telling the truth. But now, something had changed.

Something about his father's murder was scaring Gavin silly, causing him to change his story, meaning he was wasting their time. Bill had a good mind to charge him for it, but he knew he'd likely have a fight with Rob on his hands, and he really did need some kind of proof before he went sticking his oar in.

Honestly, though, he didn't care what happened to Gavin. Rob was the real prize, and this chance to get close to him and his unit was not one he was going to waste.

He was close to something. He knew it. After Vincent Kane's revelation, he knew he was on the right track. He just needed to prove it.

Once inside the PSU offices, Bill stalked over to his PC to check his messages but only got partway there before his DCI, Paige Clements, stuck her head out her office door. "Bill?" She waved him over.

A little annoyed that he'd not even managed to check his messages and emails, Bill walked across the room and into her office. "Guv," he said, closing the door behind him.

Paige, a woman in her fifties who reminded him of a former girlfriend's mother, retook her seat behind her desk and got comfortable. She waved at the chairs opposite, offering them to him. "Take a seat."

"Thanks," he said, and sat.

Paige took a moment to peer at him, as if she were reading his aura or something, weighing him up, before she spoke. "How'd it go?"

"Fine. The kid's lying and DI Loxley is letting him get away with it, but if I keep close, I might just find what I'm looking for. Maybe I'll be able to catch two for the price of one? By the way, this is a genius idea, embedding me within the

EMSOU to get a better look at how they operate, so I can keep a close eye on Lox—"

"Bill," Paige interrupted him. Her voice was calm if not a bit demeaning. "You're there to keep a close eye on Gavin and see if there's anything to add to the investigation into Major Oak. Remember that. You're not there for Loxley."

Bill scoffed. She could have chosen any other PSU officers to do this. But no, she chose him, and he already had his hands full with other case work. There was only one reason why she would do that "That's not why you chose me. You asked me because of Loxley, and you know it."

"I'm *not* sure I do."

"I beg to differ."

"Feel free, Bill. But the fact remains that we have an ongoing investigation into the former EMSOU team, and this is a significant new development in that case. Don't screw this up for me."

Bill blew air threw his lips in exasperation at her patronising tone. He took a long breath to calm his nerves. It wouldn't do him any good to return the favour. He needed to be the grown-up in this exchange. "I won't. I'm on it, don't worry. But I *will* be looking into Loxley too."

Paige sighed. "I know you will, and I know you think you have a breakthrough after what Kane told you about him meeting one of his brothers, but that's circumstantial evidence at best, heard through a third party, without hard proof. A third party, by the way, who has a certain reputation when it comes to the police and his meddling. I shouldn't need to remind you of that."

"I know what I'm doing," Bill replied, doing his best to keep calm.

"I hope so, because it sounds like you're skating pretty close to the line on this, Bill. Don't make me regret this."

"You won't. All I need is some solid evidence. That's it. I'm so close, guv. So close. I can almost touch it. Just one slip-up. That's all it'll take, and I'll have him."

"Bill, please. Focus on Lee and the allegations that Gavin levelled against his dad. That's all. Everything else is secondary. I'm warning you, Bill. Don't screw this up."

Bill could hear the note of warning that his DCI was levelling at him and nodded. She was right. He needed to be careful. He hadn't worked on this for all this time, only to have it fall flat because he'd taken some risks or shortcuts. He needed to do this right. "Yeah, sure."

"Good on yeh. Alright, off you go. And make sure to report back with any developments."

***

Paige watched him go, grumbling to himself as he left her office and returned to his desk.

Was she doing the right thing, giving this to him, of all people? He wasn't the most trustworthy officer on her team, but what he did have, was an obsession that she could use to her advantage. He had a personal investment in the EMSOU in the shape of Rob Loxley.

And, with the lack of personnel that her—and all—departments were dealing with, he was the best of the bunch.

Most of the time, Bill's obsession was something of a liability, but there were a few occasions when it came in useful, and she hoped this was one of them.

13

"Shelley Garrett?" Rob asked as he walked into the side room back at the Lodge.

Inside, a middle-aged couple were sitting on one of the sofas, holding hands. The man leaned in to his partner, talking quietly and calmly to her as she sniffed and dabbed at her eyes with the tissue she held.

As Rob and Ellen walked in, they both looked up.

"Yes?" the woman asked, getting to her feet. The man followed suit.

"Hello," Rob said and stepped inside, letting Ellen follow him in before he closed the door. "I'm Detective Inspector Loxley, and this is Detective Constable Dale. We appreciate you coming in today. I know this must be a difficult time for you."

"It's come as something of a shock," Shelley confirmed with another sniff.

"Hi, I'm Louis Jefferson, Shelley's partner," the man said, offering his hand. Rob shook it.

"Is Gavin okay?" Shelley asked.

"He's fine. He's at the Custody Suite. He'll be well looked after."

"When will you let him go?" Shelley pressed.

"After we've charged him, which will be later today. There's a process with these things which needs to be followed. I know you're eager to see him but—"

"Can I?" Shelley cut in.

Rob grimaced. "I'll see what I can do. I should be able to get you a phone call, at least."

"That would be good, thank you." She shook her head. "I can't believe he's done this. It's not like him at all."

Rob noticed the man's expression, which seemed to suggest otherwise.

"Are you sure?" Rob pressed. "Has he been acting strangely at all recently?"

Louis grunted and rolled his eyes.

Shelley sighed. "This year, it's been...well, tough."

"In what way?" Rob asked and moved to another sofa. Ellen joined him. "Please, sit."

They did as he asked. "Well, it all started going wrong when Lee and I split up," Shelley admitted. "Probably a bit before then, if I'm honest. When we were arguing, probably. Then, after we separated, Gavin became angry and reclusive. He sided with his dad more than me, because I was the one who left."

"And, why did you leave? If you don't mind me asking?"

"No, no. It's fine." She took a breath before diving in. "It was his job... Your job. It's so full on, we just never had any time together. He'd be working all hours, getting home late and wouldn't discuss his day. He'd be angry or grumpy, and he'd always refuse to talk about it. It was hellish, and in the end, I had enough. I'd reconnected with Louis online too, and that made me see what I could have."

"We were together at school for a while before Shelley met Lee, but separated."

"I was lonely, at home, waiting for Lee to get back from work, only for him to snap at me and go to bed without talking to me. I needed companionship. I needed someone to talk to, and Louis became that person for me. And over time, I fell in love again."

"I got a second chance," Louis said, looking more than a little smug.

"But Gavin took this badly," Ellen stated.

"Very. I tried to make him see things from my point of view, but he only saw betrayal. I was stabbing his dad in the back. I couldn't give up though. I wasn't going to lose my son over this. It's taken all year to get to a stage where he'll stay with us for a few nights, and now this happens. I..." She sighed.

"So, your relationship with Gavin has been improving?"

"It has," she answered. "We get along okay now, and Gavin's less angry than he was. He's had relapses in the past when things happen to set him back, but he's not had one for a while."

"What about his relationship with his dad?" Rob asked.

"That's had its troubles," Shelley answered. "He sided with him initially, but Lee eventually got a younger girlfriend, and that caused a few issues. We saw Gavin more then. But I think things with Lee and Justine have been improving too. Just the other day, he said how much fun he had with them last weekend. It seemed like things were going well for him. He came to mine, as planned, but when he asked to go and stay at his dad's, Lee said that Gavin had to wait, and he never says that. Lee said that he and Justine had some things to work on, and he needed some time. I think that affected him more than he let on."

"Things to work on?" Rob asked, curious.

"I have no idea," Shelley replied. "Lee's relationship with Justine has been…" She looked like she was choosing her words carefully. "Tumultuous, as far as I know, but I think they were getting on better more recently so, I don't know."

"Okay," Rob said. "If Gavin was upset that he hadn't seen his dad, I suppose that goes someway to explaining why he lashed out. Do you know why he was carrying a knife around with him?"

Shelley shook her head, exasperated. "No. I had no idea he'd started doing that again."

"This wasn't his first time?"

"Nope. He went through a phase of doing it months ago, but we caught him and convinced him it was a bad idea."

"Or so we thought," Louis added.

"Yeah," Shelley agreed.

"Why did he start carrying one, to begin with?" Ellen asked.

"We never really found out," Shelley replied. "It was after one of his relapses, probably the worst one since our break up. He…" Shelley paused and thought back. "Yeah, it was about seven or eight months ago, I think. He suddenly started staying at ours more and refused to see his dad for a couple of weeks. Lee convinced him to go back eventually, but it took a while. We tried talking to him, trying to find out what had happened, but we never really got to the bottom of it, and Lee said he had no idea, either. Gavin just locked himself in his room for days, and when he went out after that, we noticed some kitchen knives had gone missing. Once we realised what he was doing, we had a chat and kept a closer eye on him, and it seemed to have stopped."

"Was he being bullied maybe?" Ellen asked. "Was he attacked?"

"I honestly don't know," Shelley answered.

Rob said, "The weapon he used to stab the girl wasn't a kitchen knife. It was a flick knife."

"They're illegal, aren't they?" Louis asked.

"They are. But they still circulate, and you can buy them if you know where to look. The internet being the obvious place."

Shelley sniffed back some tears. "Then, he must have bought it after we stopped him carrying a knife. Oh god," Shelley exclaimed, unable to hold off the sob any longer. She buried her head in her hands.

"I'm sorry," Rob said.

Lifting her head, Shelley wiped her eyes and blew her nose. "I just don't understand. He's a good kid. He doesn't deserve to be locked up, and I'm sure he was acting out of fear and self-preservation when he stabbed that girl."

"I sympathise, I do. And I think you're probably right," Rob replied. "But, it's for the courts to decide, not us. What I will say is that the court will take everything into account, including the death of his father, how he stayed to help the girl and that he admitted his guilt. If he's lucky, he might not even see jail time. But I can't promise that."

"I know," Shelley said, resigned to whatever fate had in store for them.

"I'd like to ask you about Lee if that's okay?" Rob pressed.

"Of course."

"You don't know why he would be going all the way up to Clumber Park at that time of night, do you?"

"Sorry, no. I've got no idea," she answered. "He never did that when we were together."

"You're sure?"

"Absolutely. Do you know who…shot him?"

"Not yet. But we're following up on leads. We'll find them." Rob paused as he considered his words. "During the first interview, on the night of the attack, Gavin claimed that his dad was working for a gang. He said that Lee was corrupt and that he needed to tell us. But the following day, after he found out about his father's murder, he retracted that statement, saying he was just angry and upset with his dad. Do you know anything about this?"

Shelley frowned in thought before answering "Well, Gavin was upset with his dad, I know that. He was angry that Lee didn't want to see him. He'd get off the phone in a mood and start slamming doors and snapping at us. It was all a little over the top, but he's been through a lot this past year."

"And the corruption that Gavin mentioned?"

"I don't know the details," Shelley replied. "Certainly, there wasn't any talk of that before we split up. It seemed to appear after. All I can say is that I have heard rumours. As to their authenticity, I don't know. But I'd suggest that you speak with Gemma Flint. She's more up on this than I am. I know her from the police socials I went to with Lee. She's been a good friend, and I've hated seeing her lose her job.

She's a straight arrow, as good as they come. She wouldn't be on the take from some scummy gang. I think it's shameful how your lot pushed her out."

"You talking about the former DCI, Gemma Flint, who worked on the same unit as Lee?"

"That's her," Shelley confirmed. "She might be able to help. She believes she's a victim of police corruption and was pushed out of the job."

Rob smiled in appreciation. "That's very helpful. Thank you for trusting me."

"Mmm," she muttered. "I'll admit, after everything that happened, I'm not the biggest fan of the police. But I think you might be one of the good 'uns."

14

Nick led the way into the empty interview room and offered a seat to Guy. "Do you think he'll go for it?"

"He'd be an idiot not to, wouldn't he?" Guy answered. "He seemed nervous and worried about being charged when we spoke to him yesterday, so I think we've got a good chance of getting through to him."

Nick nodded in agreement. "Yeah, hopefully." He settled into the chair beside his colleague while they waited for Ambrose to show up. He gave Guy a look, eyeing his shock of light brown hair and keen eyes. He'd not met him before joining the unit and had yet to really talk to him or find out more about his background. All he knew was that Nailer had invited him to join the unit.

Figuring they had a few minutes to kill, he decided to dive in.

"So, how did you get started in the force?"

"Hmm? Me? I applied, like everyone else." He smiled and seemed to think for a moment. "I had an uncle… Well, not a real uncle, just a family friend, really, who always wanted to be an officer. He loved the police and watched cop shows and stuff, but he couldn't get past the application procedure. He kept getting rejected. Health reasons, I think. Anyway, he was always around when I was young, and I think my interest in joining came from there. At least, I *think* that's where it came from. Anyway, he was thrilled when I got in. I was only a PCSO to begin with before I moved up to being a full PC and then applied to join CID. It's a fairly standard path, I think. No fast-tracking here."

"No, me neither," Nick said. "I used to be in the Army, but once I finished my tour and passed out, I needed something to fill the void, you know? The police seemed like the best option."

"And then you applied to join CID?"

"Heh. Well, it wasn't actually my first choice. I had planned to go into firearms, but my Sergeant suggested I join CID. He suggested I had the right kind of mind for it."

"And, do you?"

"Dunno. I'm not sure what that means. But I do enjoy my job. I've done my firearms training too, so I've got that, and I keep it up to date, but yeah, I love the investigation aspect too."

"Then you made the right choice."

"I think so. I was assigned to Loxley when I joined CID, and got to know Nailer and the others from there."

"Cool. I know Nailer from working on a couple of cases together as a PC and then DC. I didn't expect him to ask me to join the EMSOU, but, here I am."

"Cool," Nick nodded. "So, are you from Nottingham?"

"Not the city. I grew up in Retford, actually."

"Oh. Same as Rob?"

"Is that where he's from?"

"Yeah. You don't know his family, do you?"

Guy smiled. "The Masons? No. Not personally. I have heard of them, though, and that's about as close as I want to get."

"I don't blame you," Nick agreed. "If half the stories I've heard about that family are true, then frankly, Rob's lucky to get out of there."

"That bad?"

"Oh, yeah. You don't want to get on the wrong side of them, that's for sure."

"I'll keep that in mind," Guy said as the door to the room opened, and a custody officer brought in Ambrose Gordon. Nick watched as he was guided around the table and told where to sit. He seemed a little calmer today, although he didn't look very impressed to be speaking to them again. Once Ambrose was settled, he glanced across the table.

"Do I need my lawyer?"

"Hopefully not," Nick replied, wondering if he'd insist on his duty solicitor being in the room, delaying this further.

"Okay," he answered hesitantly. He seemed unsure but didn't protest.

"How was your night?" Nick began.

"Shit," Ambrose answered.

Nick nodded. "Yeah, those beds are not comfortable. I'm sorry you had to find out about them."

Ambrose grunted.

"I take it you're not very happy to be here, right?" He needed to start gently and lead him slowly along the path to where he needed him.

Ambrose shrugged. "I guess."

"That's understandable. I get it. This is your first arrest, and it's a daunting experience. You were probably scared and worried about what it might mean or what the consequences of it might be, right? Was there any way back from here? Was this the life you'd chosen, or wanted? I get it. It's huge."

The kid grunted again, his eyes wandering over them and the room, as if searching for a way out.

"Are you concerned?" Nick pressed.

Ambrose sighed, closed his eyes and took a moment to himself before looking up and answering. "Dunno... Maybe..."

"Well, let me tell you where you are and the choice you have before you, because the truth is, it's not too late. You've not ruined your life. Not yet, at least. But you do need to be careful. This is a long and slippery path you've started down, and if you're not careful, you might suddenly find yourself further along it than you thought."

"Alright."

Nick gave him an appraising look. He seemed to be listening and taking in what he was saying, which was a good start. "The people you're spending time with, the likes of Dodders, Lev, and K, these are people we've had in here before. This isn't their first time, and I very much doubt it will be their last. They're much further down that path than you, making it much harder for them to climb out. They're in bed with some very dangerous people. People who commit murder as a regular part of their business. And yeah, sure, you might think I'm blowing it out of all proportion, but I can show you proof. I can tell you who we believe Dodders works for and the kind of men these guys are. I don't think you'll like them very much."

Ambrose stared at him, listening to everything Nick was saying.

"But hey, look, the choice is yours, really," Nick continued. "I can't make these decisions for you, but what I can tell you is that there are smart choices and, well, shall we say less smart choices? There are things we can offer you, too. Obviously, if you just want out, you can cut ties and such, and we might be able to help you. But maybe you can't do that, not if they know where you live."

"And maybe I do nothing and see what happens. I might be fine."

"That's a risk you can take, sure. But that was an awful lot of drugs and drug money we found in that room, so if Dodders is going down for it, I think you'll go down for it too."

"I didn't..."

Nick shook his head. "The jury will see that mound of drugs and extrapolate all the lives it would have ruined. All around the world, people die because of this stuff all the time. That money wasn't just drugs money. It was blood money. So, believe me when I tell you that if you let this play out without considering other options, then I can't protect you. You'll be at the mercy of the jury and whether they think you're guilty or not. I don't know if they'll care that this is your first arrest or not. Maybe they will, or maybe they won't. Who can say? There are other options, of course..." Nick paused, pretending to debate something internally. "But I can see you're already decided, right? No. There's no need to go into those. You're not interested in a deal."

"No, I mean yes, but..."

"No, no, it's fine. I won't waste your time." Nick went to get up, and Guy started to follow.

"Wait!"

Nick froze as he looked over at Ambrose. "What? Do you want to hear some other options?"

"Yeah."

"Okay then. Am I right in assuming that Dodders..." Nick sighed. "Do I have to use that nickname? His name's Cedric. Did you know that?"

Ambrose smirked.

"I know. Pretty goofy name for a gang leader, right?"

Ambrose shrugged, still refusing to say anything bad about the infamous Dodders.

"Anyway, do they know where you live? Who your family are?"

"Yeah," Ambrose replied.

"That makes it tough to leave, when they can just turn up on your doorstep."

"I guess."

Nick nodded. "No. I know it does, so that would mean full protective custody, a new identity and a new life. But for that, you're going to have to cooperate fully, hold nothing back, and you're going to need to know something good. Something useful."

The kid grunted. "I'm not sure I want to do that..."

"That's fine, I get it. That option's no good for you and too much of a risk. Fine. So, how about this? How about we let you go? We'll release you without charge, and probably one of the others too, like K, and all we ask in return is that you send us anything you find out. Anything useful, such as identities, locations, and activities. Anything that could lead to an arrest, and anything you can find out about Cedric's superiors. Any intel about the Mason gang would be great, and in return, we'll pay you for that info. The better the info, the better the money. How does that sound?"

Ambrose frowned in thought and then smiled.

15

Making their way back up to the EMSOU office, with Ellen close behind, Rob found himself dreading walking through the door. Would Bill be there already, waiting for him, ready to doggedly follow him about for the day, undermining him and upsetting people?

It seemed there was little he could do about it. The PSU had a vested interest in the case, after all. He'd need to bite his tongue and do his best to get along with Bill, even though the so-called 'Sheriff' was working hard to at least ruin his career and, at worst, get him arrested.

And all the while, he needed to somehow untangle this latest case and find out who killed Lee Garrett. He had no idea if he'd be able to manage it and worried that the answer would be a hitman for a gang. But if that was the case, then this might be another murder without an arrest. Worse still, he worried that if it was a gang thing, was it the Masons again? He desperately hoped not.

But, thankfully, they'd managed to interview Shelley without Bill there. That was something, at least. The idea of Bill being upset because they'd completed the interview without him made Rob smile.

"We need to speak with this former DCI," Ellen said conversationally as they approached their office.

"Gemma Flint," Rob remarked, remembering the DCI's name. "That we do. I want to see if Tucker's heard anything new from the other aspects of the case, as well."

"Here's hoping," Ellen agreed. "We could do with a breakthrough."

Rob reached the door to the EMSOU office and slowed as he stepped inside. He was pleased to see that the room was mercifully free of Bill's presence but was under no illusion that this would last. Bill would be here shortly once he'd finished reporting in and would no doubt make his presence felt.

As Rob crossed the room, making for his desk, his phone rang. Dropping his stuff on the chair, he pulled out his mobile and noted the caller ID. It was Nick.

"Nick. You alright?"

"Aye. Just a quick call. We thought you should know that we've managed to convince Ambrose Gordon to become an informant."

"Oh, well done. What's your next step?"

"We'll let him go without charge, him and the girl, Carmela. But we'll need to charge Cedric and Cleveland and hand it off to the CPS. So, we'll be busy for a while yet."

"Okay, good work and good luck with that paperwork. You have my sympathies."

Nick chuckled. "Thanks." He hung up.

He looked up to find Tucker and Ellen walking towards his desk.

"Aye up," Tucker said. "I hear the damned Sheriff joined you during Gavin's interview."

"Yeah, he did," Rob confirmed. "Looks like the PSU saw fit to send him as the liaison for this case."

"Because of the investigation into the former EMSOU officers?"

"Yep," Rob answered. "He'll probably be here any moment."

"Smug bastard."

Rob smiled. "You're not the one he's got it in for."

"True." Tucker shrugged. "But he's gonna cause all of us trouble, the little shit. He's a nightmare."

"I know," Rob agreed, enjoying Tucker's potty mouth.

"You should have seen him in the interview with Gavin," Ellen added. "He's got no idea at all, and the way he speaks to women… Christ on a bike."

"This'll be fun then," Tucker said.

"I need you two to keep an eye on him," Rob said. "If you think he's causing trouble, then do what you can to rein him in, okay?"

"Will do," Ellen confirmed.

"I'll take great fucking pleasure in it," Tucker agreed. "And did you get anything out of Gavin?"

Rob sighed. "He's a bit of an enigma, to be honest. On the one hand, he's honest and open about how he stabbed the girl. He admits it and is happy to accept the consequences of his actions."

"He regrets it too," Ellen added.

"You think he does?" Rob asked.

"I do. I don't think he's faking it at all. He regrets it."

"Hmm," Rob mused as he thought back to Gavin's demeanour during the interview and found he couldn't disagree with Ellen. Gavin did seem genuinely remorseful for his actions. "I think that's fair. So, he admits his actions there and regrets them, but he flat-out denies that he was telling the truth about his dad. He claims that he was upset and just trying to cause trouble. So now he says his dad wasn't corrupt and that he was lying about it."

"And what do you think?"

"Honestly?" Rob asked, but he didn't wait for an answer. "I'm not sure. I don't have that feeling of complete truthfulness I got from him when he was admitting to the stabbing. I think he was trying to cover his tracks. As for the reason why he'd do that, I suppose there could be several, based on both his and Shelley's interviews. His mother couldn't provide any details, but she noted that during the past year, there were times when Gavin's behaviour deteriorated after he'd stayed at his dad's. He'd become moody and withdrawn, easy to anger, and would just shut himself away. He'd also taken to stealing kitchen knives and carrying them around until they caught and stopped him, or so they thought. She mentioned a time early on after she separated from Lee when Gavin came to hers and refused to see his dad for a few weeks. Lee had to lure Gavin back. But, she also said they were getting on much better recently, until this last week."

"What happened last week?" asked a male voice.

Rob turned to see Bill approaching. He sighed and ground his teeth for a moment, annoyed that he'd finally appeared. But he did need to share this with Bill too. "Shelley, Lee's wife. We've just spoken to her, and she said Gavin had been getting on well with Lee and his girlfriend, Justine, recently, until this week, when Lee refused to allow Gavin over, saying he and Justine had something to sort out. It seems to have hit him hard."

"And you spoke to Shelley without me?" Bill asked accusingly.

"You weren't around, and we needed to crack on," Ellen replied.

"Did you now," Bill said, a note of disgust in his voice. "How convenient."

"That's enough," Rob snapped. "Time is of the essence on every case, so we're not hanging around waiting for you, Bill. Deal with it."

"Why did this recent rejection hit Gavin hard?" Tucker asked, changing the subject.

"Because of his history," Rob explained. "He's the child of a broken family."

"Yep," Ellen agreed. "He saw his dad getting on well with Justine, and now they're apparently having to take time to themselves to sort something out. It's not what he wants to hear when he's just getting to like Justine."

"Was that all you got out of this interview?" Bill asked in a mocking tone.

"Luckily, no. Shelley is also good friends with the former EMSOU's DCI, Gemma Flint, who took early retirement. She suggested we talk to her about this corruption."

"Did she," Bill stated. "The wife... no, *former* wife of a Superintendent, suspected of corruption, suggested we talk to her friend, a former DCI accused of corruption, about corruption?" Bill snorted. "I'm sure this will be fruitful. Next, you'll be telling me you're bringing Karl and Amelia into the EMSOU."

"Who?" Tucker asked.

"DI Karl Rothwell and DC Amelia Brady," Rob explained. "They're the ones who took Gavin's stabbing case. Karl is also a former member of the EMSOU under Lee Garrett."

"We're keeping it close to home then, I see," Tucker commented.

"That case is basically closed at this point," Rob replied. "Gavin's admitted to it, so it's just dealing with the paperwork and handing it off to the CPS. Plus, I'd rather keep Karl close but busy. He's a suspect, just like the rest of the former EMSOU."

"I guess we'll be talking to them too?" Tucker asked.

"We will," Rob confirmed. "We need to talk to DCI Gemma Flint and Justine Palmer first, and then we'll catch up with DC McKay and former DC Bowman as well."

Tucker grimaced. "All this talk of who's corrupt and who isn't, It feels like we're deviating from the main case. We need to figure out who killed Lee Garrett."

"We need to do both," Bill snapped.

Rob raised a hand, calling for calm. "We do, you're right, and that is my focus. I have a feeling that Lee's murder is closely linked to the corruption within the EMSOU. So I want to pursue both because it might be that if we can narrow down who was a bent copper, then we might also figure out who the killer is."

"Do you think the killer is a police officer?" Ellen asked.

"I've got no idea at this point," Rob replied. "And I'm loath to get drawn on this too early."

"It looks like a gang hit from the photos I've seen," Tucker stated. "But, I suppose that doesn't mean the killer isn't an officer. Any thoughts on a motive?"

"Other than Gavin's outburst, all we have is speculation, so no," Rob answered. "But if Gavin's accusation of corruption was the catalyst, then we have a corruption issue anyway because otherwise, how would that information get out to the gangs?"

"Oh, we have a corruption issue, all right," Bill commented, his voice filled with venom.

Rob ignored him. "If Gavin was the cause, then someone passed that info to people who shouldn't know."

"True," Tucker answered. "So, who knew?"

"Quite a lot of people, by the looks of things," Rob confirmed. "But we need to keep our minds open and look at this from all angles. For all we know, this has nothing to do with anyone being actually corrupt. Maybe Gemma killed Lee because she was angry that his accusations against her led to her losing her job. It could be a simple act of revenge, and we're over here trying to figure out which officers are corrupt."

"Good point," Tucker relented.

"That's bull crap," Bill muttered. "There's definitely corruption at work on this. It's rife, and I can just smell it." He turned to Rob. "There's definitely a whiff of something."

Rob did his best to ignore the jibes. He gritted his teeth in annoyance and pushed Bill's prejudice to one side. "We need to focus on next steps," he hissed.

Bill spoke up, "You and I should go and speak to this Gemma Flint, see what she's got to say for herself."

Surprisingly, Rob found that he agreed with him. They needed to interview her, and he didn't want to inflict Bill on anyone else. He was obnoxious, so Rob wanted to keep him close. Keep an eye on him. Plus, he could see Bill kicking up a stink if he assigned him to someone else.

"I agree. We'll go and visit Gemma," Rob said before turning to Ellen, "and I want you and Tucker to pay a visit to Justine for me. I want to know her side of the story, too."

"Will do, guv," Ellen confirmed.

"Excellent. Anything else for me before we set off?" Rob asked.

"Actually, yes," Tucker stated. "SOCO got in touch. They've apparently found a bullet casing at the murder scene. Seems like the murderer wasn't careful enough and left behind a clue. That said, we don't have a gun or a bullet yet, so it's of limited use until we find some more material evidence."

"Alright, that's good. A positive development," Rob confirmed.

He saw Bill pull a face in thought. "Don't own a gun, do you Rob?" Bill smirked. He was clearly revelling in poking Rob as much as he could with his constant remarks and smart comments. But this was Bill, and he was always going to do this. He just needed to accept it and ignore them. They needed to be water off a duck's back so that maybe if he realised he wasn't getting a reaction, he'd stop.

Rob sighed quietly to himself. Who was he kidding? There was no way Bill would ever stop.

With a roll of his eyes, Rob ploughed on. "Anything else?"

"We're doing the usual checks, bank records, phone records, emails, CCTV, all that kind of thing. We've had an FLO over at Lee's, with his girlfriend, Justine, while his computer and any other devices have been collected, all of which we'll be going through, with a focus on anything to do with setting up a meeting in Clumber Park. As far as I know, there's nothing yet, but this takes time.

"Okay, good work," Rob complimented him. "In the meantime, we have some old-fashioned police work to get on with. Let's get to work."

16

Scarlett smiled as she watched her friends coo over another dress that Rosie had picked out, this time a charcoal grey affair with diamond detailing that was quite beautiful. She'd not seen her friends in several months, and after weeks of online chats, WhatsApp messages and phone calls, it was lovely to actually be in the same place as them again.

The knowledge that they were just here for a couple of nights and they'd be heading home come Sunday caused some pangs of homesickness deep in her gut. But, she could also look forward to her actual wedding day and to individual visits with her friends, either with her going back down south, or them coming back up here.

She missed being so close to her mates, but she also didn't have any desire to move back home either. Chris's job was up here now, so it was far from a choice she could make alone. Moving up here had been a joint decision, and any further moves would need the same level of discussion and thought.

Besides, she was making new friends within the unit and would no doubt make more outside of it too.

In the meantime, however, she should enjoy her time with some of her oldest friends.

As she watched the girls discuss the merits of the dress, she noticed Ninette hanging back a little and not engaging quite as much as the others. She'd noticed this reticence a few times this morning, such as how her smile would fade quicker than the others or how she'd miss parts of conversations because she was lost in thought.

She knew why, of course, and couldn't really blame her for it. She was dealing with a rapist stalker, and although she'd done her best to forget it and hoped that Ninette might too, it was obviously preying on her friend's mind.

Scarlett's too.

She didn't notice Autumn break away from the group and wander over until she spoke in low tones, so no one else could hear.

"You've noticed it too, I take it?" Autumn asked.

Scarlett sighed. "Ninette? Yeah. She's clearly distracted."

"Of course she is. I would be too. That's not an easy thing to forget. I remember when you first told me while we were at uni, and how broken she was back then. To have that creep still picking at the wound all these years later? It makes me sick."

Seeing one of her friends looking over, Scarlett smiled at her. And then hissed at Autumn, "Keep your voice down." They were the only two who knew about the rape back at university, and Autumn was the only person Scarlett had told about Sebastian still messaging Ninette. She'd caught her alone earlier in the day and gone over the details, much to Autumn's horror.

"Sorry, I'm just so… That little shit. I'd rip him a new one if I saw him," Autumn blurted.

"I have no doubt about that," Scarlett muttered.

"You should do something. You really should. You have resources that I don't. You can find him, find out where he is, and—"

"And what?" Scarlett asked.

"I'm not asking you to break the law, Scar. Just to, I don't know, scare him a bit? Put the fear of God into him? We need to make sure he doesn't keep making her life hell."

Scarlett smiled. "I wish it was that easy. But there's a strict code of conduct…"

"So," Autumn said, leaning in and stressing her words. "Bend it. Find that pig, and warn him. Let him think she's come to the police about him, and now you're watching him. That's it. That's all you'd need to do. I mean, look at her. Look what that creep is doing to her."

Scarlett looked over at her friend, at how she hung back, how she struggled to laugh at all the jokes and the fear that was behind her eyes. Her heart went out to her and railed against the injustice of it all.

"I'll think about it."

17

Leaving the office, Rob grabbed a key for a pool car and made his way outside with Bill in tow. It felt a little odd having Bill follow him through the Lodge, and he got several curious glances, no doubt from those who knew about their rivalry.

But Bill kept to himself and said almost nothing as Rob finally made it outside into the car park and headed for one of the pool cars.

"We're not taking your old banger, then?" Bill asked as they climbed into the car.

Drawing up sharply, Rob paused, offended by Bill's comment. Belle, his Ford Capri and his pride and joy, was certainly not an old banger.

"Excuse me?" Rob stammered.

"That antique you drive around in thinking you look cool. I thought we'd be heading out in that."

Chewing on his lip, Rob grimaced. "Only those I consider friends get that privilege," he sneered.

Bill made a face of his own as he settled into the car. "Whatever."

Rob grunted, annoyed at Bill's disrespect. Belle had been with him for years, ever since leaving his family. In fact, it was one of the few remaining things he owned from before he left, and apart from some old photos of his missing mother, it was the thing that meant the most to him. He loved that car and hearing it being disparaged by this idiot grated, to say the least. But Bill would not get his way. He'd only insult him further, anyway.

Besides, he had nothing to prove, least of all to Bill.

Focusing on the drive, Rob pulled out of the Lodge and headed south towards the city. The Lodge was on the outskirts of north Nottingham, in the countryside just beyond the edge of the urban sprawl. Unfortunately for Rob, Gemma Flint lived in a small village on the opposite side of town, and their sat nav seemed to suggest that going through the city was the best route to take.

Rob didn't try to second guess it, and pressed on, making his way through the countryside and into the outer suburbs. They passed not too far from Top Valley, making Rob think back to the case that changed the trajectory of his career. It led to his promotion and to his new position within the East Midlands Special Operations Unit, helmed by his friend and mentor, John Nailer.

Had his former DCI, Peter Orleton, not been careless with his hobby of archery target practice on homeless people, things might be quite different.

Rob surreptitiously glanced at Bill. It was odd sitting beside the man who hated him so much and who was working hard to pin any kind of corruption on him. He felt watched. As if Bill was waiting for the slightest thing that he could pin on him so Bill could finally take him down.

He wondered what Bill would do if he succeeded in his mission? Would he find himself at a loose end, lost after having dedicated so much of his life to proving that Rob was corrupt. It was like the Batman and The Joker. They were two sides of the same coin, and neither could really exist without the other.

But who was Batman, and who was The Joker in that analogy? Rob liked to think he was Batman but felt sure Bill would take issue with that.

He realised that, on some level, he found the whole thing amusing. And given that laughter seemed in short supply right now, he took what he could get.

"You're enjoying this, aren't you," Rob suggested, allowing a smile to curl the corners of his mouth.

Bill smirked. "I take it you're not. Am I making you uncomfortable?"

Rob glanced over at Bill's tailored three-piece suit and neatly trimmed goatee beard. He was always immaculately turned out with perfectly fitted suits and polished shoes, quite different to Rob's shabby two-piece, loose-fitting tie and hair that could honestly do with a trim.

Rob pulled a face. "No more than usual."

"That was a yes, then," Bill added. "Good. You should be."

"Glad to know you care."

"Oh, I care. I care that you're on the force when you most certainly should not be and that there are people who seem to trust you. I care about that, and I will do whatever it takes to change it."

Rob sighed. "Did it ever occur to you that I might not be corrupt? That maybe you might be wrong about me, and you're wasting your time? Did you think about that?"

"I've thought about a lot of things, Rob. But let's look at the facts, shall we? You're the son of one of the county's most infamous crime lords. You changed your name and joined the police, and *claim* to be estranged from your family. You *claim* to be innocent, and yet I *know* you recently met up with your brother, Owen, in Clipstone, proving that my suspicions are right."

Rob stiffened as an ice-cold feeling ran down his spine. Bill knew about Owen's surprise visit to their temporary incident room in Clipstone? Rob cursed silently in his head, annoyed with himself for thinking he'd got away with that. Owen had turned up out of nowhere, surprising him in the car park at the back of the village hall to warn, slash threaten, him about investigating gang activities. He'd thought he was alone and that no one had seen him, but apparently, someone had, and they had reported back to Bill.

Bollocks. Bill would never leave him alone now.

He supposed it didn't matter that he had no interest in seeing his family, and would happily never have anything to do with them again. No, of course it didn't, because this was all about Bill's obsession.

As far as Bill was concerned, he *looked* guilty, he *looked* corrupt. Whether he actually was or wasn't, was immaterial. Bill had made up his mind and nothing Rob could do would change that.

"What's the matter, did I hit a nerve?" Bill asked, filling the silence that Rob had left following Bill's statement.

Christ, now he *really* looked guilty!

"No, but you did hit my boredom switch, plus my bullshit metre was off the charts, so I had to shut down for a moment." Rob smiled to himself, while Bill scoffed.

"Whatever," Bill said.

He was quiet for the rest of the drive as they passed through Nottingham and out the other side. The urban sprawl gave way to fields and hedgerows, and it wasn't long before they turned into the tiny village of Thrumpton. He soon found Gemma Flint's modest detached house and pulled up.

Bill made to get out.

"Wait," Rob snapped.

Bill paused and looked back, his expression incredulous. "What?"

"I'll do the talking. You stay out of it. No more outbursts and accusations." Rob made sure to sound pedantic. "I don't want you upsetting them."

Bill tilted his head. "I'll do as I please." He got out.

Rob sighed and muttered to himself as he climbed out. "Bollocks." Getting ahead of Bill, Rob led the way to the front door. Their knock was answered in short order as a dark-haired woman in leggings, and a t-shirt answered the door with a young child on her hip.

She took one look at them and grunted. "I wondered how long it would be before you darkened my doorstep."

"Afternoon, Mrs Flint," Rob greeted her. "I'm DI Loxley, and this is DI Rainault."

"Two inspectors? Wow, I'm flattered." She sighed. "I recognise you both, so you'd better come in. You'll be the new EMSOU, right?"

"We are," Rob confirmed.

"Who is it?" asked a male voice from further into the house.

"My lot," Gemma called back.

"Aww, shit. Again?"

"It'll be about Lee," she called out and then turned back to them. "This is about Lee, right? About his murder?"

"Still on the grapevine, I see," Rob commented.

She grumbled but led them through to the front room, where she placed her young son on the soft carpet for him to play while she perched on the edge of a soft seat. She waved at the sofa. "Go on, sit. We might as well get this over with."

A man walked in and offered his hand. "Hi, I'm Ben, Gemma's husband."

"Nice to meet you." Rob shook his hand and stated their names and ranks again.

"Two Inspectors?"

"That's what I said," Gemma commented with a smile before she turned back to them. "So, Lee was shot, right?"

"He was, yes. Sorry for your loss."

She nodded, and sighed, as if bracing herself. "No one should be killed in our line of work... My former line of work," she clarified. "But Lee..." She took another long breath. "I won't miss him. He wasn't the easiest of people to work with, and at the end... Well, you probably know what happened."

"You resigned," Rob answered, with a glance at Bill to make sure he wasn't going to butt in.

"Resigned?" Ben spluttered. "She was forced out, more like. She wasn't given a choice. She didn't want to resign, you know."

"I loved that job," Gemma added. "I gave everything to it. I barely had any maternity leave, I was so keen to get back, and this is how I'm thanked?" She shook her head, clearly exasperated. "I worked hard for Lee, I sacrificed so much for him and that unit, and after all that hard work and dedication, they threw me under the bus. He used me, and then dumped me when it suited him."

"He was the one who forced you to resign?"

"One of them. I was getting pressure from others too, but Lee was probably the main one."

"What details do you know about Lee's murder?" Rob asked.

"Not much. Just that he was shot in Clumber Park. Looks like a gang hit."

"You're right about that. That's what it looks like, and we're still looking for information. Do you have any idea who might want to kill him?"

"Only all the scrotes he's nicked through the years." She shrugged. "But no, not really." Gemma seemed to mull something over for a moment, before looking back at him. "Have you spoken to Lee's girlfriend, Justine, yet?"

"Not yet, but we will. Why? Do you think she might know something?"

"I have no idea, but, it's often those closest to you, isn't it," she suggested. Beside her, Ben shot a frown her way, but a moment later, shrugged and seemed to dismiss whatever thoughts were going through his head. Was she suggesting something about Justine?

Rob chose to move on. "And what were you doing the night of the murder?"

"I was here, watching TV," Gemma said.

"I was out with some friends," Ben answered. "I can get you their details."

"Please," Rob said.

"Have you got anything else to go on?" Gemma asked.

"We're following clues. But what you might not know is that Lee's son, Gavin, was nicked for stabbing a girl just hours before. He's copped to it and is happy to admit his guilt, but when he was first interviewed, before he knew about his dad, Gavin claimed that his dad was corrupt and in the employ of a gang." Rob paused as he watched her expression, trying to read it and her thoughts, but she was good at hiding them. "Do you have any idea why he might say that and then withdraw it once he found out his dad was dead?"

Gemma frowned. "No, I don't know why. I could guess if you like."

"So could I," Rob said. "But that's not really helpful."

"True. I was, however, always convinced there was at least one corrupt officer on the team. There were just too many coincidences, and then when Major Oak went sideways, that just cemented it for me. Someone was bent."

"We spoke to Shelley Garrett. She said we should speak to you, that you've been looking into this."

"I have a bit. It's not quite as easy to do when you're not on the force, and you have your hands full with a one-year-old, and so far, I don't really have much." She pulled a face. "Well, I don't have anything, actually. Sorry to be of no help whatsoever."

"That's okay. Any suspicions?" Rob asked.

"Well, Lee, obviously. But he's dead now, so that's not much use to you. You know, there were four members of my EMSOU killed on this op."

"I'm aware," Rob said.

"Well, did it ever occur to you that maybe the gang was using this as a way to clear house? Maybe whoever they were paying was no longer useful, so they took this opportunity to get rid of them, nice and cleanly. So maybe they're already dead."

"Sure, that's a possibility," Rob admitted. "Do you think it could have been Lee?"

Gemma shrugged. "Yeah, maybe."

"He was the one that pushed her out," Ben added. "Anyone with an ounce of empathy wouldn't do that. But someone who needed a scapegoat, might. Nah, screw him. I'm glad he's dea—"

"Ben!" Gemma snapped.

"Sorry," Ben said. "Talking ill of the dead. My bad."

"No, that's okay," Rob replied but noted how much Ben seemed to dislike Lee for what he did to Gemma. Was it enough to drive him to murder?

"Why did you step down?" Bill asked, taking Rob by surprise. "I mean, you could have fought it. You could have gone over Lee's head to more senior officers. You might still be on the force today if you'd just—"

"I did fight it," Gemma retaliated. "I didn't just walk."

"Are you sure about that?"

"What are you implying?"

"Innocent people don't give in so easily." Bill smiled.

Rob cringed at his words. He was running with the idea of them being to blame for Lee's murder, but this probably wasn't the best way to frame it.

"Screw you," Gemma barked.

"Fuck that," Ben added. "Where do you get off, coming round here with your stupid bloody questions, accusing us of murder. You're sick."

"Whoa. I'm sorry," Rob said, raising his voice and his hands before he turned to Bill. "I think we're done here." Yep, definitely not the best way to address this.

"Rather hit a nerve there, didn't I," Bill sneered.

Ben started shouting again and took to his feet. Bill followed suit.

Rob did the same and positioned himself between the two men. "That's enough, Bill!"

Bill grimaced but turned away, allowing Rob to address Mr Flint. "I apologise for his comments. I'm sorry. That was uncalled for."

"Sit down, Ben." Gemma sighed, then sat back and smirked. "Not exactly taking after your names sakes, are you?"

"Huh?" her husband grunted.

"What?" Bill asked.

Rob frowned and then smiled when it clicked. "Oh, Bill and Ben. Very good."

For a brief moment, a smile played over Rob's lips. But the chat was over, so Rob wasted no time in excusing themselves from the building. There wasn't a lot to go on here, although it did seem that both of them blamed Lee for Gemma's dismissal from the police. There was spite in Gemma's voice when she spoke about Lee and the work she did for the unit. She hated him for what he did to her. But would that be enough for Gemma or Ben to kill Lee?

It was certainly possible. People had killed for a lot less. He tried to work through that train of thought but found himself constantly derailed by Bill's line of questioning, and as they reached the car, he just had to say something.

"What the hell was that?"

"I was asking a question, a valid one, I think." Bill smiled. "You can thank me later. They clearly hated Lee."

"Just because they hated him doesn't mean they killed him. You hate me, don't you?"

Bill shrugged.

"Exactly. So when I tell you to drop it, you drop it. And that includes this ridiculous fixation with me. I will go over your head to get you removed from this case if I have to, Bill. That's a promise."

"Try it. See what happens, Judas."

"I'm not corrupt, you ignorant twat," Rob hissed, getting in close to Bill's face and speaking through gritted teeth. "I hate my bloody family. I hate who they are and what they brought me into. I want nothing to do with them, ever. They're scum. I have never gone looking for them and never will. But have I seen them over the years? Have I been wandering down a street and spotted them or happened across them? Yes, but I get the hell out of there as quick as I can because I want nothing to do with them. So if you have someone who thinks he saw me with one of them, maybe he did, but you need to get your facts straight before you go accusing me of anything. Got it!"

Bill smiled serenely. "Nice story. Have you been rehearsing it long?"

"Oh, do piss off. You don't half talk some bollocks."

"Gladly. Now, if we're done, I'd like to get back. I'm done with you for the day. I need to report in and get home."

"Oh, why? Hot date, is it?" Rob smirked and then caught a flicker of something in his eyes. "Oh, it is! Shit. Who's the lucky woman? Maybe I should call and warn her."

Bill raised a single finger as he climbed into the car and said nothing the whole way back to the station.

It was bliss.

18

"Ugh, Lord above, it's good to be out from behind that bastard desk," Tucker grumbled, stretching in the seat beside her as she drove through Nottingham.

Ellen smiled to herself, happy to be with her foul-mouthed friend once more.

"Hope you're not getting illusions of fucking grandeur from hanging out with the guv," he added.

She smiled. "No, don't worry. I don't need to hang out with Rob to know I'm superior to you in every way."

"Christ on a rusty bike, I'm going to need a skin graft on that burn."

"Damn right you are," she said with a snarky laugh.

"So, this is Justine Palmer we're going to see, right? Lee's girlfriend."

"That's right. We've had officers out to her already, including the FLO who's taken a statement. But Rob wants us to talk to her. See what's going on. Get a feel for things. You know."

"Aye, we can do that," Tucker confirmed. "Is there any specific stinky shit we're focusing on?"

"Gavin's statement, I think," she answered. "In the interview with Rob, Bill and I, he said that in the last few days before Lee was killed, he refused to allow Gavin to come round, saying that he and Justine had something to sort out. We need to know what that was."

"I see." Tucker adjusted his position in the passenger seat. "So, what was it like, being in the room with both Rob and that knicker-stealing bollock stain?"

"You mean Bill?"

"Aye. Sheriff arse ferret. Who else? The man is an offence before God."

"It was interesting, is what it was. They clearly hate each other," Ellen said, thinking back to the atmosphere in the room. "The room was tense, and Bill, well…he certainly has a way with words, but not in a good way. He just winds people up the whole time. I've got no idea how he's made it to Inspector."

"He's probably got his tongue up someone's rear end."

"What a delightful image."

"I specialise in those." Tucker smiled. "So we're going to have to put up with this grotty bell end for the next few days while he goes around fucking things up. Wonderful."

"Well, hopefully, he'll keep his distance. Rob's cordial for the most part, but makes it quite clear that he's not wanted."

"Good on 'im," Tucker muttered. "He's a good 'un."

Ellen's phone rang in its holder on the dash. She noticed it was Christobel, her partner. "Mind if I take this?"

"No, no. You go ahead."

She tapped the screen. "Hey, Chrissy."

"Hi, El. Can you talk?"

"Yeah. I'm in the car with Tucker. You're on speaker."

"Oh, okay. Hi Tuck?"

"Afternoon, love." He grunted. "How you doin'?"

"All the better for speaking to you."

"What's up?" Ellen pressed, aware that they weren't far from Justine and Lee's home in the Mapperley Park estate in Nottingham. "We're on our way to see someone."

"No, that's okay. It was just a quick call anyway. I was just wondering when you think you might be back home?"

"I'm not sure," Ellen replied. "There was talk of a drink after our shift, but I don't know if that's still happening. Depends how the case goes, I guess. If there's any more bombshells…"

"No, that's fine. Will you be late?"

"Not really, don't worry. I'll eat with you when I'm back. It'll be good to have some time together."

"It would," Christobel answered. "I'll see you later, El. We can grab a takeaway when you get in."

"Sounds good. Love you."

"Love you too," Chrissy answered and ended the call.

"I think you're in for a good night," Tucker commented with a smile. "A nice takeaway would be bloody stunning later."

"Yeah. She looks after me," Ellen replied.

She enjoyed her time with Tucker, even though there wasn't much of a filter when it came to his mouth. He could be quite inventive with his insults when he wanted to be, and for a former member of the clergy, he was about as liberal as they came. She didn't know much about his fall from grace, as he sometimes put it, but it sounded very much like Nailer found him in the gutter and inspired him to make a change.

All of which made him useful. Someone who'd experienced life on the wrong side of the tracks or grown up in the less savoury parts of society but who'd since reformed themselves could be a real asset to the police. They gave insight into the criminal fraternity, allowing the police to fully understand the people they were hunting down, and Tucker certainly seemed to fit into that category.

Ellen pulled up outside a detached house that could have been better cared for on a nice middle-class road. She eyed the neighbourhood and gave some thought to Justine, who'd be left alone in this house. "I wonder if she'll have to give this all up?"

Tucker caught her meaning. "Who knows, maybe."

They left their car and made their way up to the house. The door was answered by one of the Family Liaison Officers that was assigned to the EMSOU, Heather Knight.

"Hi. Come in," Heather said.

"How's she been?"

"Upset, understandably."

Ellen nodded. It was less than a day since Justine's partner had been brutally murdered, so it would be strange if she wasn't upset. "What does she know?"

"The basics," Heather whispered, before she started counting points off on her fingers. "Lee was shot in Clumber, and he didn't suffer. Gavin is still in custody for the stabbing. Not much else."

"Good, thank you. Where is she?"

"Through here." Heather led them through a closed door to the front room.

Ellen found Justine slumped into one of the comfortable-looking soft chairs in the lounge. She looked up as Ellen walked in, followed by Tucker and the FLO.

Justine went to get up.

"No, please. Stay where you are." They moved to the other seats in the room and sat. "We're sorry for your loss. I'm Detective Dale, and this is Detective Stafford." She gestured to Tucker. "Thank you for agreeing to see us."

"Sure, that's okay," Justine replied. She tried to smile, but it didn't really hit the mark or last very long.

Ellen chose to get started. "As you know, your partner, Lee, was found shot through the head last night on Lime Tree Avenue in Clumber Park, at about ten PM. A couple of hours earlier in Nottingham's Forest Fields estate, not too far from here, Lee's son, Gavin, stabbed a girl in a shop. He's in custody and has admitted to his crime. He should be released on bail later today, all being well. Would you like to tell us if you know anything about these events?"

"I don't really know anything other than what I've been told," Justine answered. "I don't know where this has come from or who could do this to Lee."

"Are you sure? You can't think of anyone?"

"Well, obviously, there were people who didn't like him, but no one that I know would do this. At least, I didn't think there was."

"No one. No one at all?"

"What are you saying? Do you think I killed him? I couldn't do that."

"I didn't suggest you could, but we do need to ask some difficult questions, Justine."

She sighed. "I know. It's just, it's been a lot, you know? I couldn't do this. I couldn't hurt Lee. I loved him. Him *and* Gavin."

"He's not your son, though, is he," Tucker stated.

"No. He's Shelley's son," Justine answered. "But I loved him anyway."

"Okay," Ellen said. "As you're aware, we found Lee on the road leading into Clumber Park, Lime Tree Avenue. Do you know why he might have been up there? Did you know he was going up there? It's a fair drive from here. Was it to meet someone?"

"I don't know," Justine replied. "I didn't know that was where he was going. He just said he had a work thing and that he'd be back later. I didn't question it. He's always taking phone calls and getting called out at all times of day. I didn't think anything about it."

"So this was nothing unusual?"

"Not at all."

"Well, we've spoken to Shelley, obviously, as she was Lee's estranged wife and Gavin's mother. We've also spoken to Gavin, and they've told us a few things that we'd like to clear up. Shelley told us that a few months after her split from Lee, there was a time when Gavin came back from staying with Lee and you, and he seemed distraught and upset. He stayed away for a few weeks until Lee managed to coax him back. Do you remember that?"

Justine sighed. "You see, the thing is, our relationship, mine and Lee's, was quite a passionate one. Fiery, really.

Things were great at the start and more recently, but there was a time in the middle when we were fighting quite a lot. Naturally, we did our best to keep it away from Gavin, but that wasn't always possible, and there were a few occasions when he probably heard a little too much. But I don't think that's a crime. It was probably after one of those that Gavin chose to stay away."

"I see," Ellen said. "So he didn't like you fighting."

"What child does like their parents fighting?"

"Fair point. So, what about more recently? You said you were getting on better, and yet Lee told Gavin to stay away in the last few days, as he had something to sort out with you. But if you were getting on better, what changed? Did Lee upset you?"

Justine sighed again, as if she didn't want to answer, but felt she had little choice.

"Whatever it was," Ellen continued, "Gavin has taken it badly, and acted out, injuring that girl."

"He doesn't know what it was," Justine answered. "Lee never found out either." She paused again, seeming troubled and unsure.

"It's okay," Ellen suggested. "If we can help…"

"There's not a lot you can do, but you should know." Justine took another deep breath and closed her eyes for a moment. Ellen spotted a tear fall from one eye before it rolled down her cheek. "It started earlier this week when I found his second phone. I didn't know he had a second phone, so I thought it was odd right away, and I just had this funny feeling, right. I couldn't place it, but it felt wrong. So I broke into his phone."

"You broke in?" Ellen asked.

"Um, hacked, I guess. I know the passwords he uses, so it wasn't hard. I just used variations on them until one worked. Easy, really. Then I went hunting." She looked up at Ellen. "There's only a handful of reasons why someone has a secret second phone, you know, and very few of them are good."

"Yeah, we know all about burner phones," Ellen replied, referring to the cheap phones with pay-as-you-go SIMs that criminals often used and discarded to avoid tracking and detection.

"Yeah, well, this one was used for something else. He was having an affair."

"An affair?" Ellen asked, surprised. She checked to make sure Tucker was making a note of this. He was. "With who?"

"I couldn't believe it. I was shocked. There was a months-long text chat, plus voice mails. He'd been sleeping with another woman behind my back."

"Who was it?" Ellen asked again.

"Gemma Flint. His DCI. They were shagging!"

"Gemma? Are you sure?"

"There were pictures of her... Selfies that she sent him, you know? Christ. It had been going on for months. It started around...well, when we were at a low point. About seven or eight months ago? Something like that."

Ellen frowned, wondering how this would fit in with what they already knew. Wasn't Lee supposed to have pushed Gemma to leave the EMSOU? How did that work? "And, were they still seeing each other before the murder?"

"No. It stopped around the time of Operation Major Oak. Before that, it was all dirty texts and arranging meetings, but Major Oak seemed to change everything. They had a falling out and started arguing. The messages between them became angry. She started to accuse him of pinning the failed op on her, so she accused him of corruption. Lee then accused her of the same thing and threatened to go to her husband if she didn't do the right thing and take one for the team."

"He blackmailed her?"

"Yeah. He'd ruin their marriage if she didn't go down over this."

"And this is why Lee refused to have Gavin over?"

"Yeah," Justine answered with a shrug. "He knew something was wrong. I was angry at him and Gemma, but I couldn't deal with it. I needed time to think. I told him to keep Gavin away for a few days as I had some stuff to work through. I just needed time. I did end up calling Gemma, though."

"You called her? So, she knows you found out?"

"She does. I just got so angry one day that I called and shouted at her, telling her I knew everything. I probably wasn't going to do it, but I threatened to tell her husband too. Stupid idea, but in the heat of the moment, I just said it. She begged me not to, but I just hung up."

Ellen waited for Justine to follow it up with more, but she went quiet. "What happened next?"

"Nothing," Justine answered. "Lee was killed that night. Yesterday. I was probably going to talk to him this weekend and have it out with him, but that won't happen now."

"You should have told us before," Heather said from her seat across the room.

"I know, but... I'm sorry. I should have, but I didn't. I'm not sure why, but, you know now. Hopefully, it's helpful."

"Very, thank you," Ellen replied as she thought about the new angles this revelation brought to the case.

19

The drive back to the Lodge seemed to take forever. Sitting beside Rob, Bill stared out the window at the passing city, at the thousands of people going about their lives, and wished he was anywhere but in here with this obviously corrupt, or at the very least, compromised officer.

They'd had their run-ins before and swapped cross words, but Bill had always felt in control of the situation. He'd always felt like he had the upper hand. But today seemed different, and he hated himself for how he'd let Rob get in his face and have his say. The anger and venom in his outburst had been surprising. He'd never seen him like that before, and for those brief seconds, he'd been lost for words.

He was kicking himself for not standing up to him and not fighting back. He replayed Rob's rant over and over in his head, coming up with all manner of clever comebacks, but it was too late. The moment had passed, and there was no going back to it now.

Why was this case getting away from him? He'd been looking forward to this, to getting close to Rob and hopefully finding some kind of hook, a clue that might give him the insight he needed to really hammer Rob, once and for all. But somehow, it felt like he was further from his goal than ever before. He found himself getting angry and frustrated and unable to make sense of what was going on.

It was Rob. It had to be. He was getting to him somehow, getting under his skin and turning things around.

How had he guessed that he had a date tonight? He'd never mentioned it to anyone. He was so wrapped up in what he was doing he'd kind of forgotten about it himself. It had been arranged for over a week after swapping messages with this girl he'd matched with on Tinder. Given his preoccupation with this case, he wasn't sure how it would go, but he might as well give it a try.

It would keep his mother off his back, at least.

He tried to put thoughts of Rob and his date to one side and focus on the case. He had to report to Paige. She'd want to know how things were going, if they'd made any progress on the Lee Garrett murder and the corruption within the former EMSOU.

Their meeting with Gemma and her husband, Ben, had been enlightening, and their hate towards the former Superintendent was obvious. They claimed he'd pushed Gemma out, but it seemed to him that Gemma hadn't really fought them and had resigned. But why would she do that if she wasn't afraid that she'd be found out? But by resigning, she could leave with whatever pension she'd built up and stay out of prison. Surely, she'd only be afraid of losing these things if she was on the take.

Part way back, Rob's phone rang. It was attached to the dash, but Rob wasn't using it to navigate. He apparently knew the way.

Bill spotted Ellen Dale's name listed on the caller ID before Rob answered.

"Ellen," Rob greeted her. "Bill and I are driving back. You're on speaker. How did the interview go?"

Bill sneered at Rob's unsubtle warning that he was in the car with Bill, and he could hear whatever she was about to say. Dodgy, bugger, he mused.

"Good, thanks. Justine was very helpful. Turns out that in the last few days, Justine discovered that Lee had a secret second phone. She broke into it and found out that he'd been having an affair with Gemma Flint."

"What?" Rob exclaimed. "His DCI?"

"Yep. It started about seven months ago and ended when Operation Major Oak went bad."

"I knew she was hiding something," Bill exclaimed.

"Aaah," Ellen muttered. "I take it Gemma didn't mention this to you during your chat with her?"

"No," Rob replied. "She didn't."

"Aaah, well. Apparently, they started arguing after the operation, with both of them blaming each other for the failure. That ended with Lee threatening to reveal all if Gemma didn't take one for the team and resign. So that's what she did. Justine found all this out a few days ago and had been working herself up to confront Lee about it. That's why Lee didn't want to see Gavin. Justine was upset and not talking to him, so he knew something was wrong, and he didn't want to upset his son. Anyway, according to Justine, she called and shouted at Gemma down the phone after she found out, threatening to tell her husband. This was yesterday. Then a few hours later, Lee turns up dead after a secret meeting in Clumber Park."

"Christ. Right then. Did you get the phone?"

"We did. Justine gave it to us," Ellen confirmed. "We'll be going through it to see what else is on there. But Lee having a second, secret phone doesn't look good for him."

"No, it does not," Rob agreed. "We need to find out who Lee went to meet. Was it Gemma, or was it someone else?"

"We were already checking phone records and email accounts," Tucker answered from the other end of the line, "but there didn't seem to be much. I'm willing to bet this mobile will shed some light on that."

"Okay, good work. Hopefully, this will be the breakthrough we need." Rob ended the call.

Bill nodded in agreement and thought back to the hate Gemma and her husband seemed to have towards the victim.

It was all very suspicious, and Bill felt that Gemma might have something to do with it. But was this affair the limit of it, or did recent events turn Gemma from a bitter former lover into a murderer? Whatever the case, it was looking more and more likely that he was right.

"I'll happily accept your apology and your admission that I was right about Gemma when you're ready to give it," Bill said, feeling smug that he'd spotted Gemma's deception before Rob. So much for him being a good detective.

But Rob snorted with mirth. "We're a way off from that, yet, Bill. Just because she hid her affair doesn't make her a murderer."

"Are you sure about that?"

"Quite sure. But if you happen to be right, I'll happily give you credit."

Bill grunted and remained silent for the remainder of the trip, unsure how to take Rob's admission that he might be right. Besides, he had other things to concentrate on.

Back at the Lodge, Bill climbed out of the car. "I'm off to my office to report in." He fixed Rob with a glare. "I'll see you tomorrow."

"Hope your date goes well," Rob answered with a smile and then strode off, snickering as he went. Bill watched him go, feeling nothing but hate and revulsion towards him. How was it that a compromised officer like Rob had made it to DI, the same rank he was, and why did so few others seem to see the problem with him? He was, at the very least, a liability and, at worst, actively working against the police and undermining their efforts. Was this how the Masons had evaded capture for so long?

Isaac Mason, the Godfather of the firm, had never seen jail time, and neither had three of his four sons. Rob, obviously, who claimed to be estranged from the family, had never been to jail. But neither had Sean, the eldest, and Oliver, the next eldest. Only Owen, son number three, the one closest in age to Rob—who was the youngest—had been arrested. He'd been held in custody for a short time, decades ago, but it wasn't long before he was out again.

Despite this, the Masons remained something of an enigma. Isaac and Sean were local public figures, always involved in charity events, giving money to worthwhile causes. They were well-liked within the community around Retford and north Nottinghamshire. They ran numerous legitimate businesses, from car washes to nail salons, garages, construction firms and more. All of them were legit, although Bill suspected they also served as fronts for less savoury activities and ways for the firm to launder their money.

Within the police and certain other circles, however, the Masons were linked to organised crime. Certainly, the criminal underworld seemed to know that you didn't cross the Masons. Before Isaac took over the firm decades ago, it was run by his father, Rob's grandfather, Manny Mason. Manny was a known criminal. An old-school British gangster who did everything from robbing banks to blackmail, extortion, prostitution, protection and even some drug running. That was until the fateful raid that put Manny in both a wheelchair and in prison.

According to those around at the time, and Bill had spoken to many of them, everything changed that day. It was as if the Mason Firm had just disappeared. Several of Manny's old-school supporters turned up dead or just disappeared entirely, but nothing was ever linked back to Isaac.

It was obvious to Bill that Isaac had probably been clearing house as he took over. But he had no proof. Just like he had no evidence that Rob or any of his family was actively involved in any kind of criminality.

But that wouldn't stop him from digging and doing his best to find out the truth, no matter what it took.

Rob would go down one day.

Snapping out of his daydream, Bill made his way into the Lodge and up to the PSU office, where he went to see his DCI, Paige Clements.

"Welcome back," Paige greeted him. "So, you survived your day with the fearsome Rob Loxley, then?"

"Of course," he confirmed. "That was never in doubt, ma'am. But you know my thoughts about him, and those have not changed. He's most certainly compromised and probably corrupt, working from within the police to undermine our efforts and keep the Masons in business. I will find—"

"Bill," Paige cut in, "I know you think this, and I'm not interested right now. I appreciate your dedication, but what I am interested in is the corruption of Lee Garrett and the EMSOU that he presided over. Was Lee corrupt? Was it someone else? And how deep did that corruption go?"

"That's hard to tell, but I accompanied Rob on his interview of Gemma Flint this afternoon while two other officers spoke with Lee's girlfriend, Justine Palmer. We discovered an affair between Gemma and Lee, that turned bad following the failure of Operation Major Oak. It looks like Garrett then forced Gemma out of the force, blackmailing her into resigning. But apart from Gavin's retracted statement, there's nothing yet regarding a gang connection."

"Do you think Gavin was lying?"

Bill considered this for a moment, thinking back to their interview with him. "I think there's more to Gavin's story than he's letting on. Was he lying? I'm not sure, maybe. He was certainly upset with his father, which could have led to his outburst in the interview."

"So, you think Gemma might be the killer?"

"Well, both Gemma and Justine have good reasons to hurt him due to the affair and Gemma's resignation. Gemma is certainly suspicious, though. She and her husband, Ben, both seem to hate Lee for what he did. I wouldn't put it past them to do this."

"Okay, keep looking and focus on the corruption. We'll leave the murder to the current EMSOU, okay?"

"Of course."

"Right then, I take it you're done for the day?"

"I am," he confirmed, his mind still racing.

"Any plans?" she asked, leaning back in her chair while fiddling with a pen in her hand.

Bill narrowed his eyes, wondering why she'd asked. "I'm going out for dinner, but that's all."

"Oh, a date?"

"Something like that."

"Lucky you," Paige said with a smile. "Have fun. I'll see you tomorrow. Don't stay up too late."

Bill raised an eyebrow. She was worse than his mother.

20

Glad to be away from Bill, Rob strode through the Lodge, making for the EMSOU office while reflecting on the afternoon. Bill was as annoying and self-righteous as ever, and he was also something of a liability. His people skills left much to be desired. Rob honestly believed that if he wasn't careful, Bill could end up alienating a potentially useful witness if he continued accusing everyone of Lee's murder.

He seemed to get an idea in his head about someone's guilt and then wouldn't shift from it for anything.

Was it possible that Gemma was guilty of Lee's murder? Certainly. She had a strong motive, and so did her husband. But this would be a crime of passion, and the clinical nature of the murder didn't suggest that emotion was involved.

Rob frowned as he thought about that some more.

Gemma was a DCI until she resigned and was well aware of how police investigations worked. She would know what they would look for and was certainly capable of manipulating the scene or staging things to make them look like something else… Like a gang hit, for instance.

That would feed into the idea that Lee was corrupt and turn attention away from her, even with the affair.

After all, she had to be aware that they would find out about her dalliance with Lee at some point. There was no way that she believed she was getting through this without that particular bombshell going off.

Rob grimaced as he worked through these ideas and wondered if Bill had done something similar? Shit, maybe Bill was right, and he'd end up having to admit to the idiot that he'd solved it.

God, he hoped that wouldn't be the case. He'd never live that one down.

"Rob, hey." It was DI Karl Rothwell, and he seemed to be hanging around in the corridor close to the EMSOU office.

"Karl," Rob began with a smile. "How's the case against Gavin coming along?"

"Good. We're finalising the details. You know how it goes with all this paperwork. Amelia is working on it now."

"And you left her to it, did you?"

"Perks of being a higher rank." He grinned.

Rob grunted. "So, what's going to happen with Gavin? Is he being remanded in custody, or will he be out on bail?"

"Bail, by the looks of things. We don't believe he's a threat to the wider public, and his cooperation on this case has been amazing. What with that and his dad being murdered, I'm not sure he'll even see jail time. The girl he stabbed will be okay too."

"Hmm. And he's being released tonight?"

"He is, unless you have any objections. But you'll need to be quick in applying for an extension."

Rob shook his head. "No, I don't think so. Is that why you're hanging around here? You wanted to update me?"

"Kinda," Karl answered. "I did want to update you, but there's something else… Can we go somewhere to talk?"

Rob paused as they reached the entrance to the EMSOU office. He glanced in to see Ellen and Tucker at their desks and Nailer in the corner office. There wasn't much privacy in there, so he led him to a nearby side room.

"Coffee?" Rob asked, wandering over to the machine on a nearby unit.

"Oh, um, yeah. Thanks."

"So, it's been a busy day for you," Rob remarked as he grabbed some disposable cups and keyed in his choices into the machine.

"Yeah, It has. I'll be glad to get home."

"Do you live with your girlfriend? Michelle, was it?"

"Michelle, yeah. And no, she's got her own place, but we spend a lot of time at each other's," he answered while taking a seat. "It works, so…"

"Certainly."

"Yeah, I'll see her later tonight. What about you?" Karl asked. "Any wife, or partner on the scene?"

Rob smiled to himself. "No. No one right now. I'm too busy and... This career isn't kind to relationships. It tends to kill them, so. I just don't want to put someone through that."

"That's very noble of you."

"It's just practical. There's nothing noble about it." Rob grabbed the coffee and joined Karl in a nearby seat, placing the drinks on the low table between them.

"Right then, what's up?" he asked once he was settled.

"It's just... Something's been bothering me, and I need to tell you. It's important, and I'm an idiot for not telling you sooner."

Rob suppressed the urge to raise an eyebrow. "Alright, go on."

Karl sighed. "I met up with Lee last weekend. He wanted to see me, so we had lunch. Something seemed to be on his mind—bothering him—but it took a while for him to come out and say it. He started by saying he was worried about Gavin and his behaviour, and... Well, we know how that went."

"Aye, we do," Rob agreed.

"Yeah, well, he went on to say that he needed to tell someone because it's been bothering him, this thing he wanted to tell me. But he was worried. He was upset, so I tried to reassure him and said he could tell me, no matter what it was. I wanted to help." Karl sighed. "It's weird because we were never very close. We were workmates, and we'd attended the same drink nights, but that's all. Anyway, he finally gets to the point and admits that he's been passing information to a gang. A powerful criminal gang. I was shocked. I didn't believe him at first. I thought he was having me on. But no, he wasn't. I asked why and if they were paying him, but he said no. He explained that they'd kidnapped Gavin. They took him, hurt him, and threatened to kill him if Lee didn't do what they wanted. He agreed, naturally, and they released Gavin."

Rob listened in shock to what Karl was telling him, and for a moment, he didn't quite know what to say or ask. "They threatened to kill Gavin?"

"They beat him up, but didn't hit his face, only his body, so he could hide the bruises. They did a number on him, that's for sure."

Rob frowned. "When was this?"

"I think he said it was about seven, maybe eight months ago?"

Rob thought back to his chat with Shelley and remembered she'd said Gavin came and stayed at theirs for a few weeks around then and refused to see Lee. It all made sense. "That's when Gavin started carrying a knife around."

"That's right," Karl agreed. "This was the behaviour that Lee was worried about. Gavin had started doing it again more recently, and it was stressing him. Anyway, when we spoke, Lee insisted he was no longer working for this gang. He went to great pains to stress how it was all in the past, and he was just concerned by how Gavin was acting."

"Did you believe him? Do you think he had stopped?"

"I don't know." Karl sighed. "I'd love to say yes, but I'm not sure it works like that once they've sunk their claws into you. I'm sorry I didn't tell you sooner, but Lee made me promise to keep it a secret. He said that no matter what happened to him, I couldn't tell anyone. Otherwise, *my* life would be in danger. I was furious with him for putting me into that position, but he said he needed to talk to someone. He said he was sorry, and as long as I kept quiet, I'd be fine." Karl's voice started to crack from the emotion. "I'm sorry, but I didn't know what to do. When Lee turned up dead, I knew it was the gang. I wanted to tell you, but I couldn't."

"So what changed?"

Karl took a long calming breath and got control of his emotions. "Seeing Gavin. He's made some mistakes, but he's defiant and honest. He admitted to that stabbing and chose to face the consequences. I needed to do the same. Lee might have told me to say nothing, but if I don't, then nothing changes. I can't do that. This has to stop. This might be the stupidest thing I've ever done, but at least it's the right thing."

Rob sighed and leaned back into the sofa. "Bloody hell." He shook his head and let it sink in, until a thought occurred to him. "By the way, do you know which gang we're talking about here?"

"The Masons," Karl replied, his tone flat.

Rob's heart sank. He closed his eyes and took a moment to steady his breathing. Of course, it was the Masons. Why would it be anyone else? "Alright, so they blackmailed Lee Garrett by kidnapping his son and threatening to kill him if Lee didn't work for them. Which he did. Afterwards, Gavin was so terrified by the ordeal that he started carrying a knife around to defend himself."

"That's right," Karl confirmed. "I hope this doesn't tarnish Lee's legacy too much. I don't think he ever meant to hurt anyone, but what could he do? The Masons had shown him they could hurt him and his family."

"No, I agree. Once they do that, there really is no other option." It was one of the other reasons why Rob refused to get involved with anyone. Once his family found out, how long would it be before they did this to him? "As for Lee's legacy, I don't know about that. I guess we'll have to see."

"Okay," Karl muttered quietly.

"Was there anyone else, or was Lee the only one working for the Masons?"

"Well, he only talked about himself, but if I'm being honest, I think there might have been one other."

"One more corrupt officer on the unit?"

"Yeah. I think it might have been Isobel Dickerson."

"Really? She saved at least two other officers and got killed herself during the botched raid. Are you sure?"

"No. I'm not sure. But I had my suspicions based on her actions before the raid. I think that, when the raid happened and she saw her friends dying, she had a change of heart and wanted to fight back."

"Okay, we'll take a look at it."

"So, what are you going to do?"

"Honestly, I'm not sure," Rob said. Karl might have opened his heart to him, but he wasn't part of this investigation, so there was no need to discuss details with him. He decided to be vague. "I need to think about this."

"You need to be careful," Karl warned him. "The Masons are dangerous."

"Oh, I know. Don't worry about that." Rob sighed. They *were* dangerous, and the more he learned, the more he hated them. Violence and misery seemed to surround the Masons, and his connection to them made the threat they posed very real. But he wouldn't allow that threat to hamper this investigation. He'd get to the bottom of this, one way or another. First, he needed to verify what Karl had told him, and there was one way he could hopefully do that tonight.

"So, what do we do?" Karl asked.

He looked up. "I'll tell you what we're going to do. We need to get down to the Custody Suite to charge and release Gavin."

"What?" Karl looked perplexed.

Rob nodded to the clock on the nearby wall. "I've just seen the time. We need to get a move on."

"We?"

Rob smiled. "I'm going with you."

21

Walking through the corridors of the Custody Suite, heading towards reception and freedom, Ambrose felt a growing sense of unease in his belly. His gut twisted and tied itself in knots as he thought about the deal he'd made with the detectives that had interviewed him. They walked in front and behind, guiding him to the exit.

He'd turned the idea over and over in his mind, trying to look at it from every angle, but he still wasn't entirely sure he'd made the right choice. The only thing he was certain of was that he did not want to go to prison.

He'd heard stories from Dodders, Lev and the others about the crazy shit they'd got up to while inside.

He remembered laughing along with the joke while, deep down, feeling scared and worried. It sounded like hell. A paranoid, violent nightmare from which there was no escape.

Some of those tales haunted his dreams, waking him in the middle of the night and making him question his choices. Why was he hanging around with these guys? Where had it all changed and gone wrong.

And here he was, in custody, and the police were dangling the offer of freedom before him if he'd do something for them in return.

The money sounded good. He liked that idea of getting paid for info, and he'd already come up with some ideas for the kind of things he could pass along. But he couldn't help but wonder what would happen to him if he got caught. Dodders and the others frequently hurt people they considered rats, and here he was, agreeing to become the very thing his gang mates hated.

But what could he do? It wasn't as if he had much choice in the matter, not when the threat of prison loomed before him.

He did not want to go to prison.

There was no way he was going to end up in one of those cells, fearing that rival gang members might come knocking and stab him to death with a shiv.

"Remember," the detective behind him said. He couldn't remember his name. "Don't say a word to anybody about our agreement, not if you value your life."

"I won't, don't you worry," Ambrose agreed. "I ain't saying nothin'."

"And you've got the number to call when you have something for us?"

"Aye, it's saved under 'Dick' in my phone."

Ambrose didn't need to turn to know that the detective was rolling his eyes behind him. "Of course, it is," the man answered. "We won't contact you, but we will expect a call from you at least once a month with an update. But if you don't come back to us with anything useful in three months, we'll review our agreement."

"And you might take action against me," Ambrose added. "I know, I got it. Don't fret it, fam."

"Don't you worry. I'm not fretting anything. You're the one that's got the hard job."

Ambrose grunted at the idea. He'd got himself into this situation, and it was down to him to get himself out of it, somehow, if that was even possible.

"We've already released Carmela, so she might be out there, waiting for you, but we're going to charge Mr Dodson and Mr Levine."

Ambrose listened and nodded along while staring ahead as the detective in front opened the door and allowed him through.

This second detective briefly locked eyes with him, giving him a cool stare that chilled Ambrose, sending a shiver down his spine. He pressed on and walked out into reception. He couldn't quite believe they were just letting him walk out of there, and for a moment, he stopped and looked back.

"Go on, off you go," the more talkative detective said before they closed the door. He glanced at the custody officer behind the reception. She smiled back before continuing on with her work. A handful of people were sitting in the reception, but they paid him no mind, and he didn't recognise anyone. It was curious, though, because he felt suddenly vulnerable as if everyone could read his mind and knew he was now a grass.

Steeling himself for the trip home, he turned and marched to the exit. It opened easily, and the warmth of the building was instantly replaced with a cool breeze. He shivered but stepped out anyway. He needed to get home.

"Just you, is it?"

Ambrose turned to see Carmela Kerr, who he knew better as K. She had her back to the wall while taking a drag from a cigarette. She pulled the smoke down into her lungs with a hiss before breathing it out in a billowing cloud.

For a brief moment, Ambrose was frozen to the spot, worried that she'd somehow already guessed that he was now working for the enemy. But that was silly. How would she know?

"Cat got your tongue, Rice?" she asked, using his nickname. It was born from his love of egg fried rice from the local Chinese takeaway, and it wasn't long before the name just stuck.

"No, just, you took me by surprise. That's all."

"You're jumpy, Rice. Something wrong?"

Had she noticed something was off? He needed to reassure her. "I just wasn't expecting to get out. Are Dodders and Lev out too?"

"Nope," she answered quickly and narrowed her eyes. "Just me and you." Did she suspect?

"Shit," he muttered. "Are they… You know…"

"Going down?" she asked, but then shrugged. "No idea. How'd it go? It's your first time, right?"

"Yeah. It was okay. Scary, though. I thought I was going down, for sure."

"And what did you say?"

He could answer this one. He still felt hot and nervous, though. Would she notice him sweating? "I did like you guys said I should. I answered no comment to everything."

"I see…" She sounded suspicious.

"I did. I promise," he answered. "I promise."

She threw her cigarette onto the floor, stepped on it and ground it into the concrete with a twist of her foot. "So, they didn't try to get to you? They didn't offer you anything? They usually offer shit to newbies like you."

"Oh, yeah. They offered stuff," Ambrose confirmed. "They wanted all sorts from me, but I just did as you told me. I just said no comment. Next thing I know, they're walking me out. I've got no idea what changed." He could feel his confidence growing as he continued to defend his honour. There was no way she was drawing it out of him like this.

"What did they want?" she pressed.

"Anything. They were asking me all sorts, trying to get me to rat on you and the others. But I ain't about that. I didn't give them nothin'." He smiled, pleased with his answer.

Carmela stared at him for a moment, before nodding slowly. "Alright. Let's get out of here, this place stinks of bacon."

Ambrose smiled to himself and set off beside her, feeling like he'd passed the test. Maybe this wouldn't be so difficult after all.

22

Having parked up in the Custody Suite car park, Rob walked towards reception with Karl and noticed two of the four gang members they'd arrested yesterday in Worksop walking away from the building.

Rob slowed to watch them go, remembering Nick had said they'd turned one of them into an informant. They'd no doubt let two of them go to make sure it wasn't too suspicious while keeping two others in and charging them with the crime.

He hoped their gamble worked. It was always a risk, turning a gang member into an informant. There had been several cases of gang members using this situation to grass up other gangs, so the police arrested their rivals. The informant's gang could then expand and grow, taking over enemy territory with little risk to themselves because they were useful to the police.

He hoped that letting these two go wouldn't end up biting them on the arse later or get the informant into trouble. The informant was taking a much bigger risk than they were, after all. If the gang found out he'd turned into a grass they'd almost certainly seriously hurt or even kill him without a moment's hesitation.

Time would tell.

He followed Karl into the building. They made their way through security and walked along corridors before finally reaching the central desk at the crux of the four wings. The evening was drawing in, and there wasn't much light coming through the skylights above the desk anymore.

Rob waited while Karl spoke with the custody officer and arranged for the formal charging to take place. When a suitable moment presented itself, Rob leaned in. "If you don't mind, I'd like one last quick chat with Gavin before we charge him."

Karl turned to frown at him. "Oh?"

"Hope you don't mind. I have a couple of questions."

Karl paused for a beat and glanced at Gavin before answering. "No, of course not. That's fine. Do you want me to join you or…"

"No, thank you," Rob replied and smiled.

It didn't take long to arrange, and soon Gavin was led into a nearby interview room, where he sat and waited. Rob joined him and took the seat opposite, dismissing the custody officer who'd remained in the room.

Gavin was no threat.

The young man stared at Rob. "What's up?"

"A little birdy's told me that you were kidnapped by the gang that your father works for about seven months ago.

Apparently, that's how they broke him, by beating you up and threatening to kill you. Is that right?"

"No. That's nonsense. That's a lie. Who told you that?"

"So that didn't happen?" Rob asked, sceptical.

"No, it didn't."

"You're sure about that? You weren't beaten up?"

With his brow knitted, Gavin shook his head. "Of course, I'm sure. I'd know if I'd been kidnapped and beaten to a pulp. It, did, not, happen," he said, enunciating each word. "Which idiot is saying that?"

Rob frowned. "I'm not at liberty to say, I'm afraid. But it does fit with what others told me; that around seven months ago, you refused to go to your dad's for a few weeks until he could convince you to go back. Do you want to explain why two people have independently told us this? Was it because you'd been kidnapped and hurt?"

"Seven months ago? Christ, I can't remember. I was probably upset at my dad over something. It wouldn't be the first time." He seemed exasperated that Rob would even ask him about it.

"So it wasn't because you'd been beaten up."

"No. I wasn't beaten up. Have you spoken to my mum? Did she say I turned up with a black eye or anything?"

"Well, no," Rob admitted.

"Of course she didn't," Gavin jumped in, "because it didn't happen."

"But what if they didn't touch your face? Then you could hide it."

Gavin laughed. "Have you heard yourself? This is insane. It's obvious lies. Why can't you see this? Look, I'll tell you again. My dad was not corrupt. I was just lashing out when I said that, but it's not true. I screwed up. That's it."

"And you don't know who killed your dad?" Rob asked.

"No. No idea. Isn't that your job? Shouldn't you have made some progress by now?"

Rob grimaced, feeling a little uncomfortable. "We're all working hard to find out who killed him. You have my word on that. But, to be clear, you don't know who killed him or why someone might want to kill him, right?"

"I don't know who killed him," Gavin stated clearly. "As for why… Well, he was a police officer, so he's probably pissed a lot of criminals off."

Rob bit his lip. It was possible, sure. But he doubted it. It had been years since Lee had been a front-line officer, making arrests and dealing directly with criminals. So that idea just didn't ring true for him. What was becoming obvious, though, was how pointless this conversation was. Gavin wasn't going to accept anything Rob suggested, and it seemed like there was little he could do to change the young man's mind.

"Okay, fine. We're done. Let's get you charged and out of here, okay?"

"Sure, thanks." Gavin seemed to relax, and his whole attitude changed, becoming warmer and easier.

Back out in the main lobby of the unit, Rob watched as the custody officers charged Gavin with GBH against the girl he'd stabbed and released him on bail with certain conditions, all of which were outlined on the sentencing sheet which was handed to him. Gavin would be under a curfew and must report to his local station at least once a week until his court date.

Rob leaned against the wall as he watched, with Karl nearby.

"It's been a busy weekend," Rob said.

"It has. But I've got the day off tomorrow," Karl mused with a smile.

"Lucky you," Rob replied absentmindedly. "Got anything planned?"

"Nah," Karl answered. "Michelle's working, so I've been left to my own devices. I might be at a bit of a loose end, actually."

"Do you get a lie in?"

"Oh yes," Karl confirmed. "I'm looking forward to that."

"I bet," Rob replied with a smile, feeling a little jealous that he'd be working on a Sunday. But he didn't mind too much. This case needed work, so it would be all hands on deck… Rob paused his train of thought and glanced over at Karl, wondering why he'd said he was at a loose end. But then a thought occurred. Karl had already said how much he missed working with the EMSOU, so was he expecting an invite to help out?

Rob looked away and shook his head to himself. No chance.

"Well, enjoy it," Rob said. "I'd rather have a day off than be working on a Sunday."

Karl grunted but didn't seem to agree.

Moments later, the process was done, and Gavin could leave. For a moment, he seemed a little lost, as if unsure what to do.

Rob stepped forward. "Fancy a lift home? I can take you to your mother's."

"Aaah, yeah. Sounds good." He didn't seem sure.

"Or somewhere else? Justine is at your dad's place."

"No, my mum's will be fine. Thank you."

Rob eyed him and the hesitation in Gavin's voice. He seemed uncertain or maybe worried. "Would you like me to get an officer to stand on the doorstep?"

"Aaah, yeah, okay, sounds good," Gavin replied, looking a little happier.

Now, why would that be, Rob wondered as he plucked his phone out of his pocket.

23

Rob drove east through the city, winding his way through the New Basford estate to Nottingham Road and headed south. He was joined on the ride only by Gavin, having left Karl back at the suite. They'd travelled there in separate cars, knowing they wouldn't be returning to the Lodge, so Karl didn't need to catch a ride with Rob.

Slumped in the front passenger seat, Gavin seemed to turtle, keeping his hands in his lap and hanging his head. But his eyes were alert and flicked around the car, taking in everything around him.

They were in Belle, Rob's Black 1985 Ford Capri, which probably seemed like a museum piece to Gavin.

"It's an old car," Rob said, glancing at Gavin.

He briefly met Rob's gaze and nodded. "I guessed. No Bluetooth or anything."

Rob laughed. "No. Cars had radios and tape decks back then. It probably seems a little basic, right?"

"A bit."

"It's not got all the mod cons of a police pool car, but the drive is so much better, in my opinion. You really feel the road and the power of the engine. You should try driving an older car. That's how you really learn. These modern cars practically drive themselves."

Gavin continued to nod along, listening, but his expression was slightly incredulous. "You're really into this, aren't you."

"Yeah," Rob admitted. "I take good care of Belle, and she—"

"Belle?" Gavin asked, butting in. "You named your car?"

"I did," Rob said, feeling a mild flush of embarrassment. He chose not to go into the sentimental reasoning behind the name, preferring to keep that very personal information to himself.

"It's a bit like a mustang, isn't it."

"It is," Rob agreed. "It was billed as the British version of that car."

"Cool."

"Very cool." Rob grinned as they drove by Forest Fields, going past the road with the off-licence where Gavin had stabbed the girl. He looked down the road as they passed it. Rob did the same, spotting the tell-tale blue and white police tape still attached to the shop front before it was suddenly gone again as they continued south. Soon they'd head east into the Mapperley Park area, where Gavin's mother lived, and Rob could drop him off.

"How you feeling?" Rob asked, as Gavin dropped his gaze to his lap.

"I'm okay. Wish I hadn't been such an idiot, like, but... What's done is done."

"It is," Rob agreed. "But you did the right thing. You didn't leg it, you confessed, and you've bent over backwards to help us. It's appreciated, and I'm sure the judge will agree."

"I hope so."

"I just wish you'd be a little more helpful with your dad's case."

Gavin grunted.

"We're here to support you, Gavin. If you'd just help us out, I'm sure everything would be fine."

"Nothing's going to be fine now. Not now... Not after... This."

He seemed a little emotional, but given this was his first time returning to the scene of his crime and the loss of his father, it was probably to be expected.

It was bringing it all home to him. He'd screwed up. But was there more to it, than that?

"No, I guess not. But if you're worried about anything, maybe we can help? We're quite good at protecting people, you know. If that's what you need." He wasn't sure if this was the issue, but something was bothering Gavin, and Rob couldn't help but wonder if there really was a gang angle to this.

"I'm good," Gavin answered quickly.

"As long as you're sure."

"I'm sure."

Moments later, they turned into his mother's road and parked right outside her house was a police car, just as Rob had hoped.

"See, you'll be fine."

"Mmm," Gavin muttered. He didn't sound convinced.

Rob parked up, and once they were out of the car, led him to his front door, where an officer was standing guard.

"Sir," the constable said. "I've introduced myself to the family. They know I'm out here."

"Thank you," Rob answered and knocked on the door. It was opened moments later by Shelley.

"Gavin! Oh god," she gasped, and pulled her son in for a hug. "I'm so sorry. Are you okay? How are you? Did they treat you alright?"

"I'm fine, Mum." Gavin sounded annoyed by his mother's fussing. He managed to free himself from her hugs and kisses, and pushed past her into the house. "I need a drink."

"Oh, okay, well, that's fine." She seemed to want to follow after him and fuss, but she hesitated, sensing he probably needed some space. She turned back to Rob. "Thank you. Thank you so much for bringing him home."

"My pleasure."

Rob watched Gavin walk to the kitchen at the back of the house, hunting for food and drink. Shelley's boyfriend, Louis, appeared as Gavin passed. They swapped a one-word greeting, with Gavin barely looking at his potential future stepfather.

"Can you…" Shelley said, and nodded to the kitchen.

"Yeah," he agreed, and followed Gavin down the hallway.

"Is he okay?" Shelley asked, turning back to Rob.

"He's fine. He's been charged with GBH, and should have his day in court in the next few weeks. But with the loss of his dad, his general cooperation, and given the girl survived with no lasting damage, I suspect they might go easy on him." Rob shrugged. "Don't quote me on that, though."

"I won't. What's all this about?" She pointed to the uniformed officer in his bright yellow high-vis vest.

"Gavin seemed a little worried about coming home, so we assured him we'd put an officer on the door, just in case," Rob explained. "He'll watch the house for you tonight."

"That's very kind. Do you think he's in trouble, then?"

"I don't know," Rob admitted. "Possibly. So don't go opening the door to anyone you don't know."

A look of concern crossed her face. "You think that's a possibility?"

"I'm not trying to scare you. I just want you to be careful. I'm sure everything will be fine. Don't worry."

"It's a little late for that."

"And that's why we have an officer here," Rob said. "You'll be fine. And it goes without saying that Gavin needs to stay inside. His terms of bail have him on a curfew anyway. It's all on his sentencing sheet. He'll show you."

"Okay," she said. "And what about Lee? Anything new there?"

"You should have been visited by an FLO," Rob stated, keen to make sure the team were doing what they should.

"Yeah, she visited. She's not here now, though."

"No. That's fine. As for Lee, the investigation is still very much ongoing, so I can't say much. We're speaking to witnesses and trying to piece it all together. Rest assured, as soon as we have something concrete we can come to you with, we will."

"So you don't know if he was corrupt, then?" she asked.

"It's hard to say for sure, and I can't really offer an opinion," Rob answered.

"Okay," Shelley said, seeming to drop this line of questioning. "I have one thing I'm concerned about, though," she added. "Justine."

"Why?"

"She wants to see Gavin tomorrow, and I'm just... I'm not sure if that's appropriate. She's not his mother or anything.

She's not even old enough to be his mother. There's only nine years between them."

Rob pressed his lips together in thought before answering. "I understand, and it's not for me to really say one way or another, but Gavin is nineteen and quite capable of making his own choices. So, maybe ask him if he wants to see her. You can't stop him if he does. She'll only text him directly anyway, now he's got his phone back."

"No, I know," she admitted. "But, she might be a bad influence on him."

"How so?" Rob asked with a frown, unsure what she meant.

"Well, Lee changed when he got together with her. I think it could have been her that changed him. She was a bad influence."

"I'm not—" Rob began, not really agreeing with her.

"I know," she cut in. "I can't really explain it. It doesn't make much sense to me either, but there's just something about her that I didn't like. She seems better now than she used to be, but... I don't know. I'm not sure. Maybe I'm wrong. I just know that Lee changed when he started dating her."

Rob wondered if there was a note of jealousy there or not. Did she resent him for finding happiness with a woman over twenty years his junior?

"Sorry, just ignore me." Shelley sighed. She must have seen the scepticism in his face. "It's been a difficult few days, and I'm just tired."

"That's okay," Rob reassured her. "We all have days like that. I'm going to need a few days off to recover after all this is over, too."

"I bet," she sympathised. "It can't be an easy job."

"No, it's not. But it has its benefits too." As he answered, a thought occurred to him. "Actually, I do have a question for you."

"Mmm."

"Yeah. So, you mentioned that there was a time when Gavin came back and hid in his room for a week or two, and you hardly saw him, right?"

"Yeah," she agreed.

"Did he seem in pain to you, during that time?"

"I, don't know... I suppose he could have been. He didn't really talk to me about it. He just spent a lot of time in bed. I thought he was ill, maybe? Why? What have you learned?"

"We're not sure, at this time. But thank you anyway."

"Okay."

"Anyway," Rob reached into his pocket and plucked out a business card, "here. This is the number for my work mobile. You can always reach me on it. Call if there's anything you need to speak to me about."

"Thanks, I will," she confirmed. "Maybe I'll let him choose what to do about Justine." She shrugged. "You're right. He is old enough."

"I think that's your best option."

"Thank you."

Rob said farewell as he felt his phone buzz in his pocket with a notification. He checked it to find a message from Nick, asking if he wanted to join them for a few drinks in town.

24

Standing outside All Bar One, on the edge of the Lace Market in Nottingham, Bill checked himself in the window one more time, peering at his reflection and adjusting his shirt. He felt irritable and impatient, wanting to get this over and done with rather than enjoy it.

He was keen to get back to work tomorrow and try to turn things around after everything seemed to get away from him today. He still couldn't quite understand why he felt like this, apart from things with Rob and the new EMSOU not going as he'd hoped. He thought Rob would be more nervous around him, and he'd be more in control. But control seemed to be the one thing he didn't have. He had none of it, and that made him anxious.

Tonight had been something he'd been looking forward to, until all this had kicked off. He'd swapped messages with his date, Susie, and she seemed nice enough. She was certainly good-looking, but then, he had standards. There was no way he'd be seen dead with anyone who didn't care as much about their appearance as he did. First impressions were key, after all, and it was always important to look good. He wondered what she'd be wearing and if he'd recognise her when she arrived. He'd texted her with a description of his outfit and where he'd be waiting, so between that and his profile photos, she should be able to pick him out from the crowd.

It was Saturday night, after all, and while it was busy, it wasn't quite as bad as a Friday.

Bill checked his smartwatch and noted with slight dismay that she was a few minutes late. He preferred people to be punctual, but he decided to let her off. He supposed it was a woman's prerogative to be a little late.

As he allowed his gaze to wander over the evening crowds, looking for Susie, he suddenly spotted a few faces he recognised and froze to the spot.

Across the street, a short distance up from where he was standing, he saw Rob with Nick, Guy, Ellen, and Tucker, walking as a group towards him. For a moment, he panicked, unsure what to do. He didn't want them to see him out, and he certainly didn't want them to see him and his date. He'd never live it down.

But as he watched with growing horror, they turned into the Cross Keys Pub on the other side of Weekday Cross road. They were talking and laughing amongst themselves and didn't notice him at all. As they disappeared inside, Bill felt his heartrate ease, but his curiosity grow. They'd gone out without him, no doubt, to discuss the case, and he wouldn't be there to participate.

Clenching his fists, he felt his anger at their deception rise. It felt like his blood was starting to simmer. How dare they leave him out of this?

"Bill, is it?"

Shocked by the sudden mention of his name, Bill jumped and turned to see a pretty woman beside him, smiling expectantly. He recognised Susie from her Tinder profile.

"Oh, Susie. You caught me by surprise."

"I'm sorry." Nervously, she brushed a loose strand of hair behind her ear. She smiled, and he found himself admiring her for a moment. She did look nice, although she'd chosen to wear trousers tonight, which somehow disappointed him.

"That's okay." Bill glanced over at the Cross Keys, finding himself torn as to what he should do. Stay on the date, or dump her and start watching them? But maybe he could do both. If they got a window seat, he could keep an eye on the pub and enjoy his meal too.

"Everything okay?"

Bill turned to her. "Yes, fine," he snapped. "Why wouldn't it be?"

She flinched ever so slightly, but Bill didn't really register it as he waved her towards the bar's entrance. They walked inside and were shown to their table in the centre of the main bar. Bill sneered at the position. He couldn't keep an eye on the pub from here.

Susie went to sit, but Bill glanced around, spotting a table at the window where another couple was starting to get up and leave.

"I'd like to sit over there," he said, pointing. The waitress seemed to freeze for a moment as she processed this information and glanced at Susie, who was halfway to sitting down.

"Oh, but, um, that table isn't ready," the waitress said.

"This is fine," Susie added, going to sit again.

"No," Bill said, his words pulling her back. He turned to the waitress. "We'll wait while you clear it. I'd like a window seat."

"Okay, fine," the waitress said. "If that's what you'd prefer."

"It is," he snapped, offering the waitress a joyless smile. Why did so few wait staff realise that the customer was always right.

Looking flustered, the waitress strolled to the table by the window, allowing the previous couple time to vacate their seats. Bill followed once Susie had extricated herself from the seat she'd chosen as her own. She smiled at him, but he wasn't sure how genuine it was. He didn't much care. He had bigger things to think about than what she thought of him. Bill didn't return the smile, and walked over to the table.

The departing couple briefly got in his way, slowing him down as he approached. He sighed loudly, triggering dirty looks from both before he got by. Susie had ducked around the other side of the departing couple and reached the table first, and to Bill's dismay, she went for the seat facing the Cross Key's pub.

"I want to sit there," he stated, bringing his date up short as she went to sit for a second time. She froze and stared up at him, but he didn't pay too much attention to her expression as he checked out the view he had of the pub. It was perfect. He smiled to himself.

"Okay, sorry," Susie said before she moved around to the other side of the table. His date and the waitress seemed to swap a glance out of the corner of his eye, but he paid little attention to it as he took his seat and doubled checked his view.

The waitress offered them the drinks menu and said they could order via the QR code at the table.

Susie thanked the waitress, and she left. Susie coughed, catching Bill's attention. He looked across at her, and she smiled.

"You're right. This is a nicer table," she commented. "It's good to have a view."

"It is," he agreed and studied her face for a moment, spotting some clumping of the Mascara on her eyelashes. He ground his teeth.

"So, you're a police officer?" she asked.

With constant glances across the road, Bill sighed. Unfortunately, he needed to talk to her when all he wanted to do was sit and wait for Rob and the others, so he could follow them. Well, follow Rob mainly, just in case he ended up meeting anyone he shouldn't.

"I am," Bill answered his date. "I work for the Police Standards Unit. I hunt down corrupt cops."

"Oh, I see. That's been in the news a lot lately, hasn't it."

"Police corruption? Yes, it has. It's a constant thorn in our side, but we must maintain standards so we can serve the public to the best of our ability. Without the public's trust, the police cannot function and do its job. We need that trust, and it's my mission to make sure we keep Nottinghamshire police clean of any kind of corruption. It's an important job."

"You certainly sound dedicated to it," she said.

"That's because I am. You don't reach the rank of Inspector without doing a good job."

"That's impressive," she said with a smile.

Her compliment buoyed him up, and he enjoyed the recognition of his hard work and dedication. He returned her smile, feeling good about himself. "Thank you. It's nice to be recognised. I take my job seriously."

"I can see that," she replied and left her words hanging. Bill wasn't sure where the conversation was going, and for a moment, a silence grew between them until she filled it. "I'm a teacher, by the way."

"I saw on your profile," Bill confirmed, remembering. He'd made sure to re-read her profile before meeting up to keep her information fresh in his mind.

"Mmm," she muttered. Again there was a silence until she filled it. "I teach primary school kids, which has its challenges too, but it's very fulfilling at the same time. I get a lot out of it."

"I get a great sense of achievement when I finally bring down a corrupt cop I've been chasing," he stated. "After months of hard work and investigation, there's nothing quite like slamming those cuffs on and seeing the look in their eyes as they realise the game is up. It's a great feeling."

"I'm sure it is," she said, but her voice sounded stilted.

"So, you're a teacher," he mused. He was staring out the window and missed her looking up with interest and fading hope. "Schools these days, they don't have a clue. They don't teach life skills at all. They just teach algebra and long division. Who uses that? Teachers have no idea, I tell yeh. I had some bloody stupid ones." He shook his head, a little lost in his monologue. "Those who can, do, those who can't, teach." He stared out the window at the Cross Keys, wondering what Loxley and the others were discussing and what he was missing out on. Rob was almost certainly stringing his work colleagues on with a tale about how he was being victimised by the PSU breathing down his neck. The idiot. Bill bit his lip, and after a few moments mulling over what the EMSOU group would be talking about, he realised that Susie wasn't talking.

He glanced over to find she was tapping away on her phone. He couldn't really remember what they'd been talking about, but this was intolerable. How rude of her to sit there on her phone. He was disgusted.

He sighed loudly. Her eyes flicked up briefly before returning to her phone.

"Is everything okay for you?" Bill looked up at the waitress. She wore a shit-eating smile. "Would you like to order drinks with me or use the QR code?"

Bill coughed to get Susie's attention. He smiled at her when she looked up, but it was all for show. "I presume you're okay to split the bill?"

Susie screwed her mouth up, stared at him for a long moment, and then looked up at the waitress. "We'll need five minutes," she said, and stood up. "I'm going to the bathroom."

She grabbed her bag and walked off. Bill looked up at the waitress. "Sorry, I'm sure she won't be long."

The young server looked off in the direction that Susie had gone and then back down at Bill. "Yeah... I'll give you a few minutes." She walked away.

Bill shrugged and went back to staring out the window. A moment later, Susie walked by on the street, giving him the finger.

For a brief moment, shock and adrenaline raced through his body as he registered what had happened. He looked off in the direction she'd left the table and realised she'd walked to the exit. When he looked back out the window, Susie was long gone.

Bill slumped into his chair and chewed his lip in frustration before his eyes returned to the pub.

Well, he mused, she was boring anyway. But as it turned out, the night might not be such a waste after all. Taking a breath and putting Susie out of his mind, he took a long look at the menu. Bill picked out the Duck Gyoza starter, with Fish and Chips as the main. Within moments he'd used the QR code to place his order and settled in for the night.

25

The barman placed the first of their drinks down before Rob.

"Thanks," he said and turned to Nick. "Well done on getting Ambrose to turn informant. If he can shed some light on the Masons' business, that would be great."

"It was touch and go there for a while," Nick replied. "I wasn't sure he was going to go for it. But we caught a break, so I guess we'll see."

"You released two of them, right? To throw the others off the scent."

"Yeah, Ambrose and the girl. It would have looked odd had we just released one."

"You did right," Rob complimented him. "I just hope it works out for us. How did Ambrose seem to you? Was he game for it?"

"I don't know about that. He seemed nervous, to be honest."

"Aaah. Well, hopefully, he doesn't blow it."

"Provided he doesn't say anything, he'll be fine," Nick said. "He just needs to keep his mouth shut."

"That would be a solid start," Rob agreed as the barman placed the last of the round before them.

Once he'd paid, Rob stood three pints together on the bar in a triangle and carefully picked them up with the front pint clamped between his fingers. Nick grabbed the other two, and they returned to the table where Ellen, Tucker and Guy were sitting and talking.

Rob passed out the drinks and took a seat.

"So, how was it?" Guy asked after taking a sip of his beer. "You spent most of the day hanging out with the delightful Sheriff. I'm surprised you're not curled up and whimpering in bed."

"I'm made of sterner stuff than that," Rob replied. "It was fine, though. Honestly, he's a bit of a dick. But it's not as if I didn't already know that."

"So you didn't learn anything new then?"

"About Bill? Not really. He was rude and pushy with potential suspects, almost alienating them entirely. I had to step in when we were talking to Gemma and Ben, though. I thought Ben was about to lamp him one."

"Holy hell," Tucker commented. "He's such a wazzock."

"I know."

"Has the willy-womble still got it in for you?"

Rob nodded. "Oh yes, he still thinks I'm Mr Big. He'll die on that particular hill. I ended up speaking my mind to him, though, at the end of the day. I'm afraid to say I lost it a bit and had a go at him. But he deserved it, the idiot. I hope his date is a disaster."

"Date?" Ellen asked.

"He's on a date?" Nick added.

"I think so. He said he was busy, so I made a joke suggesting he had a hot date, and he went very quiet."

"Oh, I wish I could see that. I'd pay money to be a fly on the wall in that restaurant."

"I know," Rob agreed. "Poor girl, whoever she is. She's got no idea what she's letting herself in for."

"Well, at least she'll have a story to tell," Ellen said, grinning. "In fact, he might put her off men altogether, so there'll be more for us vagitarians to choose from."

"Honestly, it wouldn't surprise me," Rob agreed.

"Me neither," Nick added and then addressed the group. "So, how did your day go on the Garrett case?"

"We ended with a revelation," Ellen stated.

"Two, actually," Rob added.

"Two?" Ellen asked, surprised.

"Yep," Rob confirmed with a smile. "You go first, though."

"Intriguing," she said mysteriously and cleared her throat. "We went to speak with Justine, Lee's girlfriend, and she told us that she discovered a secret phone that Lee had. She unlocked it and discovered that he'd been having an affair with his DCI, Gemma Flint, before the Major Oak investigation. But it all turned sour when that op went sideways. They argued, and Lee threatened to tell her husband about their affair if Gemma didn't take one for the team and resign. So she did. Justine then phoned Gemma and threatened to do the same just before Lee was murdered."

"So both Justine and Gemma have a motive for killing him," Nick stated. "And Gemma knows our procedures."

"And how to manipulate them," Rob added. "But the revelations didn't stop there. DI Karl Rothman, another of Lee's subordinates, came to see me at the Lodge. We had a private chat, and he told me that he'd spoken to Lee recently, and Lee had admitted to him that he had worked for a criminal gang in the past, passing information to them."

"So he *was* corrupt," Ellen exclaimed.

"Karl told you that?" Nick asked.

"Yeah. Apparently, Lee needed to share it with someone because keeping it to himself was becoming too much to bear. But he told Nick not to tell anyone because if it got out that he knew, then he'd be in danger. It's possible that Lee was also in trouble and needed someone to know the truth."

"Which gang was this?" Tucker asked.

"Guess," Rob answered, his voice even.

"Oh."

"Yeah, that one," Rob confirmed. "The Masons, again. They're just everywhere right now. I can't seem to escape them."

"So Lee was working for the Masons, once upon a time," Nick said. "Do we know when? How long for? Anything?"

"Karl was unsure about those details, but Lee said he didn't work for them anymore. Karl didn't really believe that, though, and I don't think I do, either."

"But if he had stopped, it would give the gang a motive to kill him."

"It would," Rob agreed. "That was part of Karl's point."

"What about Major Oak?" Guy asked. "Was he working for them, then?"

"Again, I don't know. But now I think about it, I suppose that could have been a turning point. When three of Lee's team were killed, it could have made him rethink his actions and pull out."

"Which in turn, would trigger the gang," Nick added. "They find a shooter and kill him to teach any other defector a lesson. You don't walk away from the Masons."

"Not easily, at least," Rob agreed, aware of his own situation. "But that's not all Karl told me. He said that the gang recruited Lee by kidnapping Gavin and threatening to kill him. This in turn made Gavin paranoid..."

"Aaah," Nick said. "Yes. So then he starts carrying a knife around to protect himself. That makes sense. It also explains why Gavin clammed up and retracted his statement about his dad being corrupt. He assumed the Masons learned about it and killed his dad in retaliation. Gavin took it as a warning."

"It's a working hypothesis," Rob agreed. "But that all depends on us being right about the gang angle rather than it being a disgruntled or former lover."

"We can't rule those out," Ellen said. "It's usually someone closest to you that kills you, not a stranger."

"Absolutely," Rob agreed. "And until we have some hard evidence that points the finger more clearly, we're in the dark about all this. So keep an open mind and a clear head, guys." Rob raised his drink. "I'll let you off tonight, though, as long as you come in bright-eyed and bushy-tailed tomorrow."

"You're too kind," Nick said with a smile.

"So, are we going to take in a few pubs tonight? We could tour around the Lace Market," Tucker suggested.

"I'm not sure about that," Ellen grumbled.

"This won't be a late one for me," Guy added.

"Lightweights," Tucker shot back.

As they spoke, a pretty face at the bar caught Rob's attention. It was Matilda Greenwood, and she was ordering a drink. He gazed at her for a long moment, noticing that her hair was down and how it softened her look, even with the pencil skirt and heels.

He had to admit to himself that she made his heart flutter.

For a tantalising moment, he considered getting up and going to talk to her before looking around the table at his unit and feeling bad for considering leaving them.

But they wouldn't mind. He'd spent plenty of evenings with them since joining the unit, and the topic of conversation had moved on from the case to more mundane matters. They didn't need him here.

He glanced back at Matilda and found her looking right at him. She smiled and waved. His stomach did a somersault.

Rob smiled back and glanced at his team. Suddenly, echoing through his head, he heard Scarlett's telling him to take a chance. If she were here right now, she'd be kicking him off his chair and ordering him to go and speak to her.

He briefly wondered how Scarlett's weekend was going with her friends and found he missed her drive and fierceness. She was a key member of the group, and it just wasn't the same without her.

Rob went to get up.

Nick gave him a look. "Everything alright?"

Rob nodded. "Yeah, I'm fine. Just spotted someone I know. Shouldn't be too long."

Nick scanned the bar. "Oh, take your time," he answered and bobbed his eyebrows at him suggestively.

"Shut it, you." Rob wandered over to Matilda. She turned to greet him and held up an arm to pull him in for a hug.

"Hiya."

"Hey." He obliged and hugged her back, enjoying the brief moment of closeness and the waft of her perfume.

"How are you?" she asked once they'd separated. "It's good to see you out and about."

"I'm just with the guys, grabbing a quick drink before turning in. I'm working tomorrow."

"Me too," Matilda commiserated. "Working Sundays sucks."

"You'll get no argument from me on that one. Not as bad as Christmas, though."

"True," she confirmed. "I've done that before."

"Are you here alone?" Rob asked. There wasn't anyone at the bar with her that he recognised.

"No," she answered and pointed to another table. "I'm with some workmates, but they can get along fine without me."

Rob recognised some of them. "We both had the same idea, then. A quickie before bed." He realised the innuendo the moment he'd said it, but it was too late.

She raised an eyebrow and smirked. "Something like that. Can I get you a drink, or are you okay?" She nodded to the half-drunk pint.

"I'm fine. I don't want a hangover tomorrow."

"Okay." She paid for her large glass of white wine before settling onto a bar stool. Rob followed suit. "I think I heard about the case you're working on. It's the Clumber Murder, right?"

"That's the one," Rob confirmed. He couldn't reveal too much, even if she was, to some extent, a work colleague.

"Sounds like a gang hit, maybe? Or a professional hit of some kind, anyway."

"That's a possibility, but we have several lines of enquiry, and I want to keep an open mind."

"Of course you do. You can't work off of hearsay and rumours."

"No, I certainly can't. Sorry, I can't really talk about it much. You understand?"

"Of course." Matilda's eyes were drawn to somewhere just behind him.

"What about to me?" said another female voice he recognised. He turned to see Mary Day, the reporter he'd recently worked with, standing beside him. Her auburn hair framed her striking face in the pub's warm light, making her eyes sparkle with mischief. "Can you say more to me? Off the record, of course."

Rob smiled and shifted uncomfortably on his stool. "Aaah, no. Sorry."

"Shame." She smiled.

"What are you doing here?"

"Really, Rob?" Mary asked. "Is it not obvious? I'd be a shit reporter if I didn't know where the police hung out after work."

"Fair point," Rob answered.

"What? Did you think I followed you here or something? Sorry to burst your handsome little bubble, but I wasn't pining for you, Loxley. Not this time. I just happened to spot my favourite Special Ops Dick and thought I'd come and rub up against him to see what popped out." She gave him an innocent smile followed by a less innocent wink. "But, if you've got nothing to tell me..."

"Sorry," Rob replied, feeling like a deer trapped in two pairs of headlights, unsure of where to turn or look.

"That's okay." She glanced over at Matilda. "Are you going to introduce me to your lovely lady friend?"

"This is Matilda. She's one of the local Duty Solicitors."

Matilda offered her hand. "Pleasure to meet you."

"Likewise," Mary answered.

"We were just having a *quiet* drink," Matilda stated, making her meaning clear.

"Oh, okay. I get the hint. You're not interested in this being a menage a trois. No problem. I'll catch you later, Loxley." With a last cheeky smile, Mary swanned off across the bar.

Rob kept his eyes on his drink as Matilda watched her go.

She turned back to him. "Pretty woman."

"I guess," Rob answered.

"Provocative, too. She was full of double entendres. But I guess that's how she throws people off guard."

"Well, it works, I can tell you. She's good at her job."

"How do you know her?"

"She turned up on our last big case over in Clipstone. Now, I don't usually have a lot of time for the press. But she was nice, rather than an idiot, unlike some reporters I know of, and we kind of got talking. So I ended up agreeing to help her with one of her stories. But that's all."

"Cool," she replied. "I suppose you end up working with some interesting characters in your line of work."

"I bet you do too," Rob shot back. "We're both scraping the bottom of the human barrel when it comes to our jobs."

"I see all levels of the barrel," Matilda answered. "From those that society forgot to those who've basically won the game of capitalism."

"I can imagine. And you still seem well-adjusted. Well done, that's no mean feat."

She laughed. "Thanks, I think. I've got good people around me, though, including my work colleagues. Speaking of which, I take it Scarlett's still shopping with her friends?"

"If she's got any sense, she'll be out getting drunk and enjoying her time off by now. But yeah, I suppose so. I've not heard from her, but I didn't expect to. She'll be having too much fun with her mates to think about work. And no, I'm not jealous. How dare you suggest such a thing," he said in mock outrage, before letting a cheeky grin spread over his face.

She laughed. "Well, as long as you're jealous of her time off, and not the bridesmaid dress shopping, otherwise I'm going to worry."

"You mean to say, you don't think I'd look simply divine in a slinky dress?" he quipped.

"I'll withhold judgement until I see it for myself."

Rob raised his eyebrows. "That's never going to happen."

"Shame," she answered with a smile.

Rob smiled, enjoying the moment of levity. It was nice spending a little time away from the stresses of work to enjoy a drink with Matilda again. They'd done it once before, and he had fond memories of that night, so this would make it twice. "It's good to see you away from an interview room."

"You too," she agreed, running her fingers through her hair. "Cheers."

They clinked glasses.

26

Sitting in the middle of the living room's threadbare sofa with the small dining table up against the wall and the muted TV in the corner, Ambrose listened to his mother's ranting.

She'd hugged him when he'd first arrived home, smothering him with kisses. Since then, she'd followed him around the flat, not leaving him for five minutes unless he visited the bathroom. And even then, she hovered, waiting for him to reappear.

But her initial joy at his return had turned into a self-righteous rant about how he was throwing his life away. This, she said, was cold hard proof that if he didn't stop right now, there would soon come the point of no return. He'd either get himself killed or thrown into the slammer, and that would be the end for him.

She didn't understand.

He had a job to do now, an important job for the police, but it was also a job he couldn't tell her about. She might not be involved in the gangs, but his mum was an incorrigible gossip. So he had little doubt that should he admit he was passing info to the police, she'd soon blab it to the wrong person, and it would be common knowledge all over the estate within hours.

He had to keep quiet and only speak to that pig, Nick.

"I'm struggling to understand you, Ambrose. I really am. I don't know what got into your head about hanging out with these guys. They're idiots, sweetheart. They don't care about you. They just want to use you for their business, that's all. I'm telling you, you'll end up dead. You'll get shot or something, and then I'll be alone. I do not want a policeman coming to my door with terrible news, Ambrose. I don't. I can't handle it."

"You don't understand," he muttered, frustrated, with a zinger of a headache creeping into the edges of his skull.

"Nonsense, I understand perfectly. You spent the night in a cell, young man. A cell! Do you get that? You were arrested. You could have gone to prison, but you escaped by the skin of your teeth. You've been given a second chance. You do see that, right? That you have a second chance to do the right thing? But if you go back to them, if you insist on going back to that gang, I don't... I'll..."

"You'll do what?"

"I don't know. I don't know what I'll do, but I can tell you this, I don't want you here, in this house, bringing their crap home. I don't want it. I don't. Do you understand me?"

There was an almighty bang behind him.

Ambrose turned to see the flat's front door fly open and slam into the wall. Before he could react, three big men charged into the front room. His mother screamed.

"Grab him," one said. "I'll deal with her."

Two others rushed and grabbed him, while the third went for his mum.

"Hey, what? No. Leave her alone!" he shouted as they forced him to the floor. "Get off me."

"Ambrose," his mum shouted. "Ambrose. No. You leave him alone. Don't hurt him. Please."

Ambrose raged, fighting the two men, but he simply wasn't strong enough. They put him onto his front and tried to secure his wrists. He bellowed and roared in protest, fighting them as best he could. One of them punched him, knocking his head into the floor and dazing him.

He felt his wrists being secured with a zip tie, but he couldn't stop them. Then he was up, back onto his feet. The movement seemed to help, and he managed to shake the daze off. Nearby, his mother was whimpering. He looked over to see her slumped onto the floor holding her bleeding face, the third man standing over her. Had he hit her?

"You don't breathe a word of this to anyone, bitch. If you speak to the police, a neighbour, anyone, he dies. Got it?"

She nodded as she cried. "I understand."

He grabbed her by the throat and slammed her head back against the wall. "You'd better. I do not want to come back here and teach you a lesson about how to respect your betters. But I will if I have to, and you won't like it. Got it?"

She nodded furiously.

He dropped her. Ambrose hated seeing them hurt his mother.

With enough of his faculties back, he realised he needed to fight for his life. "You leave her alone, you fucking bastard."

The man turned and made a face. "I'm impressed you're still fighting. That's good. I like a bit of fight."

"Let me go. I'll show you fight," he shouted.

"Too noisy." The man stepped forward and punched him hard in the face.

Reality slipped away, leaving nothing but fleeting dreams and darkness.

27

"No, no, no," Lucy said. "You're having another. This is a celebration. You're marrying my big brother, and this is one of your last nights of freedom, missy!"

Scarlett accepted the drink with a resigned smile and took a mouthful. Her friends cheered.

"I can't believe Chris is getting married," Lucy added. "But I'm glad it's to you."

"Hear, hear," Autumn said. "It couldn't happen to a nicer person."

"I can't believe you're first out of all of us," Cara scoffed.

"That's only because you thought it would be you," Rosie snarked back. "Have you dropped enough hints?"

"Tell him to pull his finger out," Scarlett added. "He needs to put a ring on it if he wants to keep you."

"Aww, don't be mean," Cara said. "Tim's lovely. I'm sure he'll propose soon, especially once he's been to your wedding."

"That's months away." Scarlett pulled a face. "He needs to do something before then."

Cara shrugged. "Hopefully."

Rosie snorted. "Tell him if he doesn't hurry up, I'll pop over and have a word with him."

"O-Oh, the big scary lady is coming over," Scarlett and her friends laughed.

Rosie made claw shapes with her hands and attempted a somewhat weak-sounding roar, which only made them laugh even more.

"You all need to find someone soon," Scarlett said. "I want to have more nights out like this and go to more weddings."

"I'm not ready to settle down yet," Lucy replied, sounding scandalised.

"Yeah, but you're a baby," Autumn commented. Lucy was only about five years younger than Scarlett and her friends, but she was clearly enjoying her single life and making the most of it. "You've got time."

"Thank you. Yes, I have, and I intend to enjoy it," Lucy replied. "I'm not in a rush."

"Good for you." Rosie raised her glass. Scarlett grabbed her wine and joined in with this latest round of cheers before taking a drink.

It was lovely spending time with her friends, and it had also been a very successful day's shopping. They'd narrowed the choice of dress down to two, one of which Ninette had picked, the other was one Cara had found. The issue was that Scarlett liked both, and right now, she wasn't sure which to choose, which meant there'd be a second gathering once she'd made up her mind.

No one was complaining about that, though, and plans were already afoot to arrange it.

Looking around the table, she realised Ninette hadn't returned from the bathroom. She'd been gone for a while. Scarlett checked her watch. Fifteen minutes. Even with a queue, that was ridiculous.

Frowning, she leaned her chair back and looked across the bar towards the toilet door. She couldn't see Ninette there, and a sweep across the bar also failed to reveal her. Where was she?

Scarlett checked her phone, but there weren't any messages saying she'd headed home. She wouldn't have been very surprised if she had abandoned them and made her way back. She'd been aloof all day, only partially joining in with the day's activities. The time she'd been most engaged was when she'd picked out the dress that made the cut into the final two, but other than that, she'd been quiet, withdrawn and kept to herself.

Scarlett understood why, of course. She was worried about Sebastian and the toxic messages he'd been sending her, but she was safe here with them, and Scarlett had hoped Ninette would let her hair down and relax. Unfortunately, she didn't seem quite capable of that.

Where had she gone?

With her curiosity getting the better of her, she went to get up and leaned into Autumn. "I'm going to check on Ninette."

"Okay," Autumn said. "Do you want me to come…"

"No. You're alright. You stay here." Scarlett straightened up to her full height, feeling momentarily dizzy. But the concern for her friend had already had a sobering effect, allowing the vertigo to fade. She walked confidently across the bar, threading between the groups of revellers until she reached the door that led to the bathrooms. She pressed through, passing more people, and spotted the two doors. Male and female. The hallway was quiet and, right at that moment, empty.

At the far end was a service door that presumably led outside. Above it was a smashed CCTV camera. She frowned as she spotted something on the floor below. The unease in her belly grew as she approached the service door to find bits of glass and electronics scattered over the floor below the camera.

A pang of worry made her stomach cramp. Scarlett turned and walked back to the bathrooms. As she went to open the door to the ladies, another woman stepped out first, beating her to it. Scarlett pushed past and walked inside. There was a small queue, but nothing crazy. She ignored it and walked into the main area with the sinks on one side and the stalls opposite.

There was no sign of her friend.

Her unease ratcheted up a notch. "Ninette? Are you in here?"

The women in the queue all turned to look at the crazy blonde.

"Apparently not," one of them said after a moment when it became clear no one was answering.

"What does she look like?" another asked.

"Dark hair, dark blue dress. In fact, like this." She pulled her phone out, opened the gallery, and displayed a photo of her, taken today. She showed it to the ladies in the queue, but none of them recognised her.

"Sorry, not seen her," one of them said. "What's happened? Has she gone missing?"

"I don't know, maybe?"

"Are you sure she wasn't just desperate and used the mens?"

"I've done that before," another woman added.

It was a good shout, so she ran from the ladies' room and into the mens'.

"Oi, oi," one of the guys inside said. "I think you've got the wrong room, love."

"Or the right one," another crooned, grinning like an idiot.

"Ninette? Are you in here?" Scarlett shouted. "Ninette?"

"Is that a girl?" came a voice from a stall.

"You mean there's two fillies in here," the first man said.

But there was no reply from Ninette or any female voice, as Scarlett's concern deepened, and a mild panic began to set in. She ran from stall to stall, opening the doors or jumping to see over the top, much to the dismay of the men inside.

She didn't care.

Ninette wasn't in here, though, so she ran back to the ladies and did the same thing, checking all the stalls.

"Hey, you can't do that!" one woman cried out.

"I'm a police officer, so I'll look where I like," Scarlett said in a moment of frustration. "A friend has gone missing. I'm trying to find her."

The protesting woman went quiet as Scarlett ran from the toilets and crossed the main room again, this time taking a circuitous route that took in the full stretch of the bar and gave her a good look at everyone in there.

Fully sober, she made her way back to the table empty-handed.

Ninette wasn't in here.

"She's gone," Scarlett told the table, getting their attention.

"What?" Autumn asked.

"Who?" Lucy added.

"Ninette. She's disappeared. I can't find her. I've looked in both bathrooms and all the stalls, but she's not there, and I can't see her out here, either."

Everyone jumped up, and within moments they were organising searches while Scarlett tried Ninette's phone. It didn't connect, suggesting it was turned off.

"Might she have gone home?" Autumn suggested. "To yours, I mean?"

"She hasn't got a key," Scarlett answered. "So I don't know how she'd get in."

"Worth checking, though, right?"

"Of course. Come on, let's help the others."

28

Rob ambled down Quay Place, the road leading to his apartment, holding open a polystyrene clamshell food container in one hand. Displayed within it was a half-eaten doner kebab, complete with strips of lamb, salad and garlic sauce. In the cool night air, the heat was fading from the meal, and Rob was starting to feel a little full, but the smell from the takeaway kept luring him back, as he stabbed another strip of meat and ate it.

Ahead, the large modern, three-story apartment blocks on the edge of the river Trent loomed before him. They were a welcome sight for his weary legs.

He'd had a lovely night chatting to Matilda in the Cross Keys pub. They'd talked and laughed, enjoying each other's company, until she had to go. They'd said goodbye with an awkward hug, and Rob felt a tinge of sadness that he couldn't spend any more time with her tonight.

As he bit into another plastic fork full of doner, he mused on how a relationship with Matilda might work if he were to pursue it. They were very much on the opposite sides of a key part of the job, but that didn't mean they couldn't make a go of things. Would there need to be a declared conflict of interest?

On the other hand, having a friendly solicitor might just help them out sometimes.

He did like her, but was this something that Matilda wanted as well? Was he jumping the gun by assuming she was interested in being more than just a friend? Scarlett seemed to think so, but that didn't mean she was right.

But these were all minor inconveniences in the grand scheme of things. His biggest hurdle was himself, which would also be the first he'd need to cross. Did he really want to have a girlfriend when things were just starting to heat up with his family?

He'd avoided this very thing for years out of self-preservation to prevent anyone from getting a hold over him. With his family being who they were, there was an ever-present threat of blackmail, and he was keen to avoid it at all costs. He'd worked long and hard to get where he was, and he did not want to lose it all now.

And even if he put that issue to one side, he'd need to be upfront and honest about his family situation and allow Matilda to choose whether she wanted to take him on, and the baggage he brought with him.

He'd always assumed that few people would agree to such a thing, but he'd never reached that point before, either. He had no idea how Matilda would react and wasn't even sure how much she knew about his family. She never asked him about them, and he'd never volunteered the information. It wasn't something he liked talking about, but he knew he'd have to if he went down this road.

Rob sighed as he munched on another calorific mouthful of this poor excuse for a meal. It was tasty, though, especially after a few pints when he had a bit of a walk to get home.

As he wandered along the road towards his apartment, a taxi passed him and then pulled up a short distance ahead. As he watched, the door opened, and a young woman climbed out. It was his neighbour, Erika. She paid for the taxi and closed the door before turning to look for him.

"Hey," she said cheerily. "Who's the dirty stop out, now?"

"Me," Rob answered, around his mouthful.

She grinned. "Damn right. Oooh, what have you got there?"

"Doner," he muttered.

"Chilli sauce?"

"Garlic."

"Shame. Still, can I have a bite?" Her hungry eyes flicked between him and the remains of the meal.

Feeling full anyway, he handed it to her. "Feel free. I'm done anyway."

"Oooh, lovely. This'll hit the spot nicely. She grabbed the fork and started picking at the salad. "Night out, was it?"

"With a few guys from the office," he confirmed. "We had a couple of drinks, but that's it. Nothing heavy."

"Nice."

"You? Were you out on a date?"

"Nope. I was round a friend's. We had a quiet night in and a few glasses of wine. It was nice." She took a mouthful of doner and moaned in delight. "Oh, that's good."

"I didn't take you for someone that ate a doner kebab. You surprise me."

She smiled. "Oh, I'm full of surprises."

"I bet." Rob smiled as he neared the main door to the building. He glanced left to check on Belle and make sure she was still parked where he'd left her. She was and looked majestic in the evening light. He spotted another car parked nearby and a man leaning up against it.

Probably waiting to pick someone up.

When he turned back to the door, Erika had already opened it. Rob walked over, grabbed the door, and noticed another man standing a short distance up the road in the other direction.

It was odd, but he wasn't concerned.

"What you up to tomorrow?" Erika asked as he closed the door and looked up the street in the direction he'd come. A couple of people walked this way and that, but the night was otherwise quiet.

"Working," Rob answered as they turned towards the stairs.

"Really? On a Sunday?"

"The life of a police officer," he mused as they walked up the stairs to the first floor. "It's not a job with sociable hours."

"Apparently not. Hi," Erika said to Mr Wilkins from the top floor as he wandered down the stairs.

"Oh, it's you. Hello Erika," he said. "You made it inside, I take it?"

Erika frowned. "Yeeeeaaah?"

"Good, good. I can't be doing with all this racket."

"Oh, okay. Sorry."

Mr Wilkins smiled at Rob as he passed. "These young un's, ay." He rolled his eyes. "Always up to somethin'."

"Oh, absolutely," Rob agreed.

"I'll see you later," their neighbour said and carried on downstairs. Erika watched him go with a bewildered look but then shrugged and climbed the last few steps.

"He's funny," Erika mused. "Noise? I've not made any noise."

"No?" Rob asked as he stepped onto their landing.

"I've been out, and so have you."

Rob thought about that for a moment and furrowed his brow. Sensing something, he turned to look at his door.

It was slightly ajar.

"Erika, go inside."

"Your door's open," Erika stated.

"I know. I'd like you to go into your apartment, please," he insisted.

"And leave you to deal with this alone?" She took a step closer and lowered her voice. "Like hell I will. You might need me."

Rob grimaced. As a police officer, he didn't like it. But she was her own woman, she was quite capable of looking after herself, and having backup was probably sensible. "Fine, but stay behind me."

"Don't you worry about that," Erika replied reassuringly.

Looking back at his front door, Rob took a long breath before striding towards it. He gripped the handle and stepped quickly inside, hoping to catch any intruder unaware.

Two steps into his open-plan apartment, Rob came up short. He froze to the spot as Erika bumped into his back. There was a small crowd in his front room.

He recognised four of them right away, although they were all older than he'd remembered them.

His dad, Isaac, sat facing him in one of the soft single-seater chairs. His oldest brother, Sean, perched on the sofa close by. The middle of his three older brothers, Oliver, stood beside his dad with his arms crossed, and Owen, the youngest of the three, was standing closest to him, just a few feet away. Several more suited and booted thugs were standing around the room, watching him with keen eyes and threatening expressions.

"Shit," he hissed.

"Rob! Is that any way to greet your family?" his dad said.

"What are you doing here?"

"I came to see you. We all did. Who's this?" His dad pointed to Erika standing behind him.

Rob had honestly forgotten she was there, watching this play out. Suddenly filled with concern, he turned. "Go back to your apartment."

"No. I ain't leaving. Who are these guys?"

"Please, just go. Don't worry about me. They're family." He tried to direct her towards the door. She resisted at first but then relented.

"Wait," Owen growled and moved to block her. "Is this a good idea?" He was talking to their dad.

"Get out of the way," Rob rumbled, warning him.

Owen turned to Rob, squaring up to him. "What's that little bro? You trying to threaten me?"

"I ain't so little anymore."

"The fuck you say?"

"Owen." His dad's quiet voice cut through to Owen, who suddenly stopped and glanced over.

"Let her go," his dad said.

Owen grizzled but relented, backing away. Rob smiled at him as Erika moved to the door. "Go home, lock the door, stay there."

"Are you sure you're alright?"

"I'm fine. Go," Rob insisted. Erika backed out. Owen grabbed the door and slammed it shut.

Rob shared a hate-filled look with Owen. He allowed a slight smile to play over his lips before he turned back to his father, who was still relaxing in his soft chair. "And to what do I owe the pleasure?"

His dad smiled. "You've done well for yourself, Rob. I hear you've risen through the ranks. You're a DI now. That's impressive. Very impressive."

"I take my job seriously," Rob replied.

"I can see that." His dad lifted a framed picture from where it had been sitting beside him. It was his Graduate Diploma in Professional Police Practice. A quick look revealed his dad had removed it from its home on the wall. "I've very proud of you and everything you've achieved. You're a credit to the Mason name."

"Shame you changed it, Loxley," Owen mocked.

"Was it embarrassment?" Oliver asked.

"It doesn't matter," his dad said before placing the frame on the table before him. "That's not why we're here. Sean?"

"For the record, I think this is a waste of time," Sean stated, still perched on the edge of the sofa. He looked eager to leave.

"Do it." His dad's voice was low and full of menace.

Sean sighed. "Fine." He stood up and seemed to consider his words. He glanced around the apartment. "Nice place you have here."

"I do alright," Rob said.

"Do you?" Sean asked, wandering out from the seating area and coming closer. "You're still driving that piece of crap Mum got you, I see."

Rob ground his teeth together in restrained fury. "So what?"

"You could do so much better for yourself, Rob. So much better. You could have anything you wanted. Anything. Think about that for a moment. No more money troubles. No more scrimping and saving. You'd be rich…like us."

"Let me guess," Rob said, seeing where Sean was going with this. He was about as subtle as a wrecking ball. "You can make it happen, right? You can give me all the money I could ever want. All I'd have to do, is what? The occasional favour? Passing a piece of information to you now and again? Is that it? Is that what Lee Garrett did for you?"

"Don't turn your nose up at this too quickly, little bro. You should take your time, and think about it. You could change your life." Sean added.

"Want me to persuade him for you, Dad?" Owen asked. "I could bring that pretty little neighbour back in here, if you like, show her a good time? What do you think?"

"Owen," their dad warned. "Quiet."

"Don't be so crude," Sean added. "There's no need for...alternative methods of persuasion."

"Make your choice, Robert," his dad said. "There will be no violence here today, no matter what you choose. I'd rather you didn't disappoint me, son, as you have so many times before, but I'm beyond being upset over such things."

"Then why are you here?"

"I just need to hear it from your own mouth."

"You are pathetic," Rob said. "You really thought that you could come here, break into my home, make a few threats, and then I'd agree to be your lap dog?" Rob shook his head. "You thought wrong."

His dad, Isaac, stared at him for a long moment with cold, dead eyes, long since devoid of vitality or compassion. "Very well." Isaac stood with a little help from Oliver, who passed him his walking cane. Once he was up, his dad raised his head to look at him again. "You never fail to disappoint, Robert."

With a deft move of the cane, he knocked the frame containing his diploma onto the floor.

"Oops," he said. "Clumsy." Taking a step, he then slammed the end of his walking stick into the glass, covering it in a spiderweb crack. "You might need a new one of those."

Rob balled his fists and ground his teeth. Inside, his mind raced as adrenaline coursed through his body, screaming at him to do something, anything. But he held that rage in check, channelling it into thoughts and fantasies of the day he finally threw them behind bars. That day could not come soon enough. His dad walked right up and placed his hand on Rob's shoulder. He leaned in. "We'll be watching you, Robert."

"I know," he replied before narrowing his eyes. "I've always known. Now get your hand off me."

His dad smiled and then patted him on the shoulder. "Good evening, son. I'm sure I'll see you soon."

Rob turned and watched them walk out before following them onto the landing. He wanted to be sure they left Erika alone and didn't knock on her door. In short order, they were soon back in their cars and driving away. He watched them go, taking deep breaths to calm his nerves.

Once they were out of sight, his pulse slowed, and he returned to his apartment, locking the door behind him. He sat on one of the stools at the breakfast bar, closed his eyes, and concentrated on slowing his breathing.

His black cat, Muffin, jumped up onto the bar and meowed loudly, before padding closer. Rob smiled and stroked him. "Where were you hiding, hey? Did they scare you? I bet they did. Good boy for keeping out the way."

He gave Muffin some fuss, enjoying his affection and the calming effect the cat had on him. At least he was okay and had the good sense to hide.

He'd not seen his brothers or father much since he'd left the family, and never all in the same place. He was frankly shocked that they all turned up here and tried to stage an intervention. He was even more amazed that he'd managed to survive it. The Masons were known for their unforgiving and violent ways within the criminal fraternity, but then, he supposed this was different.

He was one of them. He was family.

Maybe that changed things.

At least in the short term, it seemed to. But he was under no illusion that his defiance would go unchecked for much longer. They were making a play for him, clearly. They'd seen his rise in fortune and rank, and they wanted a part of that. They saw an opportunity and wondered if they could capitalise on it. But there was no way in hell he was going to betray himself, his morals or those who cared for him. As far as he was concerned, Nailer, Scarlett and the others were his family now, not the Masons.

Would they try to turn him again, he wondered? Would they try some other tactic? What lengths would they go to, to try and get to him?

There was a knock at the door.

29

Exasperated, tired and frustrated, Erika looked through the peephole in her door for the second time in as many minutes and breathed a sigh of relief.

The coast was clear. They were gone, or so she hoped. She could make out Rob's door, which was closed, just across the way. This wasn't over until she was one hundred percent sure. She needed to be absolutely certain, which meant she needed to check.

"Again?" the man behind her asked. "I don't think anyone's there."

She ignored him as she pulled away from the peephole and took a second to steel her nerves. Turning back to the man sitting in her kitchen, she pitched her voice and tone carefully.

"Please, can you just wait there for one moment? I need to check something."

"But," the man countered.

"Just one moment, please," she insisted.

"Okay, okay."

Without giving him a chance to protest further, she stepped out her front door and closed it behind her. With that secure, she approached the window that looked out the back of the building. The black cars that had been parked there were gone.

Good, she thought, then darted across to Rob's door, knocked and waited.

Moments later, a shadow crossed the glass in the peephole, and then the door opened partway, revealing Rob. He seemed drained, as if the experience he'd just been through had sapped all his energy.

"Hey," he said.

"Are they gone?"

"They're gone," he confirmed. "Sorry about that, it's um… It was family stuff."

"I wondered. They didn't seem friendly."

"Don't worry about it," he answered, dismissing her concern. "It's nothing for you to be concerned with."

"Are you sure?"

"Yeah, you're fine." He smiled. "Thanks for checking on me."

She grinned and nodded. "How's Muffin?"

"He's fine. He hid from them, but he's been to say hello now they're gone."

"Good. Well, if you're sure you're okay?"

"I am," he confirmed. "Night."

"Night." Stepping away as he closed the door, she mused on this latest turn of events and what it might mean for her.

She hadn't expected to run into his family so soon, and it was certainly a concern that they'd seen her face. She considered herself lucky that things had played out the way they had because it all could have gone very badly wrong.

Speaking of things going wrong, she turned back to her door and sighed to herself in preparation. There was one last thing to deal with.

Taking a breath, Erika walked back into her apartment. She smiled at the man in her kitchen, making sure to look a little sheepish.

"What was that all about?" Bill Rainault asked.

30

Rob yawned as he wandered through the corridors of Sherwood Lodge, making his way to the EMSOU office. He grimaced, scowling internally to himself for daring to yawn after the night he'd had.

Despite managing to calm down, something which was aided by Muffin's purring and attentions, his mind had continued to churn through the events of the night and the day before. He couldn't help linking the sudden appearance of his family at his apartment with the Garrett case and wondered what he'd managed to get himself into.

Was Lee's murder committed or sanctioned by his family? Had they been the ones to torture Gavin to coerce Lee into working for them? What about the kids they'd arrested at the drugs sting? Were they linked to all this? Had their sting against them set this whole thing off, causing the Masons to lash out?

And when he wasn't thinking about that, his mind jumped to the lovely night he'd had with Matilda and the thoughts he'd entertained of a relationship before his father had reminded him, they were watching.

The result of all this internal conflict was that he barely slept a wink and eventually decided to give up and come to work a little early. At least he could do something useful in there.

And now he was yawning? After hours of tossing and turning in bed, trying and failing to get any kind of meaningful sleep, *now* he was yawning. *Now* his body was telling him he was tired and needed sleep! No shit! He needed sleep hours ago, but it didn't do him much good then. But now he'd made his choice, he refused to change his mind.

Muttering and grumbling under his breath, Rob opened the EMSOU office door and walked in. He was several steps into the room when he realised he wasn't alone.

Scarlett was sitting at her desk, totally absorbed in whatever she was doing on her computer. With dark rings beneath her eyes and her blonde hair pulled back into a messy ponytail, she looked about as exhausted as he felt.

Her eyes flicked over to him before she continued to focus on her screen.

"Morning," she said, but there was little joy in it.

Rob glanced around the room, looking for anyone else, but she was alone for now. It wouldn't be too long before the others started to arrive, but for now, it was just the pair of them.

But this was odd. Why was she in?

"You weren't due in 'til Monday," Rob stated. "Everything okay?"

"Not really, no," she muttered. "Things are pretty fucking shit, actually."

Rob noted the raw emotion that coloured her voice. She was upset.

"Okay." He approached her desk. "Can I help? What happened?"

Chewing on her lip, Scarlett closed her eyes. Clenching her fists, she took a deep breath before she looked up at him. "Sorry. Look, I shouldn't be doing this, but I couldn't just sit around waiting. I'm a detective, for god's sake. I should..." Her voice cracked, and she sniffed back tears. "I should have done something. If I'd paid more attention, maybe she'd still be..." She drew up short and took a long breath. "I'm sorry, I'm rambling."

"That's okay." Whatever it was, it was serious. "What happened?"

"We were out last night, visiting a few bars. You know, just having fun. And, Ninette..."

"Your friend?"

"Yeah, she..." Scarlett paused and sniffed. "Okay, so this goes back a little while so I'd better start at the beginning. Ninette was a friend from university, and while she was there, she was raped by a monster called Sebastian. We reported it and did what we needed to, but in the end, he got away with it."

"He got away with it? How?"

"Honestly, I'm not sure. They gave us reasons, like not enough evidence and such, but that's bullshit. Personally, I think money talks. Sebastian came from a wealthy, well-thought-of family, and I think, for whatever reason, that worked in his favour. We were devastated when we found out it had been thrown out of court. Anyway, the one positive that came out of it was that everyone believed us. Sebastian's reputation at the university was ruined, and he ended up leaving. But what I didn't know, and didn't find out until Friday, was that he's been in contact with Ninette. He's been sending her messages, ranting and raving at her, saying how she ruined his life and he wishes she was dead. That kind of thing."

"I'm sorry," Rob said.

"That's okay," Scarlett muttered. "She told me Friday night before everyone else arrived. It wasn't the start I had planned for the weekend, but Ninette was a mess. He'd just messaged her before she got to me, and she was upset. She had to tell someone, and given I'd stood by her through the whole thing at uni, it made sense for her to tell me."

"I see. So, why are you here today?"

"Because she's gone missing."

"What? When?"

"Last night. We were out, having a few drinks. I noticed Ninette hadn't come back from the bathroom, so I went looking for her. But we couldn't find her. She wasn't anywhere in the bar, she wasn't at home. She'd disappeared. Her phone's off too, so we can't call her. We've tried everything."

"I hope you reported it," Rob said.

"Absolutely. As soon as we looked all around the bar, we called it in. A team over in Central is looking into it, but..."

"But you wanted to help?"

"Earlier on, I was talking to one of my other friends, Autumn, about these messages. She was at uni with us and knew about the rape. We know that Sebastian moved away from Surrey, but we don't know where, and both Ninette and Autumn have been trying to persuade me to find out where he is. I've resisted, because it's against the rules, but then this happens."

"I understand," Rob said. He nodded to her computer. "Did you find him? This Sebastian?"

Scarlett nodded. "The bastard lives over in Lincoln."

"Just over the border," Rob muttered as he briefly thought through the best way to handle this. In the end, there was only ever one answer. "What can I do to help?"

"Nothing. I don't need your help. I shouldn't be doing this, so I don't want you involved. Besides, it sounds like you're busy with the Clumber case."

"I am," Rob confirmed and thought about what he had to deal with today as they tried to track down Lee Garrett's killer. A frown creased his brow as he considered the facts and his family's efforts to bring him into the gang. Was this part of that too? Were they somehow linked to the disappearance of Scarlett's friend?

Rob briefly closed his eyes and wondered if he wasn't actually going a little crazy. His family's exploits were making him paranoid, to the point of seeing their influence in everything, even if there was no evidence.

He needed to get a grip!

Pushing that to one side for the moment, he focused on the here and now. He'd worry about the wider implications later. His friend needed him.

"You're right. I am busy, but not so busy that I can't help you. I can be of use here."

"I appreciate the offer, I really do, but the answer is still no. I'll do this alone. No one will notice me dashing off to Lincoln, but they will notice you if you're not at the morning briefing."

She was right, of course.

"This is risky, Scarlett."

"I'll be fine. I'm not scared of that idiot. I'm just going to pay him a visit. I'm a detective, and we have a missing person who has a history with a local man. He should be expecting someone to call round."

"That's what has me worried."

"You're not coming," Scarlett snapped. "And that's final."

"If anyone else finds out about this..."

"I know. I'll be in trouble. I don't care. She's my friend, and I need to help her." She grabbed her coat. "I'll see you later."

Rob sighed. It felt like she was slipping away from him. "No, I can't. I'm going with you. I can't..."

Scarlett stopped, spun on her heel and raised a finger at him. "No! Stop. Rob, I like and respect you, but seriously, piss off." She turned and stormed out, leaving Rob stunned.

He stared at the door with a growing feeling of unease. He did not like where this was going.

31

Rob chewed the end of a pen, rolling it back and forth between his teeth as his mind wandered. Sitting slouched in his chair, with the rest of the team arriving and logging into their PCs, he kept playing the conversation with Scarlett over and over again in his head, wondering if he'd done the right thing.

Nick had already been over to say hi. He'd noticed the mood Rob was in and asked him how he was. Rob had done his best to brush it off and insist there was nothing wrong. He refrained from mentioning anything about Scarlett, as it would only provoke questions and incriminate her.

She might be only trying to help find her friend, but she was operating outside the bounds of her job and accessing information that had nothing to do with what she should be working on.

Rob, however, did understand why she was doing it and sympathised. If he were in her position, he'd likely be doing the same.

He was in no place to judge.

And so, he continued to chew on his pen, feeling terrible for letting Scarlett go off on her own but well aware that he had little choice in the matter. He couldn't go galivanting off on a damn fool idealistic crusade when they were neck deep in the Garrett case. Not without some serious questions being asked, at the very least.

And then there was his family and their sudden appearance at his place last night. Did they have anything to do with the disappearance of Scarlett's friend? Or, was it a revenge kidnapping by the rapist who lived no more than forty minutes drive away? Was he keeping an eye on this Ninette? Did he know she was visiting and took the opportunity to pay her a visit?

Or was it as he feared, and the Masons were going after Rob, through Scarlett?

Christ, he hoped not. Because if they were, he dared not think about what Ninette would be going through. Not that either option was good, of course, but he didn't know Ninette's rapist.

However, he did know the Masons and what they were capable of.

Movement at the office door drew Rob's attention as it opened again. For a brief moment, he hoped it might be Scarlett, back after changing her mind.

But no. It was Bill. He wandered in, letting his gaze track over the room and the faces of the team as they looked up. Bill didn't seem too concerned, and after a moment's pause, he focused on Rob and wandered over.

Rob smiled. "Morning? How'd the hot date go?" He made sure to project his voice, so the others could hear.

Bill grimaced. "None of your business."

"Not well then," Rob stated. "No kiss at the end of the night."

"Shut up y—" Bill stopped and looked away. He took a moment to himself before he addressed Rob again in a calmer tone. "That is not any of your concern, Loxley. I suggest you remain focused on the case at hand rather than on how my evening was spent."

"Oh, don't worry, I will," Rob replied with a smile.

"Now, now, children," Nailer said as he walked over, having left his office. "Let's play nice, shall we? Remember, Bill, you're only here because I agreed that it would be okay with your DCI. If your presence here is causing too much of a distraction or becomes problematic, I have no issue with having you removed."

Rob watched Bill's face as Nailer reprimanded him, enjoying the lip quiver as Bill wanted desperately to say something but didn't. To his credit, Bill just took it and nodded at the end of Nailer's dressing down.

"I understand, sir," Bill said in confirmation.

"Good," Nailer finished. "Now, if we're done here, we have a family who desperately needs our help. So, shall we put aside any petty squabbles and get on with it?"

"Of course, guv," Rob answered.

"Yes, sir," Bill added.

"That's what I like to hear," Nailer confirmed. "Right then, let's crack on. Incident room, now. Morning briefing. Move it or lose it."

Rob got to his feet and summoned the rest of the unit into the side room, where a large whiteboard had been plastered with photos, maps and notes about the case. Pictures of Lee Garrett, laid out in the grass up at Clumber, were clustered to one side. There was a picture of the bullet casing that had been discovered, as well as tyre tracks and footprints. There were also photos of Lee when he was alive, his son Gavin, and related images, such as a print of the stabbing CCTV footage.

Finally, there were photos of the entire former East Midlands Special Operations Unit, including the two they'd yet to speak to, Wally MacKay and Rebeka Bowman. Most of them had notes written beside them.

They had plenty of digging still to do, it seemed. Rob greeted Nick, Guy, Ellen and Tucker as they walked in and took their seats, talking amongst themselves.

"We had a good time last night," Tucker said, directing his words towards Bill. "Shame you couldn't join us, but I guess you were busy?"

Bill grunted but said nothing.

"I take it the date went swimmingly and we should be expecting our wedding invitations imminently?"

Ellen slapped him on the back of the head.

"That's enough," Nailer barked. "Don't make me regret asking you to join this team."

"Sir," Tucker said, sitting back in his chair. "Behaving now, sir."

"Glad to hear it. Right then, I've been through your reports so far, so let's get this straight, shall we? We have Gavin Garrett stabbing a girl over in Forest Fields, apparently in self-defence, but he went way overboard. Later, in his interview, he claims his dad, a serving but at the time, off sick, Detective Superintendent, is corrupt. Later that same night, Lee Garrett goes to Clumber Park, and is shot. Do we know why he was there? What he was doing in Clumber at that time of night?"

"We think he was meeting someone," Rob states. "We don't know who, but if he was corrupt then it would fit that he was meeting his contact."

"Fine," Nailer replied. "Which leads us to the biggest question in this case. Who was that person? Who did he meet, who killed him and why? I understand we have several theories on this, from it being a gang hit, because maybe they were clearing house, to it being a warning to Gavin, because of what he said. And then there's the possibility that it was a crime of passion by one of his former teammates on the former EMSOU. I'm aware that you've spoken to Gemma and Justine recently, and it seems there was an affair going on between Lee and Gemma, his DCI, that Justine discovered just days before his murder. Both are potential suspects and have motives to kill him."

"I also had Karl Rothman from that team speak to me last night," Rob said. "He told me that he met with Lee last Saturday for lunch. This was at Lee's request, apparently. During this meeting, Lee admitted to Karl that he had taken bribes from a gang in return for information. But this was all in the past. Karl didn't believe that last part, and neither do I. Gangs don't just stop using a valuable asset like a Super."

"No, they don't," Nailer agreed. "What else did he say?"

"That the gang tortured Gavin to get Lee on board, and that's why he was paranoid and carrying a knife around."

"And why did Lee tell Karl this?" Nailer wore a frown as he spoke. "Seems a bit random."

"Apparently he never said, but Karl suspects that he knew something was up, and that maybe he believed something would soon happen to him. So he wanted to offload. I have no idea if this is right, but it makes sense."

"Alright, that's useful. But does it bring us closer to figuring out who killed Lee? This is the most important thing right now, and it feels like we're no closer to the answer than we were yesterday. It's all very well having these theories and ideas, but we need to work out who did it, and we need proof. If it was a gang hit, then which gang member was it?" Nailer's voice was passionate as he urged his team to work harder. "Come on, people. The victim's family are desperate to know what happened to Lee. Corrupt or not, he was a husband, a boyfriend and a father. No one deserves to be executed, and everyone deserves justice. Right then, what's next? Where are we going with this investigation, Rob?"

"The most immediate thing is to finish off questioning the remaining two former EMSOU officers, Wally MacKay and Rebeka Bowman. That and regular old policing work of going through the evidence gathered so far and seeing what we can find. We should also reinterview some of those we've already spoken to now we have more information. Gemma, for instance. She never mentioned her affair with Lee when we spoke to her."

"Alright, good work. Anything else. Nick, Guy? How's the case going against those dealers?"

"Good," Nick answered. "We turned one into a potential informant and set him loose with the girl from the gang. The other two will be charged with drug-related offences this morning, so they'll be off the streets for a little while."

"Great," Nailer said. "There is one other thing I need to bring to your attention. It seems that a woman called Ninette

Clarke, who is a good friend of our colleague, Scarlett Stutely, went missing last night under mysterious circumstances. There's a team over at Central looking into it, so we'll leave them to it, and I'll keep you updated."

Muttering broke out through the room as Nailer spoke, until he raised his voice." Hey, that's enough. Gossiping won't help. We'll obviously support Scarlett during this time, and I expect you to all act responsibly."

"Guv," several of them said.

"Okay, then. This is good policing by all of you, but it looks like we have plenty of work to do. Keep me updated on how things are going with any new developments, and let's bring this home today. Okay?"

32

How she drove from Nottingham to Lincoln without crashing, Scarlett would never really know. After finding out Sebastian's address and telling Rob to piss off, her drive east passed in a chaotic mess of maddening thoughts as she tried to process what had happened.

She was taking a huge risk doing this, but there was simply no way she could sit at home, or anywhere, and let others try to find Ninette when she had a very clear and obvious lead that needed to be followed up as soon as possible.

She'd felt like a criminal, walking into the office before anyone else was there and then accessing the PNC to find what she wanted.

That moment when she'd typed Sebastian's name into the search function, matched the relevant listing and found his address would be one she'd never forget. Finding out he was in the next county over was a moment of pure horror. Of course he was local. It made perfect sense, in a sick kind of way.

So, was he doing more than just sending her creepy messages? Was he tracking her somehow? Following her and biding his time. Did he think her trip up here would be a perfect chance to strike? A chance for him to take his revenge for Ninette apparently ruining his life?

But as she contemplated what she'd say when he opened his door, how she'd handle this, and what she'd do to him, a nagging doubt played at the edges of her mind, making her wonder if she wasn't making a huge mistake and jumping the gun entirely.

What if she was wrong? What would she do if there was no sign of Ninette at all, making this not only a wasted journey but a liability should Sebastian opt to complain about police harassment?

Could he end her career because she wouldn't wait and let the team at Central do their thing?

But how much did her career matter next to the life of her good friend? Honestly, it didn't matter, and as the thought of being fired or worse played across her mind, she found she didn't care. It was more important for her to find Ninette alive and well than it was for her to still be a detective at the end of all this.

That's why she gave in to both her conscience and Autumn's very persuasive words. She'd been urging her to use the resources at her disposal all day, and that only increased once Ninette had gone missing.

Scarlett pulled onto the road where Sebastian lived and drove along it, noting the house numbers as she went.

Nearing her target, she suddenly spotted a police car parked a short distance past Sebastian's house. Scarlett cursed. Had Central already sent someone? Was she too late?

For a moment, she considered driving by and heading home, but as she stared up the road and where that led, she knew she couldn't do it. Ninette might be in there right now, desperate for help.

She couldn't leave. She had to at least try.

She was a detective, for Christ's sake!

She pulled in and parked up. She'd try to blag it and get in anyway. If these uniforms were just here to guard the house, they probably wouldn't think twice about a detective coming to chat with him. That's what she hoped, anyway.

Getting out, Scarlett walked up the street as confidently as she could and stepped up to the passenger side window. She knocked and flashed her ID, before recognising Sergeant Megan Jolly looking back at her.

Megan lowered the window. "May I help you, detective?"

Scarlett frowned. They were Mansfield coppers, so what were they doing here, in Lincoln? "Aren't you a little out of area?"

"We were sent here by Inspector Loxley, Constable Stutely."

"So, are you here...for me?"

"For you? No. Not at all. I'm not sure what you're talking about. We're just…here. You know, to keep an eye out for trouble."

PC Tom Reid, in the driver's seat, leaned a little closer. "We're not here for you," he said. "You've not done anything wrong."

"Absolutely," Megan agreed. "But say, if you were to get into a spot of bother for whatever reason, then we're quite close by, aren't we."

Scarlett smiled. Rob had sent them here as a backup to keep an eye on her. He really wouldn't take no for an answer, would he?

"You certainly are," Scarlett agreed.

"Carry on, Constable," the sergeant said.

"Yes, ma'am." Buoyed by Rob's support, Scarlett turned back to the house, and with a renewed sense of purpose, she marched to the gate and up to the door, where she knocked insistently.

With her chest heaving as her adrenaline spiked, she stared at the door, willing it to open. Come on, she silently urged. Come on.

The door unlocked and then opened. With her ID already out, Scarlett thrust it towards his face. She recognised Sebastian and his smug features right away. "Police," she barked and stepped into the doorway, pushing it wide. "I need a word."

"Scarlett? What? How the...?" Sebastian stammered as his eyes tick-tocked back and forth between her ID and her face. He looked like he'd just woken up and was wearing slippers, t-shirt and pyjama bottoms. "I don't..."

Putting away her ID, she grabbed him by the scruff of his neck and forced him back into his house. Closing the door behind them.

"Hey, what the..."

"Shut it," she warned him. "I need to look round your house."

"What? Why? How did you find..." He shook his head. "What's going on?"

He seemed genuinely shocked and confused, and that worried her. She pushed him up against the wall and put a finger in his face. "You stay right here and don't move. I've got a police car with backup outside, so don't you dare try anything. Got it?"

"Yeah, sure. That's fine."

She narrowed her eyes at him, finding him disgusting. "Does it excite you?"

"What?"

"Sending your foul messages to Ninette? Does it get you off? Is that why you do it?"

His face fell as it clicked. "Oh, shit."

"Yeah, we know," Scarlett said. "I've seen all of them. You're filth, Seb. Utter filth."

"I... She ruined my life! She destroyed it..."

"SHUT IT!" Scarlett shouted. "You don't get to talk or explain. Not to me. You stand there, and you keep your bloody mouth shut. Got it?"

"Yeah, sure."

He seemed terrified, which was a good way to start. Satisfied, she backed off and then started to march through the house, checking the front room first, then the kitchen and so on, going from room to room and then heading upstairs.

The house was clean, sparse, and very male. But it was also devoid of Ninette. Scarlett even checked the loft, but Ninette wasn't there. Finding the key in the back door, she checked the garden too, including the shed, but there was nothing.

Frustrated and angry, she marched back into the house, accidentally on purpose forgetting to wipe her feet before walking on the cream carpet.

"Have you seen Ninette?" she asked, finding Sebastian where she'd left him.

"Seen her? No. How would I see her? She's down in Surrey."

"She's been visiting me in Nottingham."

"You're in Nottingham?"

He didn't seem to be lying, much to her frustration. Was the unthinkable possible? Did he have nothing to do with this?

"Yeah, and so was Ninette until she went missing last night."

"Missing?"

"You keep repeating what I'm saying back to me. Are you a bit dim? Yes, she's missing. She disappeared last night and given your history with her, you freak, I thought I'd pay you a visit."

"You think... No. I didn't do this. I didn't take her. I've got nothing to do with it. I wouldn't."

"Didn't stop you from raping her, though, did it."

"I didn't rape her," he said, his tone serious. "We were fumbling around, drinking, having fun. She should have asserted herself more..."

Scarlett slapped him. She caught him right across the face, making his head spin.

"Shut your fucking mouth. Twats like you, you're all the same. Self-entitled idiots who think they run the world. You think you can take anything you like, well you can't, and I will be watching you. Do you understand me?"

Holding his red cheek, with his eyes wide and watering, Sebastian nodded.

She stepped in close, getting in his face to make him uncomfortable. "If I hear of one more thing," she hissed under her breath, "one more message, anything, I'll be coming for you. Do you understand?"

He nodded.

"You'd better," she spat, and brought her knee up into his groin as hard as she could.

He fell to the floor, howling.

"I wasn't here, this never happened," Scarlett snapped, and he nodded through the pain.

With her heart beating out of her chest, Scarlett left him crumpled on the floor, his hands over his groin, moaning and crying.

She slammed the front door behind her, and marched back to her car, feeling both satisfied and terrified at the same time.

She'd wanted to do that to him for years, but the question remained. Where was Ninette?

33

Back at his desk, Rob gathered his things ready for his interview with Rebeka Bowman. He shuffled uncomfortably under the watchful gaze of Bill, as he checked through his notes. Standing nearby, Bill watched with crossed arms and a face like thunder.

"So, how was *your* night?" Bill asked.

Rob briefly paused what he was doing and glanced up, meeting Bill's eyes. He appeared to be studying Rob's reaction as if the answer to this question was of great importance.

"Fine." Rob shrugged.

"Where did you go?"

What was this, twenty questions? "We were at the Cross Key's pub," Rob answered.

"On the edge of the Lace Market," Bill stated. "I know it."

"Good. I'm sure you do." Rob continued what he was doing. "Where did you go?"

"All Bar One, opposite the Cross Keys," Bill answered and smiled. "I saw you."

"Oh," Rob exclaimed as he looked up, surprised. "So, you were just over the road?" He wished he'd been a little more vigilant now. It would have been fun to see Bill out on a date.

He was curious about the sort of person Bill would be interested in. What kind of woman did he usually go for, and did these women know what they were letting themselves in for when they agreed to a date with him?

"Was it a late one?" Bill asked.

"Not really," Rob answered. "Why? Are you checking up on me?"

Bill smiled but didn't answer.

But he didn't need to. Rob knew all too well that Bill was always checking up on him, watching him, hunting for anything he could pin on him.

"Well, if you're that curious. No, we didn't stay out late. Maybe about ten PM. And just to put your mind at rest, no, I didn't drive home. I walked. So you can't pin drunk driving on me, either."

Bill shrugged.

"I had a kebab, too. I suppose that might be a crime against nutrition, but I didn't break any actual laws."

"Good for you, Loxley. You still at those apartments on the Trent?"

"Why? Do you want to pay me a visit?"

"Who says I haven't already?" He looked smug.

Rob shivered as he thought back to his family visit. Was he hinting at something? It seemed a little odd, this line of questioning, and it made him wonder if he was coming to some kind of point. "So, you're admitting to stalking me. Is that right?"

"Stalking, no. It's called investigation. You should do some, some time."

"In your case, the difference between the two is a fine line."

Bill scoffed and looked away, apparently done with his line of questioning. What was he trying to get at, Rob wondered, curious.

"Right then," Rob began, feeling annoyed and frustrated that he needed to work with Bill again today. He couldn't wait to have Scarlett back again. "Shall we?"

Bill grunted. Rob moved away from his desk to see Ellen and Tucker making their way out too. "Wally's off work today," Ellen said as they neared each other. "So, we thought we'd pay him a surprise visit at home and talk to him there. See what he has to say."

"Great. Good luck." Rob followed them out and made for some nearby side rooms. As they approached, Rob spotted PC Rebeka Bowman waiting beside a door. She was talking quietly with another woman wearing a suit. She'd be Rebeka's Police Federation representative, who would keep an eye on proceedings and advise her should she need it.

As they approached, Rebeka turned and offered a brief smile.

"PC Rebeka Bowman?" Rob asked. "I'm DI Rob Loxley, and this is DI Bill Rainault."

"Good morning," she answered, looking a little concerned. They then introduced themselves to her rep and moved into the room, closing the door behind them. They were soon settled at the table.

"Thank you for meeting with us, Rebeka," Rob began.

"My pleasure. I want to help."

"So you're aware of the investigation we're conducting?" He was keen to find out what she knew, so he could build from there.

"You mean, the Super's murder? Lee Garrett? Yeah. Everyone's heard about it. It's a nightmare. I thought this was all over, but it just keeps coming back."

"Are you talking about Operation Major Oak?"

"What else?" she answered. "Everything changed after that. It was a nightmare. I'd be dead if it wasn't for Izzy."

"DC Isobel Dickerson, you mean?"

"Yeah. She saved my ass that day, but I was done after that. I couldn't go back. It was just that everything seemed so corrupt. I'm not even sure I want to keep being a police officer if I'm surrounded by corruption."

He could feel Bill's eyes on him, making sure Rob knew what he thought about him. There was no way he'd give Bill the satisfaction of knowing that he felt uncomfortable, though. No way. With some effort, Rob focused his attention back on Rebeka. "But you didn't leave. You just went back to being a PC."

"Yeah," Rebeka answered. "I couldn't stay in CID, and after everything that happened, they supported me in moving back."

"That's good. I'm glad you're still with us. Now, you said you see corruption all around you, but did you see any within the EMSOU when you were on it?"

"I don't know, maybe? The finger was pointed at all of us at one time or another. Gemma seemed to bear the brunt of it, though, which led to her resigning."

"Do you think she was corrupt?"

"I don't know, but I don't trust anyone anymore. That's why I want to leave, but..." She sighed. "I don't know. Every time I think I've made my mind up, I get sucked back in. I'm still friendly with some of the officers on CID, and they want me to go back and be a detective again, but I don't know if it's the right thing for me to do."

"Which officers?" Bill asked. Rob shot him a look but didn't object to the question. He'd been burnt by Bill's outbursts before, though, so he was keen to avoid a repeat performance.

"DC Amelia Brady, mainly. We're mates."

"Amelia? As in Karl Rothwell's partner on CID?"

"Yeah, that's her. I know Karl's girlfriend too, Michelle. We hang out from time to time."

Rob narrowed his eyes. There was nothing suspicious about that on a surface level, but was there more here? "And what do you think about Karl? He was on the EMSOU with you, right?"

"Yeah. He was. He's nice enough. A hard worker."

"Corrupt?" Bill asked before Rob could continue his line of questioning. Rob cringed, hating both the question and his tone. Still, it could have been worse, so he let it go to see how Rebeka responded.

"I don't think so, but then, I don't trust anyone, so…"

"Okay, so you're aware of Lee's Murder," Rob said, attempting to bring this interview back on track.

"I am. He was shot, wasn't he?"

"He was. In Clumber Park. It looks like a gang hit, and we've had information that Lee might have been taking bribes from a gang at some point in the past. Do you know anything about that?"

"He was working with a gang?" She looked shocked. "No. I've not heard that before, not seriously anyway."

"But you have heard it?" Rob pressed.

"We talked and joked, just like everyone else, so it was something said in jest once or twice, but that's all. We weren't being serious. But, if he was executed by a gang, then maybe he was?"

"Do you know why he went up to Clumber? Or who he was meeting?"

"Sorry, no," she answered. "I know, I'm not much help."

"That's okay," Rob said, reassuringly.

He continued to ask questions around the core issue of Lee's murder, such as about Gavin and Justine, but Rebeka didn't know much beyond what she'd already told them, and by the time they'd exhausted their questions, they didn't feel any nearer to the truth.

Luckily, also Bill managed to keep his mouth in check and didn't insult Rebeka during the rest of their talk.

Rob took that as a win and walked back to the EMSOU office with Bill following behind. As they walked back into the office, Bill wandered off to the coffee station to one side of the room and left Rob alone for a moment as he walked back to his desk, thinking over the recent twists and turns in the case.

There was something about it all that was bothering him, specifically about the revelation that Lee had apparently been taking bribes from a gang. He wasn't sure what it was, but there was a niggling doubt there as if he was missing a piece of the puzzle.

Unsure about what it might be, he remembered Shelley saying to him that Justine wanted to see Gavin today and thought it might be an idea to speak to her before they met up. He frowned again as he focused on Justine and her insistence that she didn't know much beyond Lee's secret affair with Gemma. She seemed like a bright, intelligent woman, and her claim that she knew nothing didn't feel right.

He grabbed his phone and checked through his file. Finding Justine's number, he called.

She answered after a couple of rings. "Hello?"

"Justine Palmer? Hi, this is Detective Inspector Loxley from the Nottinghamshire police."

"Oh, hi."

"I believe you're seeing Gavin today? Is that right?"

"I am, yes. I wanted to see him and see how he's doing. I know I was only his dad's girlfriend, but I grew quite fond of Gavin, and this *is* his house."

That was a good point, Rob realised. Gavin was probably listed as the one who would inherit the house in Lee's will, not Justine. Did that play into this somehow? He couldn't be sure.

"Yes, of course. Please be aware that he's out on bail and has certain restrictions on his movements. I'm sure he'll fill you in."

"I'm sure," she agreed. "Have there been any developments?"

"We have some new leads we're following, yes, but I can't really say much more at this point. Was there anything else you remembered? Anything you want to tell me?"

"No. Nothing. Should there be?"

"No, no. But if anything else does come up, feel free to contact me, okay?" He gave her his number.

34

"I hope we didn't keep you too bastard long, last night. I don't want Chrissy coming after me," Tucker said.

Ellen smirked as she drove south, through Nottingham towards Clifton, and the home of Wally MacKay. It was Sunday, and one of Wally's off days.

"No, you didn't keep me out. She's used to my late nights by now. Besides, she enjoys her time alone too much to complain. That, and she's got our cats to keep her company."

"You're just two old cat ladies, aren't you."

"Less of the old," Ellen said. "But yes, we are. We do love our fur-babies." She noticed Tucker curl his lip in disgust, but it only made her smile more. "You should come and meet them."

"No thanks," Tucker replied. "I'll give that a miss."

Ellen nodded, knowing full well that Tucker would refuse the offer. But she didn't mind, she knew it wasn't anything personal. He just wasn't a fan of cats.

"How much use do you think this is going to be?" Ellen asked. "It feels like we're scraping the bottom of the barrel."

"Maybe. But you know as well as I do that the one piece of information that can turn a case around can come from the strangest of places."

"Yeah, I know. But, *Wally*? What kind of name is that?"

"I hope we can find him," Tucker said, with a cheeky grin plastered to his face.

"I don't see why not. We've got his address."

"Jesus Horatio Christ. Come on Ellen, wake up."

"What? What have I done now?" Feeling like she'd missed the point entirely, she scanned around the car and outside it, hunting for whatever it was she'd missed or failed to understand.

"You've only missed the entire joke. You know? Wally? We're going to find Wally?"

"But, we know where Wally... Oh. Shit. Sorry." She smiled, remembering the books from her childhood and hunting through those intricate pictures filled with people, looking for Wally's red and white jumper. "I'm an idiot."

"Oh, we got there, did we? Finally. Congratu-fuckin'-lations. Well done."

"Piss off. I'm tired. I shouldn't have stayed out for drinks last night." She shook her head. "If he opens his door, and he's wearing a red and white striped top, I'm going home because this is clearly a dream."

"That would be hilarious," Tucker answered as they neared their destination. Clifton was a suburban village on the southwest edge of Nottingham, at one end of the tram system that ran through the city. Like everywhere, it had its share of nice, quiet roads but also areas of social deprivation, plagued with anti-social behaviour. The road they ended up on seemed nice enough, with semi-detached and detached houses, rendered and painted white or cream, with the occasional pink one thrown in for good measure.

Wally's was a white one. They pulled up outside, and Ellen scanned the road, noting parked cars and pedestrians. But there was nothing suspicious going on.

"Right then, let's pay him a surprise visit, shall we?"

"Yes indeed," Tucker agreed and followed her up to the front door. Ellen knocked and waited. After a few moments, she was about to knock again when she heard a series of thuds as someone ran down the stairs inside the house.

"Hold on," a male voice called from inside.

Ellen waited. A few moments later, the door was unlocked from the inside, and it swung open, revealing a man in a pair of pyjama bottoms, pulling on a t-shirt.

"Can I help you?" He looked back and forth between them and frowned. "Wait..."

"Who is it," a female voice shouted from inside.

Ellen raised her ID and introduced herself. As she did, a pair of slender female legs appeared on the stairs. The woman descended until Ellen could see and recognise her.

Michelle, Karl's girlfriend, stared back at her, pulling the bottom of Wally's t-shirt down to hide her dignity.

"Oh, crap," Michelle hissed. "This, um. This isn't what it looks like."

Ellen made an incredulous face but said nothing.

Michelle deflated. "Okay, yes, it *is* what it looks like." She came down the remaining stairs. "Fuck. Look, Ellen, you can't tell Karl about this."

"He doesn't know then, I take it," Ellen said.

"No, of course not. He's got no idea. He thinks I'm at work. I mean, I will be at work later on, but not yet. Shit."

"I knew I recognised you," Wally said, leaning against the wall. He was quite attractive for a man, Ellen thought. The fact that she noticed said something about his looks, not that she was in the slightest bit interested. No, Michelle was much more up her street, but clearly, she didn't swing that way. Still, the t-shirt and bare legs look was doing wonders.

"Ellen, promise me you won't tell Karl that you saw me here. Please. It'll break him. He's been in bits since being removed from the Special Operations Unit. He loved that job. This would just kill him."

Ellen grimaced. "I can't make any promises, you know that. I won't go out of my way to tell him, but you know how we work by now. If it comes up during the course of the investigation and Karl needs to know, then we *will* tell him."

"You should have dumped him weeks ago," Wally said. "I told you."

"Yes, yes, yes. Shut up. You're right, and I'm wrong. Jesus, Wal. I was getting around to it. I just needed to pick my moment."

"Looks like it's been chosen for you," Wally said, before he looked up at Ellen. "I take it you're here to talk to me about DSI Garrett?"

"We are," Ellan confirmed.

"I'll take him through to the front room," Tucker said. "You can deal with her."

"Thanks." Ellen waited until the two men were out of sight. "Right, we need to speak to Wally alone, but I'd also like to have a chat with you, too. So go and get your knickers on and wait upstairs. We'll call you when we're ready, okay?"

"I'm gonna need to get to work, soon."

"We won't keep you long, and you can make a phone call to let them know you'll be late, if you like."

"Because I'm being questioned by the police? Mmm. I'm sure that'll go down great."

Ellen shrugged.

Michelle groaned. "Ugh, fine. I'll wait upstairs."

"Good. And look, I'll do my best to keep this from Karl for the moment, but I suggest you talk to him, because he's likely to find out sooner or later."

"Yeah, I know. I can do that."

"Good."

Ellen watched her make her way back upstairs and waited for the bedroom door to slam shut before taking a moment to think about how this might affect things. It seemed that several affairs were going on between members of the former EMSOU and their partners, all of which might push someone to do something stupid. This one, however, still seemed to be a secret, but for how long? Michelle needed to get ahead of this and come clean with Karl, but that was up to her. Ellen wasn't going to interfere with that, but it gave this case an extra dimension she hadn't expected. For a start, she felt bad for Karl, who had not only lost his ideal job posting, but it looked like he was now about to lose his girlfriend as well.

She felt bad for Michelle too. She wasn't a close friend, but she'd seen her on occasion at police gatherings, and dealing with this kind of thing was never easy.

Well, she couldn't worry about that now, so she banished those thoughts for the time being and focused on the task at hand.

With her head straight once more, she made her way into the front room to find Wally sitting down and Tucker browsing the shelves, and the photos that were displayed there.

"Sorry to keep you waiting, Mr MacKay, but we should have some peace and quiet now. Michelle's upstairs getting dressed, and we'll need to talk to her once we've spoken to you."

"Okay."

"You were right, by the way. This visit was to ask you what you know about Lee Garrett and his murder, if anything. He was found in Clumber Park on Friday night, having been shot in the head. He was executed in a manner that appears to be in the style of a gangland hit. Do you know anything about this?"

"I wish I did," Wally replied. "You know, back when that operation went tits up, I knew something fishy was going on. Someone on that team was on the take. I was sure of it. I tried to do some digging to find out, but I didn't learn much. No one was saying anything."

"Did you have any suspicions?"

"Several, but no proof. I know they blamed Gemma, but I don't know if that was right or wrong. Maybe it was Lee. I don't know. I'd love to know, though, so I could arrest them and make them pay for what they did. Their actions got four officers killed that night. They've got blood on their hands."

"I agree. Where were you on Friday night?"

"I spent the evening with Michelle. She went home fairly late and didn't stay overnight. Then I was here alone."

Ellen gave him a knowing look, and Wally blushed. "Okay," Ellen said. "Do you know what time she left you?"

"I think it was after eleven-thirty. Then I went to bed."

Ellen nodded, checking to make sure Tucker was taking notes before she suddenly got curious about Wally and Michelle's relationship. "And, how did you two meet? How did this thing start?"

"We were at one of the police parties. Karl was busy with his mates and ignoring Michelle. I was there alone, and we just ended up talking. We hit it off, and later that night, after a few drinks, we kissed in one of the back rooms. And that's how it started. It's been something of a whirlwind romance, and I think we've both enjoyed the secrecy, but it's time for that to stop. We're not kids anymore. I've been telling her for a while that she needs to talk to Karl so we can move on, but she's just been delaying it. I don't know why."

"I see. Well, you might now get your wish."

"It wasn't how it wanted it to go, but yeah, I might," Wally agreed.

"And what about Karl?" Ellen asked.

"What about him?"

"You worked with him for a while and knew him from some of our socials. What do you think of him?"

"He's alright. He can be a bit short and abrasive at times, and he's always busy with work or whatever. I think that's why we hit it off, Michelle and me. He's never around. It's a lot easier now I'm on a new team with different shift patterns, but even back when we were both on EMSOU, he'd always be off doing something rather than going home to Michelle. I've got no idea what he was up to, though. Putting in the overtime, I guess."

Ellen nodded, knowing how common that kind of dedication was. This job could be a monster, and relationships were its food of choice.

35

Where was Ninette?

Scarlett drove back towards Nottingham, wondering what on earth she should do now. Her friends were at home with Chris, no doubt distraught and wondering what on earth was going on. Their FLO would be visiting at some point today. They'd need to make an excuse for her, which would only work for a short time, but she'd spoken to Autumn about it, and she trusted her friend. Chris would cover for her too.

They'd come up with something.

All this time, her phone had been going crazy with texts from Chris and her mates, wondering what was going on. She'd ended up telling them all about Ninette's attack at university and what had happened. There was no way she and Autumn could keep it secret at this point, and every one of her mates had urged her to try to find Sebastian. Several had wanted to go with her, but she'd refused. And she was glad she had. She could certainly imagine Autumn wanting to give Sebastian a piece of her mind, but that could easily have spiralled out of control.

As it was, while hurting that monster was undoubtedly satisfying, she wasn't sure she'd done the right thing.

Would he report it? Was she living on borrowed time?

There was no way to know.

Since leaving Sebastian's, she'd gone to reply to Autumn several times, only to give up as she tried to compose her message. She didn't know what to say to them. They all expected Ninette to be there, hidden in Sebastian's house, chained up in the loft or something.

But there'd been nothing, and he seemed as in the dark as she was. So, where was she? Where was her friend?

She felt lost at sea and didn't know where to turn. Should she go home and see her friends and fiance? That was probably the right thing to do. They would be as desperate for information as she was, but she didn't have anything to give them.

She was still no wiser as to Ninette's location, with no leads to point her in the right direction.

Maybe she should return to the station and find Rob. She could text him and get him to meet her outside. He'd probably be able to help and point her in the right direction.

Her phone started ringing, and the screen displayed, 'Number Withheld'.

Scarlett frowned at the device, wondering who the hell would be calling her on a blocked number? She'd specifically told her friends not to call, but even if they did, they wouldn't block their number, and neither would Rob or Chris so who was it?

In a moment of impetuousness, she nearly dismissed the call, but stopped as she reached out.

Maybe she should take it.

She flicked the wobbling icon up the screen, turning it green. Then she tapped the Speaker icon.

"Hello?"

"Miss Stutely," said a male voice at the end of the line. "We need to talk. We have Ninette."

"What!" The voice cut through the fog her mind was mired in and yanked her back to reality. She veered left, off the road and up the verge, skidding to a stop. "What the hell are you talking about? Who is this?"

"Steady on now, Scarlett, and listen to me. We have your friend, Ninette, and unless you do as we say, you might never see her again. Do you understand?"

"Prove it," she snapped, angry. "I want to speak to her."

The voice sighed loudly at the end of the line. "Fine." She heard sounds of movement and then the voice of the man, but it sounded distant as if he was holding the phone at arm's length.

"Speak."

"Who, me? Hello?" Ninette said. She sounded weak, and her voice was croaky.

"Ninette? It's Scarlett. Is that you?"

"Scarlett! Yes, it's me. Help me, please. Please help. They're hurting me."

Scarlett's heart ached suddenly. They had her, and they were hurting her. "Hang on, please. I'll find you."

"Alright, that's enough of that," the man said, removing the phone from Ninette. "Do we have a deal?"

Immediately, Scarlett went to say yes, without even thinking about it. This was her friend, and she'd do anything for her. It was a no-brainer.

Nothing was worth her friend's life. Nothing.

"We..." She stopped, letting her words trail off as doubt grew.

"What's that?" the man asked.

"I, err..." As her mind raced, she realised this wasn't as simple as she'd first thought.

She'd read Rob's report on their current case this morning. She knew these people, these gangs, and what they were capable of.

Risking her career to save Ninette from Sebastian had been an easy choice and one she'd repeat in a heartbeat. No career was worth someone's life.

But it wasn't just her career she was risking anymore.

She had a good idea of which group the person on the end of the line answered to, and she knew what the gang was capable of. But she needed to be sure.

"You're with the Masons, right?"

"Aaah... I need an answer," the man replied, ignoring her question. But she heard the brief hesitation and the slight crack in his voice that betrayed him, and that was all the answer she needed. This was the Masons. The gang that Rob had been born into, and this was their way of getting to him because they wanted Rob.

They didn't want her.

It was possible they knew they'd never get him, not voluntarily, anyway. But that meant they needed leverage, and this was how they got it.

However, she'd seen this play out already. She'd read the reports and the theories surrounding the current case. She'd seen what had happened to Lee and the previous EMSOU when one of their own betrayed them. The end result was always the same.

People died.

Innocent people.

In a flash, she understood where this would go and what would happen. They'd drag her deeper and deeper, getting her to do more and more, until she eventually sold Rob and the Unit to them. People would die, that much she knew. So it wasn't as simple as the choice she'd made to hunt down Sebastian, because she'd be condemning others, probably several others, to death or ruin by agreeing to the gang's terms. She'd also be turning onto a road which she did not want to go down. She knew where that led, and what it would do to her. She'd seen what it did to others.

She'd become morally bankrupt while in the service of these monsters, and whatever she did for them, she'd have to live with that for the rest of her life.

It would ruin her and the lives of those around her.

But that would mean saying no to them, and she knew what that would mean for Ninette.

She gripped her car's steering wheel with a death grip, turning her knuckles white as she fought with herself about what the right choice was. Should she be selfish and think of only her friend, or should she thinking about the wider public and her friends in the unit? Which did she value more? What was the right choice?

She found her mind swinging madly from one side to the other, working through the consequences of each choice, and weighing them up. Neither of them was ideal, but as the seconds passed, she found herself naturally coming down on one side.

She knew what her answer had to be and punched the steering wheel in frustration.

The man on the phone spoke again. "What's it gonna be, detective?"

36

Justine gazed out her living room window, watching the street outside, waiting for Shelley's car to appear and drop Gavin off.

She'd not seen Shelley since before Lee's death, so she wondered how Shelley would be. Obviously, she didn't love Lee anymore, but did she care? Would she be upset?

Justine sighed. Maybe that wasn't any of her business.

All she knew was that the last few days had been a living nightmare. She'd cried too many times to count at this point, finding herself more upset over this than she'd thought she would be. It also left her with so many questions that she didn't have easy answers to, such as where would she live now?

This wasn't her house, and she was only Lee's girlfriend. She had no legal rights over it, and she was certain he'd not added her to this will.

The house, by rights, would belong to Gavin. Lee had divorced Shelley months ago, so she had no claim, but that didn't exactly calm Justine's nerves or answer her questions.

Instead, she just felt on edge the whole time. She'd done as Carter had asked and said nothing to the police, but she wasn't sure she'd done the right thing anymore. Maybe she should have come clean and told them the truth. Her conscience clawed at her mind, tying her gut up in knots as she fought with herself over what the right thing to do was.

And now Gavin was coming here.

She wanted to see him, and he had every right to live here. This was his family home, after all. But his presence here worried her.

He probably had questions, which was certainly understandable, but she wasn't sure she'd have the answers he wanted.

Justine sighed and chewed her lip.

She could probably have guessed how this would turn out, if she'd been honest with herself. She knew what she was getting herself into when she came here, and now she was reaping what she sowed.

But was this the end of it?

Would Lee be the only casualty of this mess, or would there be more? Certainly, if she followed her conscience, she'd be putting herself at a much greater risk. Would it be worth it?

But maybe that wasn't the right way to look at it anymore. Maybe she shouldn't be looking at things in terms of risk to herself or what she could out of any deals, and instead, she should be evaluating her actions in terms of right and wrong…

Despite the inherent risks, the concept felt alien but also comforting and uplifting. But was it right?

The sound of an engine and tyres on tarmac drew her attention back to her window. Shelley had just pulled up. She parked and got out with Gavin, who carried a backpack over his shoulder.

Seeing him sent a ripple of emotion through Justine, causing tears to pick at her eyes. She sniffed and wiped them as she got up, feeling intensely sorry for him and what he'd been through. She still needed to talk to him about what he'd done, but that could maybe wait until he was ready.

She opened the front door to find them walking towards her. Gavin slowed as he got close and attempted a smile. But she saw only sadness in his eyes.

"I'm sorry," he said. "I've let you down."

He'd successfully plucked at her heartstrings, and with a sob, she pulled him in for a hug. He hugged her back, and for a moment, she felt comfortable and safe. It was the first time she'd felt like that since Lee had last held her.

"Thank you for coming to see me," she said as she separated from him.

"I needed to come back. This was his home, so…" He gave her another sad smile.

"I understand. Go on, go inside. I'll only be a moment," Justine said, noticing that Shelley was waiting outside the door.

Gavin nodded and made his way inside.

"Hi," Justine said as she stepped closer to Shelley.

"Hey," Shelley answered. "I hope you don't mind him coming over. He wanted to."

"No, it's fine. This is *his* home now."

Shelley paused but nodded once she understood her meaning. "I guess so."

"How's he been?"

"Fine. We spoke about what happened. He's been quite open about it, and it looks like he's fully cooperated with the police. He regrets what he did and wants to help make it right, which is good."

Justine smiled. It was almost as if Shelley knew what she had done and was speaking directly to her, urging her to follow Gavin's example. If only Shelley knew. "That is good," Justine confirmed.

"I'm proud of him for that," Shelley added.

Would Lee and Gavin be proud of her if she did the right thing too? "I'll speak to him."

"You should," Shelley said. "But, look, I just wanted to say, I'm sorry for your loss. I know we've not exactly seen eye to eye, but you didn't deserve this, and neither did Lee. So if there's anything I can do for you, please just ask."

Justine smiled, a little embarrassed by the offer of help. "Thank you. I will."

"Okay. He's on a curfew, by the way, as per the terms of his bail, but he can stay here with you if that's what he wants. Or he could come back..."

"I'll make sure to let you know what he's doing," Justine confirmed, and the pair said goodbye, with Shelley actually hugging her. It was nice, if a little odd, given their tumultuous history.

With a deep breath, she made her way inside and found Gavin in the kitchen. He'd poured himself a fizzy drink and was already halfway through it.

"Are you okay?" Justine asked.

He pressed his lips into a thin line before answering. "Yeah. I think so. I'm sorry about all this. I shouldn't have been carrying that stupid knife. I was an idiot."

"That's okay. You shouldn't have been attacked."

He shrugged. "Yeah, maybe. But none of them deserved what I did. I just... I don't know what I was thinking. I thought I could use it to protect myself, but I just ended up hurting someone and getting into trouble."

"Yeah. But you did the right thing by helping the police. I'm proud of you for that."

"I shouldn't have bad-mouthed my dad, though."

"No, perhaps not. Um, why did you say that about your dad?"

"I don't know, I just…"

There was a loud knock at the front door.

"It'll be Shelley."

"Oh, crap," Gavin muttered. "What did I forget this time?"

"You're always leaving something in the car, Gavin." She followed him out into the hall and looked past him to the front door and the large dark shadow beyond the moulded glass.

That wasn't Shelley."

"Gavin, wait…"

But he'd already started opening the door. It slammed into the wall as three big men rushed inside.

"No," Justine yelled.

Under the direction of one of them, the other two grabbed Gavin. He yelled and tried to fight them off, only to get punched in the face.

"Gavin," she screamed.

His legs gave way, and the two thugs took his weight. The third man stormed across the hall to her.

She backed away in terror until she hit the wall. "I'm sorry, I'm sorry, I'm sorry," she stammered as she looked between the man before her and the two carrying Gavin out the front door. "Don't hurt me. Please, just leave me alone."

"Then be a good little girly, and keep your loud fucking mouth shut, got it?"

"Yeah, I got it," she said, shaking with utter horror, fully aware of what these men were capable of. She stared at him through tears of fright, wondering if he'd do anything to her. He sneered before making a clicking noise with his mouth, and marching out, leaving her with the shame of her inaction and complicity.

37

Rob stared at his screen, his hands hovering over this keyboard, ready to type, but his mind was elsewhere. He should be filling in the form, recording his findings about the interview he'd had with Rebeka, but he was finding it hard to concentrate. His mind kept jumping back to the meeting with his family, the night he'd had with Matilda and the worrying turn of events with Scarlett.

Sending the patrol car to keep an eye on her was the least he could do to try and keep her safe. It wasn't strictly by the rulebook, but it would have to do for now, and he trusted Sergeant Jolly to do the right thing.

But that had been ages ago. The sergeant had reported that Scarlett had left the property over an hour ago and seemed okay, but he'd yet to hear about how it had all gone. Why hadn't Scarlett called or messaged him? What had happened at Sebastian's?

His mind kept spinning from one thought to another without stopping, never letting him stop and concentrate on the task at hand.

Maybe it was useless to fight it, and he'd finish this report later.

As he chewed the inside of his cheek, mulling over his options, his eyes tracked left, roving over his desk until he looked up at Bill sitting on a nearby table, facing him.

Bill had a laptop out as well and was busy typing something.

He needed to be careful. Bill was no doubt watching him, and he'd probably have questions if Scarlett called. He'd certainly have something to say about her interfering with the kidnapping investigation and crossing into a neighbouring county to chase up a lead, that's for sure.

He felt certain Nailer would take her side, though. In fact, the entire EMSOU team would probably back Scarlett on this. But even so, she was taking a risk.

Rob's phone buzzed. He snapped it up, hoping and also fearing it was Scarlett, but then he saw Ellen's name on the screen and calmed down.

Nearby, Bill was watching him.

Rob answered the phone. "How'd it go?" Rob asked, knowing they'd been to interview Wally MacKay.

"It's been an interesting morning," Ellen replied.

"You're not bastard kidding," Tucker said in the background.

"Oh? What have you found?" Rob asked.

"I think we surprised him," Ellen answered, "because we found him at home with Michelle, Karl's girlfriend. Both were barely dressed and clearly having a fun time."

"Oh, shit," Rob muttered, keeping his voice low. "Does Karl know?"

"Wally and Michelle both say that he doesn't and have asked me to keep quiet about it. They think it will upset him."

"And they're probably right. Hmm. I'm not sure how this affects the case, though. It probably doesn't, actually, not if Karl doesn't know about it."

"I came to the same conclusion. It's not any kind of breakthrough, but it is interesting."

"I agree. Did you speak to both of them?"

"We did. Both said they knew nothing about the murder or Lee's supposed corruption."

"And what about their whereabouts on the night of the murder?"

"They both separately said the same thing, that they were both here until after eleven-thirty. I don't think they're lying, and that's over an hour after Lee was found by that park warden."

"Okay. Good work."

"Thanks."

After ending the call, Rob sat back in his chair, thinking things through.

"What was that about?" Bill asked, having got up and crossed the short distance to Rob. "Did Wally know something?"

"No, unfortunately. And he has an alibi for the night of the murder."

Bill frowned. "It sounded like DC Dale did discover something, though."

"Only that Wally is having an affair with someone," Rob answered, wondering if telling Bill about what they'd discovered was a good idea. Rob could see him blabbing to Karl and causing trouble. "It doesn't affect the case."

"Who is he seeing?" Bill pressed.

Rob sighed. He didn't have a good reason not to tell him, not one that Bill would accept or not get offended by. He didn't have a choice. "Karl's girlfriend, Michelle."

"Oh, really? That is interesting."

Rob's phone buzzed again. He pulled it out and spotted the notification from Scarlett. It said simply, 'come outside'.

Without reacting, Rob placed his phone back in his pocket as if nothing had happened. "I told you," Rob said, commenting on Bill's reaction to the affair. "But it's not really useful. It doesn't help us."

"No. Not right now. Was there anything else?"

He had a feeling that Bill was referring to what he'd looked at on his phone, but Rob dismissed it. "No, nothing."

"Okay."

"I'll see you in a moment. I just need to use the bathroom," Rob said. Bill curled his lip in disgust and returned to his seat without another word, leaving Rob to his supposed bathroom break.

Pleased to have shaken Bill for the moment, he left the office and went downstairs. He rechecked his messages, but there was nothing else from Scarlett. He sent a quick reply, letting her know he was on his way and pressed on.

At least she was alive and well. That was the main thing. But what did she find? From the text and the lack of any further updates, he thought it likely she'd failed to find Ninette. So, was it bad news, or just no news?

He'd find out soon enough.

Reaching the car park, he glanced around but couldn't see Scarlett or her car. He called her phone as he walked out, looking back and forth. She answered after a few moments.

"Rob. Hi. Are you okay? Are you alone?"

"Aye. Where are you?"

"Oh, hold on." He heard movement on the end of the line before she spoke again. "To your left."

He looked and saw her waving at him. "Gotcha," he said and hung up before striding over. She was to one side of the car park, beneath some overhanging branches in the shadows.

As he closed the gap, he could see something wasn't right. Scarlett's whole posture seemed nervous and unsure, and as he got close enough to see her face, it was obvious that she'd been crying.

"I take it your suspect was a dead end?"

"Sebastian didn't have her," she confirmed. "He didn't know anything..."

"But?" Rob sensed there was more to this.

Scarlett sighed. "But on the way back they called. They have her, Rob. The Masons. They have her, and they're using her to try and get to you, through me."

"What?! You're sure?"

"Someone called me. They let me speak to Ninette and said I needed to agree to some favours. But I couldn't do it, Rob. I just couldn't. Someone betrayed the previous EMSOU and got half the team killed. I can't risk doing the same or worse. And I'm not going to get into debt with a criminal gang. I can't."

"You did the right thing," Rob said in a reassuring tone.

"I told them to go screw themselves and then said to the bastard on the end of the phone that if he so much as hurt a single hair on Ninette's head, I'd make it my life's work to hunt him and the entire Mason family down. I said I wouldn't rest until they were either dead or behind bars."

"Wow," Rob said, stunned by her venom. "You've got some bollocks on you. That's incredible."

"Is it?" she asked as a tear fell over her cheek. "I'm not sure it is. I think I might have just condemned Ninette to—"

"You don't know that," Rob cut in before she could finish the sentence. "You have no idea how they'll react."

He wasn't lying, but it also wasn't unlikely that they'd just kill her now anyway. It was possible that Ninette knew or had seen too much. But there wasn't anything they could do about that now.

"Thanks, but I don't know if I did the right thing."

"You did," Rob reassured her. "You know as well as I do what happens if you owe one of these gangs. There's no getting out of it once you're in, you just ended up going deeper and deeper, and then people get hurt, or worse."

"I'm not sure my friends will see it that way."

"If they are truly your friends, they'll understand that this was the only choice you had. You took a stand against them. You made the hard choice, but the right choice."

"I hope so, and I hope they let Ninette go."

"There's always a chance," Rob agreed.

"A small one, maybe."

"Yeah, a small one. And you know this wasn't about you, right? Not really. They're after me. That's what this is about. Not you, me." Rob took a breath as he wrestled with the idea of telling Scarlett about his encounter with his family. He didn't like talking about these things, but he felt like she needed to know. "It's not the only play that my family have made for me in recent days, by the way."

"Oh?" Scarlett sniffed.

"They were waiting at my apartment last night when I got home. They wanted me to rejoin the family business, but I refused. I'm not going down that road. It's a very slippery slope that doesn't lead anywhere good."

Scarlett nodded. "I just hope she survives. I'm not sure what I'd do if she died, apart from devoting my life to bringing down the Masons."

Rob nodded. "And I'll be right there with you."

38

Gavin's face hurt, his shoulder ached, and he felt sure the bindings on his wrists—which he suspected to be cable ties—were cutting into his skin.

The thugs had thrown him into the back of the van where several other men were waiting and forced him to the floor. He didn't resist when they tied his wrists or covered his head with a hood or when several of them rested their feet on him. They'd only hurt him more if he did. No one spoke other than to issue orders, telling him to get down and keep quiet.

He could feel his heart beating wildly against the van floor as terror gripped him. All he could think about was the vicious attack he'd suffered last year when he'd been kidnapped and used to blackmail his dad.

And now it was happening again.

He'd been living in fear for months, carrying a knife around wherever he went, desperate to avoid a repeat performance. Would it have saved him?

Probably not.

As the van bumped and rattled down the road, the rational side of his brain was locked in battle with the primitive side, desperately trying to keep himself calm and comply with these thugs. Fighting them was useless and would only lead to more pain.

He'd do anything to avoid that.

Anything.

The drive to wherever they were going was the most uncomfortable journey of his entire life. He felt battered and bruised by the time the van came to a stop.

Scared out of his wits, the part of him that wanted to fight and flee screamed at him to do something. Anything. But he knew better than to try. He could remember what had happened when he'd tried that last time. It only led to more pain. Noticing his shallow, fast breathing, he consciously slowed it down, taking deeper lung fulls in through the nose and out through the mouth.

They were going to hurt him, there was no escaping that. He just needed to survive it. That's all he needed to focus on.

"We're here."

"Get him up."

The voices were gruff and authoritative, and they wouldn't stand for any disobedience. Gavin didn't resist and pushed himself up as they lifted him.

The rear doors opened, letting light in through his hood, but he couldn't really see anything other than areas of light and darkness.

For a second, Gavin hesitated as he suffered another flashback to the nightmare that had befallen him last year. He took a step back.

The men gripped his arms and forced him forward, out onto a gritty hard floor.

"Bring him through here," a man ordered.

"Go on, that way," another said as he was pushed forwards.

"I can't see," Gavin complained as he tried to walk. It was weird how unsteady he felt with the hood on.

A man grunted behind him, and a moment later, the hood was ripped off, along with a few hairs from his head.

"Ow," he yelped. Only for one of the men behind him to jab him in the kidney.

He made sure to keep quiet this time.

They were in an old building that reminded him of a warehouse or basement. Five men surrounded him. One held him by the arm and guided him to a nearby door. The lead man, the one who'd terrorised Justine, had dark hair and wore a black leather jacket. He opened the door and ushered them through.

"Keep your mouth shut, you little shit," Leather Jacket hissed as he passed. He found himself in a network of poorly lit interconnected rooms, with work lights creating pools of illumination amidst the shadows. Two more men were waiting behind a table to his right. He spotted several items of torture on the table, spotted with blood, both dry and fresh. Behind the men were several tall plastic barrels. The stickers on the side warned of their extremely corrosive contents. It stank in here.

"How's it going?" Leather Jacket asked the two behind the table.

"The rat's gone quiet. I think we broke him," a man in a cheque shirt and jeans answered.

"And the woman?"

"Pissed herself," Cheque Shirt answered. "We gagged her to keep her quiet. We're waiting to hear what to do with 'em."

"You'll hear soon enough," Leather Jacket answered, adjusting his gloves. "Where's that gun?"

Gavin's ear's pricked up at the mention of a gun, and he watched as Cheque Shirt whipped an oily rag off the table, revealing a pistol beneath. "Here."

Leather Jacket grabbed it and held it out to a man wearing a suit and a balaclava that showed only his eyes. "Take it."

"What? Me?" Balaclava asked.

"Fuckin' take it, shithead."

"But, I'm not wearing..." Balaclava raised his bare hands.

Leather Jacked grabbed his hand and put the gun into his palm. "Just hold it and cover us in case this idiot does anything stupid, okay?"

"Oh, okay," Balaclava answered, looking worried as he eyed the gun.

Leather Jacket pointed across the room. There was a chair nearby in the middle of the room. "Put him there."

"Move it," the man holding him grunted. He was bald and wearing dark clothing.

As Gavin stumbled across the room, he got a look into a side room where a naked young man was hanging by the wrists from a bar across the ceiling. His dark chocolate skin was mottled with bruising and slick with blood. He wasn't moving.

In the next room over, a fair-skinned, dark-haired woman was tied to a chair, wearing only her underwear and a gag. Her wide, alert eyes locked onto him, pleading with him to help her. She'd been beaten and sported several cuts and bruises, including a bleeding head wound. She'd not suffered as much as the young man had...yet.

The bald man thrust him into the chair. Gavin landed and nearly tipped it over. Baldy stepped away, and a moment later Leather Jacket appeared with Balaclava behind him, the gun ready in his hands.

Maybe this wasn't going to be a beating. Maybe this was them dealing with a few loose ends.

"Just do it," Gavin muttered, feeling defeated. "Just get it over and done with."

Leather Jacket frowned and then glanced at the man with the gun. "Oh, that? Don't worry about that. You need to worry about this." He nodded to the bald guy.

The punch came in quick and slammed into his gut. Gavin gasped as the pain wracked his body. For a moment, he couldn't breathe. He panicked. Is this how he'd die? Beaten to death in a dingy room surrounded by thugs?

Then another punch hit home, and another, and another.

The thug hit him in the chest, the gut, his sides, his legs, and even across the face. They didn't seem to care this time if they made visible marks, it was all about inflicting as much pain as they could while keeping him alive and conscious.

Halfway through, a tooth came loose, and several of the men laughed as he spat it out, along with a dollop of blood.

But then, sometime later, after the punches and kicks had blurred together, it stopped just as suddenly as it had started. Gavin hung there, limply in the chair, his world swimming as he struggled to see through his swollen face. Everything hurt. Literally everything.

When the bald man grabbed his head and lifted it so he could see Leather Jacket, that hurt too.

Leather Jacket stepped closer and took a moment to admire his friend's handiwork. "This is what happens to rats. Do you understand? Blink once for yes."

Gavin blinked.

He understood, alright. He'd spoken to the police. He'd messed up, and his father had paid the ultimate price for his error. Now his dad was dead, and there was nothing he could do. He wasn't even sure if he wanted to keep living after this. His world had been shattered into a thousand pieces, and his old life was no more.

Nothing would be the same ever again.

"Good." The man turned to Balaclava and grabbed the gun, snatching it out of his hands. "Give me that, before you do something stupid with it."

Balaclava went to protest about something but then thought better of it. He seemed to be frowning as he looked from his hands to the gun and back.

"Now," Leather Jacket said, looking back at Gavin. "I'm going to leave you here to think about what you've done while we decide what to do with you."

They stepped out of view, leaving Gavin to his pain and regrets.

39

"Here we go," Rob said, leading Scarlett into a side room close to the EMSOU office. With everything going on, she'd said she wasn't quite ready to head home and face her friends, so Rob had invited her in.

She'd been unsure, saying it would look weird for her to be here rather than with her fiance and friends, but Rob assured her that it would be okay. People dealt with grief and anxiety in different ways, and as a police officer, maybe she just needed to be closer to the action so she'd hear when something came in.

In the end, Scarlett relented and walked with Rob through the Lodge, keeping her head down.

No one had said anything, and they made it to the side room without any trouble.

"Bill's in the office, by the way," Rob said, inclining his. "Don't be surprised if he show's his face."

"I can handle Bill," Scarlett answered.

"I know. Coffee?"

"Please." She took a seat on one of the comfortable chairs and relaxed with a sigh.

Satisfied she was okay, Rob wandered over to the machine and set it going.

"So, your family showed up at your apartment last night?" she asked.

"Yep. In fact, I returned home to find they'd broken in and were sitting in my living room. I'd seen my neighbour outside and walked into the building with her. We spotted the open door and investigated. She saw them too."

"Crap. Glad you're both okay."

"We're fine. It was just a shock."

"And Muffin, I hope he's okay."

"He hid. He's not stupid."

"Good kitty. And they wanted you to become part of the firm again?"

"That's what they said, but I told them where to go. I'm not doing that."

"Not doing what?"

Rob turned in shock to find Bill had appeared in the doorway. He leaned in, looking over at Rob. "I didn't quite catch what you were talking about."

"Good." Rob smiled.

Bill's sudden appearance had shaken him. It was a reminder to be careful what he spoke about here in the Lodge, where anyone could be listening.

Bill turned to Scarlett. "Why are you here? Shouldn't you be at home?"

"Sorry, Dad," Scarlett sniped back with a meaningful look on her face.

Rob caught the brief sneer that Bill gave her in return.

"That's how you greet someone whose friend has just been kidnapped?" Rob asked, disgusted but not surprised.

Bill grimaced and then turned back to Scarlett. "I'm sorry to hear about your friend. I'm sure she'll turn up."

Scarlett raised an eyebrow. "I hope so..."

"The guys over at Central know what they're doing," Rob added, trying to comfort her. "They'll find her."

"Thanks."

They were kind words designed to comfort and reassure, but honestly, it didn't look good. Gangs like the Masons didn't mess about, and he knew that if they believed that Ninette needed to die because of what she'd seen or because they thought it would advance their cause, then they wouldn't hesitate.

They also had few clues as to where she might be. Much of the Masons operation was cloaked in secrecy, hidden from the prying eyes of the police and the general public. They were good at what they did, and Rob knew it.

Scarlett wasn't stupid, either. She knew what major gangs like the Masons were like and how difficult it was to bring them down. She was under no illusions as to how these things worked and what the chances were of seeing Ninette alive again.

Despite this, she seemed to be clinging on for the time being, perhaps hoping that this case would be one of the few where they found the victim alive.

As Rob carried a coffee over to Scarlett, Bill stepped inside and took a seat by the door.

"So, what's next, fearless leader?" Bill asked. "Wally and Rebeka turned out to be dead ends. Interesting dead ends, but dead ends all the same."

"I know," Rob replied. "I think we're missing something, We need to go through these statements again and compare their stories because something doesn't add up here. I just wish I could put my finger on it."

"Well, that's some quality policing, that is," Bill mocked. "You have a feeling? Well, wonderful, bully for you. I'm sure *that* will solve the case."

"Do you *have* to be obnoxious *all* the time," Scarlett asked. "I guess it just comes naturally to you, does it? It's just who you are. Were you abused as a child? Is there some trauma there we need to know about?"

The door flew open and Nick walked in with Justine Palmer, Lee's girlfriend. Sporting red, bloodshot eyes and smudged mascara, she held a tissue to her nose and sniffed as she walked in. Both of them stopped when they saw the room was occupied.

"Oh, sorry, I didn't realise... Scarlett? What are..." Nick shook his head.

"Nick?" Rob asked. "You can come in. It's fine. What's going on?"

"Justine needs to talk to you," he said.

"They took Gavin," she blurted out with tears falling down her cheeks. "You need to find him. They took him, right out of my home. They just burst in. I couldn't stop them."

Rob rushed over. "Hey, calm down," he said and guided her to a chair. Her voice was shaky and full of emotion. "Start from the beginning. What's going on? Who has Gavin?"

"They do, the Mason family."

Bill grunted. Rob ignored him.

"How do you know *they* have him?"

"Because they burst into my home and took him!" She'd started to sound angry.

"That's okay, I understand that. What I mean is, how do you know the people who took him were from that gang?"

"Did they tell you their family name?" Nick asked.

"Oh, no," she said, dismissing their words with a wave of her hand. "No, they didn't need to." She sighed. She seemed to be wrestling with a huge subject and unsure where to begin. "It's complicated."

"We're not going anywhere," Rob reassured her.

"Fine," she said, exhaling. "Years ago, I got into some financial difficulties and ended up being targeted by a loan shark. I got in deep, owed them a load of money and ended up doing favours for them. I couldn't pay it off. No matter what I did, I just kept getting in deeper and deeper. Then they asked me to be Lee's new girlfriend."

"They what?" Scarlett asked. "You're kidding."

Justine shook her head. "I was told that if I did this, if I could get close to him, gather info and manipulate him into working with the firm, I'd finally pay off my debt. So I did it. I was single, I needed the money and I needed a way out. I was desperate."

Rob got a creepy feeling down his spine. The tactic was familiar to him. A few years back, he'd had a girlfriend who he felt sure was a Mason plant. He grew suspicious and dumped her, vowing to be more careful from that day forward. "So you seduced him?"

"I did," Justine answered. "I was to watch and talk to him. They needed to know what he was working on, but it wasn't as easy as that, and I found I kind of liked the lifestyle. I liked Lee. But my work wasn't good enough for the firm, so they took matters into their own hands and kidnapped Gavin."

"You knew?"

"I knew," Justine confirmed. "It killed me to see him hurt, but it worked and they bent Lee to their side. So then we both worked for the same people. Lee just didn't know about me."

"So he *was* corrupt," Bill exclaimed. "I knew it. I told you. I knew he was bent."

Rob frowned. He wasn't sure that Bill had insisted on this being true, but he didn't much care about that.

"So why are you coming to us now if you work for the firm?"

"Because I loved Lee, and I love Gavin. Over the past year, this whole thing changed for me. It became more than a job, it became my life, and I realised I really liked Lee and Gavin. They were always so nice to me. I just grew to love them. So when they took Gavin again, I had to say something. I can't lose Gavin too. Not after losing Lee."

"Even after the affair?" Scarlett asked.

"I don't care about the affair anymore. I just want Gavin back alive. Things had been going so well until this last week. We were in such a good place. We had a lovely day out on Saturday, just me, Lee and Gavin. We went to Sherwood Pines and did some cycling and stuff. It was lovely." She took a breath. "I'll never forget that day."

"Saturday?" Rob asked. "You were with Lee all day?"

"Yeah..."

Rob frowned. "And there was no one else with you. You didn't see anyone you knew or who Lee knew?"

"No, no one," Justine replied. "Why?"

The door to the room slammed open, and Guy appeared. "Guv, you need to come with me."

"What, now?"

"Yes, now."

Rob turned back to Justine, Nick and the others. "Wait here. I'll be back." He got up and followed Guy out of the room. "What's going on?"

"You've got an urgent call."

"A call? From who?"

"DS Pittman."

"Pittman?" Rob thought he recognised the name. "Philip Pittman? The undercover officer handler?"

"Cover officer. Yes, that's him. He says he needs to talk to you about something urgently. It can't wait." He led Rob back into the EMSOU office and pointed to Rob's desk. "You can take it there. I'll transfer it over. Oh, and by the way, SOCO found the bullet."

"The one that killed Lee?"

"That's the one," Guy confirmed with a smile.

"Brilliant, thanks." He was about to walk to his desk when a thought occurred to him. He turned back. "Guy, can you do me a favour?"

"Sure, Guv. What is it?"

"Can you get CCTV from Sherwood Pines for last Saturday? Not yesterday, the week before. Ideally, from all day, but mainly around lunchtime. Can you do that?"

"Yeah, sure. Not sure what they'll have up there, but I can ask."

"Please," Rob urged.

"You got a hunch or something?" Guy enquired.

"Yeah, something like that. Thank you." Rob approached his desk and snatched up the phone. Another thought occurred to him, and he realised he needed to make another call and check something. He'd do that after this.

Once Guy had transferred it, he took the waiting call.

"This is Rob Loxley…"

40

Walking up Castle Boulevard just outside of the prestigious Park estate, Michelle approached Karl's three-story, red brick townhouse with its recessed front door and tiny front yard behind a low metal fence. She'd been here plenty of times before, spending many fun nights with him, but today, things were different.

Today, she needed to talk to him and probably upset him. She'd lived a lie with him for long enough, and it was time to be a grown-up about this. It might not be fun or easy, but people ended relationships all the time.

There'd be no coming back here after today, of that she was sure. He'd throw her out. So she'd brought an empty sports bag to collect all her things while she waited for Karl to return home.

Pulling out her key, she unlocked the front door and stepped inside.

"Karl?" she called out. "Are you here?"

There was no answer, and the house was silent. She was alone.

Perfect. She set about her work, going from room to room, grabbing her things and stuffing them into the hold-all. There were clothes in the bedroom, shoes, toiletries and other nick-nacks. She rifled through drawers, plucking out her things as she remembered the fun times she'd had in here. But those were just memories now, and she had no interest in any more fun times with Karl.

Surely he'd noticed that they weren't being as intimate as they used to be?

In the next drawer down, she spotted an oily rag, and scowled at it. She'd never seen it before, and it certainly didn't belong in here. Curious, she plucked it out between finger and thumb to avoid getting too dirty, and something heavy dropped back into the drawer.

She gasped. It was a gun.

She didn't know he owned a gun. What the hell? She went to touch it but then thought better of it.

She didn't have time for this, but seeing that thing in the drawer, only strengthened her resolve that she needed to leave.

Downstairs she grabbed some books that were hers, her Kindle and some chargers before moving to the kitchen and choosing a few bits from the fridge and cupboards. She found more shoes downstairs too, and a couple of coats that she laid on top of the bag. It was heavy, but she'd manage.

And now came the hard part. She needed to wait.

After half an hour, she texted him, asking him if he was coming home. The day had drawn on, and the evening was closing in, so he shouldn't be too long.

After another ten minutes of waiting with no message, she decided she needed some Dutch courage and raided the fridge, pouring herself a large glass of white wine. Leaning on the island in the kitchen, she took a gulp to steady her nerves. After a few more sips, her shaking hands eased up, and she started to feel a little more confident about what she needed to do.

Forty minutes later, Michelle was well into her second glass when the front door opened and then slammed shut.

She grimaced. He never slammed the door. Something had upset him.

She heard movement in the hallway. "Shell?" he called out.

"I'm through here," she answered, taking another sip.

Here we go.

Moments later, Karl walked into the kitchen. He was already frowning, but his brow furrowed more when he saw the bag on the island. "What's going on? All your stuff's gone from by the door. What are you doing?"

"Yeah, sorry…"

"You've opened my wine. I was saving that. What the hell, Shell?"

Michelle pulled a face, pressing her lips into a thin line as she considered her words. He was upset, and it scared her. "We need to talk."

"Damn right, what's all this?" He pointed to the bag.

"It's my stuff."

"Your stuff? I don't understand."

She placed the glass back down on the counter a little too forcefully, and the bottom broke off the stem.

"Oh...fuck!" She'd spilt some of the wine too.

"What the hell are you doing," Karl snapped. "What's got into you?" He approached and went to help, grabbing a cloth from the side. He reached out to wipe her down, but she saw him coming and pushed him away.

"Give me that." She snatched the cloth and dabbed at her top.

"What the hell's wrong with you. I was only going to help."

"I don't need your help with this. I'm quite capable of dealing with some spilt wine."

"What is this, Michelle? What's going on?"

After wiping at her top, she threw the cloth into the nearby sink and thought about the call she'd taken earlier, and the question the detective had asked. It bothered her that he'd wanted to know what she'd been up to a week ago, and for some reason, she felt sure it had something to do with Karl.

"Why don't you tell me what you were doing last Saturday?" she asked.

"What?" His head snapped up, and for a long moment, he stared at her with cold eyes. She'd never seen him look at her like that before. But then it was gone, and he was back to looking confused. "Last Saturday? I don't know. Nothing? What's that got to do with anything? What were *you* doing? Working probably. You're always working these days."

She sighed. "Yeah, well. There's a reason for that."

"Oh, care to tell?"

"Is it not obvious, Karl?"

"Apparently not," he spat.

"We're done, Karl. This, us, it's over. I'm dumping you. I've gathered my things, so I'll be out of your hair from now on. No need for me to come back."

"What the hell? You're dumping me? You can't do that. What the fuck?"

"I can, and I am. We're over. Done."

"Why?"

She wanted to answer truthfully. She was so tempted, but she resisted. "Because I've had enough, Karl. I'm fed up."

"No."

"What?" What was he talking about? She could feel her adrenaline spike as he denied her.

"I said no. We're not done. You can't dump me. This is ridiculous. You're fed up? What does that even mean?"

How dare he deny her feelings! "It means I don't love you anymore. I don't want to be with you. I want to be..." She pulled back at the last second. In her fit of anger and spite, she'd nearly told him.

"Want to be what, Michelle? What do you want, huh? What?"

She bit her lip to keep from saying it, but her whole body wanted to say it.

"Tell me," he yelled.

She threw the glass into the sink, smashing it. "I'm seeing someone else."

"You're fucking what?"

"You heard me. You'd find out soon enough anyway, so why hide it? I don't love you anymore, Karl. I'm leaving, and I'm not coming back. You should be thankful that I stayed to tell you. I could have just left and blocked your number or something."

"You can't leave me..."

"I can, and I am. I'm glad, actually. Glad to be leaving. You've changed. You're not the same man I knew back when we got together."

"And you're a whiny bitch who clearly can't keep it in her knickers. Whore."

"Fuck off," she spat. "You think I'm a whore? That's rich coming from a limp dicked idiot like you who thinks it's big to keep a gun in his underwear drawer. You're a pathetic excuse for a man."

"What," he said, his tone low and serious. There was an edge to his voice suddenly.

"You heard me, you—"

"No. What are you talking about? What gun?"

She gave him an incredulous look. "What gun? The gun upstairs, you idiot."

He grabbed her by the throat and slammed her into the cupboards.

She gasped, shocked to her core. "You're hurting me."

"I know, that's the point." His whole demeanour had changed to the point she barely recognised him, and for the first time in his company, she was scared of him. "Now you tell me, what the fucking hell are you talking about? What gun?"

There was a loud bang on the front door.

41

Rob banged on the door with the base of his fist.

"Karl, this is the police. Open up." There was no reply, not that he expected to get one. Rob turned to a uniformed officer behind them. "Are you sure you saw him going in here?" The first on the scene, the officer had been told to wait at a distance for the team to arrive.

"One hundred percent," the man answered. "I know Karl. It was him. And that's his car."

Rob glanced where the man pointed and recognised the car. They were here in force with the entire road blocked off and a team of uniformed officers behind Nick, Bill and himself. With no sign of danger, Rob had chosen to take the lead, but their entry team was right behind them, ready to go.

With a frown, he turned back to the door and hammered on it again. "Karl, we will break this door down if we have to. Let us in."

Behind him, Nick spoke into the radio he held. "Scarlett, Guy, are you round the back yet?"

"We're in the back garden," Scarlett answered. "Hold for one morment... Right, we're here... Oh, shit..."

"What?" Nick said, concerned.

"He's in the kitchen with Michelle at the back of the house, and he's got a knife to her throat. He's not seen us yet."

"Bollocks," Rob muttered and backed away from the door. He turned to the officer with the Enforcer—the big red battering ram they used to knock doors down—and thumbed towards the door. "All yours."

"Sir," the man in tactical police gear said and went to work.

"Scarlett," Rob said, pulling the radio to him. "Be ready. If Nick signals you using the radio, bust in and be ready to take him down."

"Copy that," Scarlett answered.

Three solid hits later, the door flew open, and the officer with the ram let them through. Rob ran in and made his way to the kitchen towards the rear of the house. He found Karl standing behind Michelle, holding a huge carving knife to her neck.

"Back off," Karl shouted. "You can't do this. I've been set up."

"Karl," Rob said, his voice calm. "I need you to calm down."

"I'm calm," he barked as if he was talking to a child. "I'm protecting myself. I just need you to understand that this is a setup. I didn't do anything."

"You're doing something right now," Rob pressed. "Let her go. Then we can talk."

"No, you won't. You'll arrest me. This isn't my fault. I didn't do anything wrong."

"Karl, you have a knife to Michelle's neck. That's not a rational thing to do and doesn't look good."

"It's stopped you from just arresting me, hasn't it?"

"We know what you did, Karl."

"What do you know?"

"You killed Lee Garrett, didn't you."

"No. Absolutely not."

"Are you sure?"

"I was...busy. I told you," he stammered but hesitated, looking unsure.

"Busy?" Rob asked. "Doing what? I mean, I remember what you told me, but I think you should share it with the group?"

Karl jerked Michelle, pressing the knife closer to her neck. Rob recognised the warning for what it was. "I was here with Michelle. It was date night."

"Except, you weren't. Were you," Rob pressed. "Because Michelle wasn't here. You lied."

"He..." Michelle went to say, but Karl jerked her again in warning.

Michelle hissed.

"You're not doing this to me, Loxley," Karl said. "I've been set up. I'm innocent, and if you come one step closer, I swear to god, I'll do it. I'll cut her throat. Do you want that on your conscience too?"

"I do have a lot on my conscience," Rob replied. It was good to keep him talking.

"I know you do. I've heard the rumours about you. I know what they say. You're the corrupt one."

Rob glanced at Bill to his right and noticed him nodding. Rob ignored him. "I'm not the one with a knife to an innocent woman's neck, am I?"

"You forced this. I'm just reacting to what you're doing. This is your fault."

Rob shook his head, exasperated and annoyed. "I didn't make you pull the knife, Karl. You did that. You're just making this worse for yourself."

"But I'm innocent."

"Let's discuss it, shall we?" Rob asked, deciding to go through the evidence and present him with facts. "Let's see if you really are innocent because I'm not so sure."

"I am."

"I understand that you think that, Karl. But I disagree because you told me, very cleverly, I might add, that you spoke with Lee a week ago yesterday to throw me off the scent. You said you met him for lunch, and he admitted to being corrupt. However, we know that's not true. You didn't meet him for lunch because Lee was out with Justine and Gavin on a day trip. We have video evidence that shows them during lunch, and guess what? You're not on it."

"So what?" Karl snapped, sounding resentful. "I must have just got the date wrong."

"Alright, how about this? When we first met at the Custody Suite, you told me you were heading home for a date night with Michelle. Thing is, we found out that Michelle was with another man that night, so you weren't with her at all, were you?"

Karl merely scowled at Rob and didn't answer. Perhaps he knew the net was closing in, and there was nothing he could do.

"But that's not all because we have resources, Karl. There are people who like to tell us things, and a little birdy that I completely trust told me that there was an officer close to the Garrett investigation who's currently in the employ of a certain gang, The Masons. And given what we already know, I think it's becoming clear who that might be, don't you think?"

Rob thought back to the phone call he'd had with Philip, the undercover officer handler, who'd passed on the info that there was a corrupt officer close to the investigation.

It was the final nail in the coffin for Karl.

"You need to let me go," Karl snapped, pressing the knife into her skin. A runnel of blood seeped from beneath the blade. Michelle squeaked in terror.

"Let her go," Rob warned.

"I didn't do anything, and the only corrupt one in here is you."

"But we're talking about you, today. This is all about you. We can talk this out." Behind his back, Rob signalled to Nick. Three short clicks of the radio later, the rear door flew open with a hit from another ram.

Scarlett, Guy, and several uniformed officers ran in.

Karl turned in shock, his grip on Michelle loosening. Rob rushed forward and grabbed Karl's arm, pulling it away from Michelle's neck as others piled in. Within moments, Karl was on the floor being cuffed while yelling in protest. Nearby, Michelle was coughing and crying as officers helped her to her feet. Scarlett was amongst them. They moved her away from Karl as he struggled beneath five men.

"Come over here," Scarlett suggested to the shaking woman. "Let's get you cleaned up and that cut on your neck looked at."

Rob walked over. "Are you okay?"

"I am now," Michelle answered. "Thank you. It was like he was someone else entirely. I didn't recognise him."

"He kept it hidden." He'd heard of plenty of similar cases where one partner was a killer, and the other had no idea.

"That reminds me," Michelle added. "You might want to check the chest of drawers upstairs in his bedroom. While I was grabbing my things, I found a gun in the second drawer from the top. I didn't touch it."

"Good. And thank you. We'll check that out." He nodded to Nick, who went to find it.

"You just relax now," Scarlett said to Michelle. "It's over. You're fine."

As Rob watched, paramedics entered the kitchen and took over tending to Michelle, and walked her out.

Scarlett turned to Rob. "She'll be okay."

"I hope so," Rob said.

"It's not mine," Karl bellowed, referring to the gun. "It's been planted. I didn't shoot him."

"You didn't?" Rob asked. "Well, we'll soon know because we found the bullet that passed through Lee's head, and I'm betting that the striations on the round will be an exact match to this gun. What do you think?"

Karl grimaced but said nothing, turning his head away in annoyance.

"Thought so," Rob muttered to himself.

"How much do you know, Karl?" Scarlett said, stepping closer. "We know you're involved, so you might as well admit it. Did they kidnap anyone else? A woman named Ninette? A young man called Ambrose?"

"I don't know what you're talking about," he muttered, keeping his head turned away.

"Karl," she snapped. "This isn't a game. People might die."

"People have died, but I didn't do it."

"I don't believe you," Scarlett muttered as she turned away. "We'll get to the bottom of this, I can promise you that." She looked up at Rob as she walked away. "I'm done with him, for now."

"I know what you mean," Rob agreed with a nod. He turned to find Bill staring at Karl.

"You're pathetic," Bill muttered to him. "You'll get exactly what you deserve, you corrupt piece of filth."

"Oi," Rob barked. "That's enough."

Bill sneered. "That's rich, coming from you."

"There's no need to gloat. It's not appropriate. We got what we need and we'll talk to him later."

"And how would you know what's appropriate?" Bill took a step closer. "Don't think for one minute that this changes things, Rob. It changes nothing. Admittedly, you've done a good job hunting this idiot down, but you're still a corrupt piece of shit, and I will bring you down too if it's the last thing I do. I promise you that."

Nearby, Karl laughed.

Rob raised an eyebrow at Bill. "Are you okay? You just gave me a compliment. Have you got a temperature? Do you need to lie down?"

"Do piss off," Bill sneered.

"Well, thank you anyway. You've certainly made me feel all warm and snuggly inside."

With a roll of his eyes, Bill turned and walked out. Rob watched him go.

"What an idiot," Scarlett said, standing beside him. For a moment, she leaned on his shoulder, resting her head against his arm. "I'm tired."

"I'm not surprised. Why don't you go home?"

"No. Not yet. I need to find Ninette. I can't go home until I've found her."

He understood, but wasn't sure how healthy it was. He'd support her, though, and keep her involved.

"We're ready to get him out of here," Nick said, pointing to Karl.

"Excellent. Let's do it." Rob led the way out, with Scarlett beside him. Behind, Nick and Guy helped the uniformed officers lead Karl through the house. They stopped in the hall as they waited for one of the vans to be made ready.

As Rob walked through the house, his phone rang. He plucked it from his pocket and checked the caller ID.

"Ellen," he said in greeting once he'd answered it. "Where did you get to? You've missed the fun."

"I've been having my own fun. I'm outside. Come and find us." She hung up.

Rob raised an eyebrow but continued walking.

"What's up?" Scarlett asked.

"Not sure. I guess we'll find out."

Once outside, he spotted Ellen and Tucker off to their right, amongst the collection of emergency vehicles. Beside them, he saw paramedics tending to someone who was sitting in the back of their ambulance. It took Rob a moment to recognise the injured man. His face was swollen and covered in blood and he looked like he was in a lot of pain. As he walked closer, he realised that it was Gavin Garrett. He'd taken a severe beating.

"Hey Scarlett," Ellen said as they approached.

"Hiya," Tucker added.

"You okay?" Ellen asked.

She shrugged. "Bearing up."

Ellen nodded and pulled her in for a hug. "We'll find your friend."

"I hope so."

"Where did you two get to?" Rob asked.

"We got held up back at the station, so we were late," Ellen replied as she stepped away from Scarlett.

"Good fucking thing, really," Tucker said.

"How so?" Rob asked.

"There was a commotion around the corner, and we were flagged down," Ellen explained. "It was Gavin. He'd been dumped."

"Where?"

"Literally just around the bastard corner," Tucker answered, pointing.

"He looks like he's taken a beating." Rob eyed Gavin's swollen face and the multiple cuts and bruises.

"That's because I have," Gavin cut in. His voice was thin and weak, and he seemed to struggle to get the words out.

"We need to take him in," the paramedic said.

"You can for me," Rob said. "We'll be in to see him later."

"No, wait. I need to tell you—huh?" Gavin said as he watched them bring Karl out of the house. He pointed. "Shit! That's him. He was there."

Rob looked at Karl and then back to Gavin. "Who? The one in the cuffs?"

"Yes, it's him. He was there when they did this." Gavin pointed to his face. "He had a gun. They gave him a gun. He pointed it at me."

"You're sure it's him?"

"Positive. I recognise the tie, the suit, his eyes. It was him. I know it."

Rob spotted Nick walking out of the building with a clear evidence bag and waved him over.

"Got it," Nick said and held up the bag with the gun in it. "We'll get it tested and see what we can lift from it. Hopefully, we get some prints off the thing."

"Hopefully." Rob pointed to the gun and turned to Gavin. "Was this the gun?"

"Looks like it," Gavin answered. "I'm not sure, maybe."

"This is a set up," Karl raged as he was guided into a car. "I'm being set up."

"Hold on a second," Scarlett said, and stepped over to Gavin. "You said, he was there. Where is there? Where did this happen to you."

"That's what I'm trying to tell you." Gavin coughed up some blood. "I can take you to it, and I wasn't the only one there."

"There were others?" Scarlett asked.

Rob's stomach sank as he realised where this was going. He had a funny feeling that the gang had let Gavin go on purpose, and hadn't been shy about letting him know where he was being kept. They wanted the police to find the bodies.

"There were others," Gavin confirmed. "Two others, a man and a woman."

"Was she about my age, with dark hair?" Scarlett had her phone out and a second later, showed him the screen. "Is this her?"

Gavin gave her an unsure shrug. "I think so, maybe? I was in another room and couldn't see her very well. I don't know. After they hit me, they hurt her. I heard them, and then later, I heard two gunshots."

Scarlett sobbed and turned away. Rob grabbed her and pulled her in, wrapping his arms around her.

"I'm sorry, I didn't mean..."

"Not your fault," Rob replied. "The woman was her friend. You said there was a man, too? A young man?"

"Yeah. A black kid, maybe in his early twenties? He'd been hung from the ceiling by his wrists. He wasn't moving when I saw him."

Rob cursed under his breath. "And you know where this is?"

Gavin nodded. "I can show you."

42

"It's been a busy weekend," Sean commented as he plucked the decanter from the drinks trolley, removed the stopper, and sniffed. He smiled at the lush, smoky scent of the whisky. Perfect, he thought and poured out two large measures.

"It has," Isaac replied from the comfortable leather seat behind him.

Very few people knowingly turned their back on Isaac, not unless they were very sure of themselves.

Sean returned from the drinks trolley and approached his father. An old man, he seemed smaller these days, as if he was shrinking, but under no circumstances would Sean ever underestimate him. His keen eyes never missed anything, and his mind remained as sharp as ever.

His dad took the drink that Sean offered him. "Thank you, son. You've always looked after your old man."

"I'm not sure giving you a whiskey is really looking after you," Sean grumbled.

"I'm a little beyond that now." Isaac smiled before taking a drink. "Mmm, lovely. Just what the doctor ordered."

"Indeed."

"Are we all cleaned up?"

"We are," Sean replied. "All the loose ends have been tied off. The police found the bodies too. So, we're done. It's just a shame it wasn't as successful as we'd hoped."

His father grunted. "It was a long shot, son. But worth doing. Rob is standing firm, and I'd expected nothing less. He's his mother's son. I'm more surprised by his partner..."

"Scarlett," Sean supplied.

"Indeed. But it seems we have another true believer on our hands with her. Her loss, I suppose."

"And what about our loss," Sean asked. "We lost a good asset."

"We have others."

"I know."

"Then don't worry." His father took another sip.

"I'm not. We have more cards to play, yet."

"Indeed we do."

43

"Yeah," Rob said. "Gavin was as good as his word. He led us to the unit where he'd been kept and tortured. We found Ninette and Ambrose there too. They'd been shot."

"Damn. What about intelligence? Any leads?" Nailer asked from where he sat opposite Rob. "Was there *anything*?"

Rob shook his head and looked across Nailer's desk. "The whole place had been hosed down not long before we got there, so I doubt it. Those guys know what they're doing. But you never know. SOCO are going over it now."

"Okay, keep me updated. And how's Scarlett? She's been through a lot."

"Scarlett will be off for a couple of weeks," Rob answered. "She needs time to digest this. She's lost a friend, so…"

"No problem," Nailer confirmed. "She can take as much time as she needs. No one should have to go through that."

"No, they shouldn't." Rob agreed. "Where was Bill this afternoon? I thought he was meant to be…"

"I sent him back to the PSU. We got our man. We're done now. There's no need for him to hang around here any longer." Nailer raised an eyebrow. "I thought you'd be happy. Not getting a liking for him, are you?"

Rob scoffed. "Not likely. He was a pain in my arse. Well, I'm glad he's gone. I can do without him looking over my shoulder the entire time."

"I thought you'd be pleased. I'll keep passing over details to the PSU, but that's as far as we go from here on out. Speaking of which, anything new?"

"No," Rob answered. "But I'm willing to bet that when the ballistics come in on the bullets used to kill Ninette and Ambrose, they'll match the gun we found in Karl's house, implicating him further."

"Of course they will. They've framed him."

Rob agreed, "He's denying killing Ninette and Ambrose, but he has admitted to killing Lee Garrett. It took a while to get that confession, but all the evidence was pointing to him. He couldn't escape it. The evidence connecting him to Ambrose and Ninette, however, is more flimsy."

"They're throwing him under the bus," Nailer mused.

"And that worries me," Rob said. "Karl was a DI, my rank, and they were willing to lose him as an asset."

"I'm not sure they *wanted* to lose him, but he *had* messed up, and we *knew* he was corrupt. He was useless from that point on."

"True. But it still worries me," Rob answered as he pondered what his family was up to. Whatever it was, it wasn't good.

"Me too. I can only conclude that they have other, better assets in place within the police."

"That was my conclusion, too," Rob agreed. "If they're willing to burn a DI, then who else do they have on the payroll? They also knew about us turning Ambrose into an informant. I can't see any other reason why they'd kidnap and torture him."

Nailer nodded. "And that does not bode well. They know too much about our operations and inner workings."

"It's enough to make you paranoid," Rob commented.

"If you're not paranoid, then you're not paying attention."

Rob couldn't agree more. It seemed they were on the same page with this, and it spoke volumes about what the Masons were willing to do to reach their goals. And one of those goals was clearly him. They wanted Rob back in the fold, and they were willing to sacrifice other well-placed assets and contacts to get him. He'd been thinking it through all night, wondering what they might do next. The way they'd tried to get to him through Scarlett was horrific, and in some way—despite Scarlett's protestations—Rob felt responsible for what had happened. If he hadn't been on this team, Ninette would still be alive today, and Scarlett wouldn't be grieving the loss of her friend.

It made Rob think about his future in the police and his place on this team. Looking across at Nailer, he realised he'd not told him about his family's visit and felt suddenly guilty. He'd always been honest with Nailer, and he felt a sudden need to come clean.

"They came to see me the other night," Rob said.

"Who?"

"My dad and brothers paid me a visit. They were in my apartment when I got home and wanted me to be part of the family again. They want me, sir. They want me, and they're willing to kill to get me."

"I know."

"I don't know what they'll try next..."

"Rob, stop. I'm proud of you," Nailer said. "You and Scarlett. You stood firm against them and didn't give in. That takes guts. They used the same tactic on Lee, but he gave in, and look where that got him. Both of you made tough choices, but the right choices."

"Probably, but I don't like this escalation. They're clearly interested in me, and I have no idea what they'll try next. I don't want to be the cause of any more death, I don't want to have us under constant PSU scrutiny, and it's not going to go away. I think I have to step down. I should resign..."

"No. You don't want to do that."

"You're right, I don't," Rob agreed, "but I don't see any other way. They'll keep coming—"

"And we'll keep fighting them," Nailer cut in. "I don't want you to resign, and I doubt very much the others will either. Scarlett doesn't blame you for what happened, and neither does anyone else. You're our biggest asset against them, and if they value you, then maybe we can use that against them."

"I'm not sure…"

"No. I've heard enough of this self-pitying crap. Get a grip, Rob. We need you."

44

Sitting in one of the mismatched chairs at the kitchen table, Erika waited while her mother pulled mugs from a cupboard while the kettle boiled.

"Go on, then," her mum said. "What happened?"

"I was just coming home from my friends, and I saw Rob outside, walking back. I stopped the taxi and walked in with him, chatting. You know, making small talk, and as we walked in, I noticed these guys were hanging around outside. I didn't think much of it as we walked in, but it makes a lot of sense in light of what happened. Anyway, we get upstairs and notice that his door's open. I thought he'd been burgled, so we sneak in, hoping to catch them." Erika paused for dramatic effect. "But it wasn't robbers."

"Don't draw this out, Erika. What happened?"

"It was his family. His dad and brothers. They were all waiting for him in his apartment."

"Oh, crap."

"Mother!" She felt scandalised. Her mum never swore in front of her.

"What? I'm just shocked." Her mum continued to make the coffee, spooning granules into the mug. "So, what happened next?"

"They kicked me out. I thought Owen was going to hurt me at one point, but his dad stopped him."

"Isaac was always pragmatic," she mused. "Sorry, go on."

"Yeah, so they kicked me out and slammed the door in my face. But when I turned around, I saw Bill Rainault coming up the stairs."

"Bill?" Her mum sounded even more surprised if that were possible.

"I know, that's what I thought. But something just came over me at that moment. I knew I had to get him out of the way before they came out, so I gave the performance of my life. You'd be proud of me, Mum."

"It sounds like it. What did you do?"

"I started by asking who he was. I mean, I knew, but he didn't know that. So I got him to show me his ID. The moment he confirmed he was a police officer, I turned the waterworks on and played the helpless-female card. I made up some cock-and-bull-story about some ex-boyfriend who was stalking me and how Rob had helped me. I basically demanded that he follow me into my apartment, my 'safe space', to take a report about what had happened." She shrugged and smiled. "He fell for it. We got into my apartment, and he sat down while I hovered near my door, listening for Rob's family. I couldn't let him go before they'd left."

"And you managed to keep him there for the duration?"

"It wasn't long, but yeah, I did. So once I knew they'd gone, I went to make sure, checked on Rob, and then basically kicked Bill out. I don't think he was too pleased with me for that."

"Wow, I'm impressed. Well done."

"I was worried for a moment there. I'd not expected to see Isaac and Rob's brothers."

"I can imagine. Rather you than me, though."

"Mmm."

The front door sounded from the hallway.

"Hello?" called out a male voice.

"In here, love," Erika's mum said.

"Hi Dad," Erika added, pleased to hear him. Seconds later, Erika's dad, John Nailer, walked into the kitchen.

"Hey, cupcake," he said to Erika. "How's things?"

"Yeah, good thanks," she answered. "You? Busy day?"

"They're always busy, you know that," he said.

"Yeah, I do."

"John," her mum said as her dad walked over and planted a kiss on her mum's lips. "Erika was just telling me how she'd been with Rob when Isaac, Sean, Oliver and Owen Mason turned up at his apartment and how she'd saved Rob from being seen with them by Bill."

"Bill was there?" Nailer asked, shocked. "Rob told me about his dad and brothers' visit, but I didn't know Bill had followed him home, too. Damn."

"I know, and your daughter saved him. You should be proud."

"I am. Well done."

"Thank you," Erika answered with a smug smile.

45

Rob stared into the half-drunk pint sitting on the bar before him. He ruminated on the weekend he'd just experienced and what it might mean for his future.

He'd not been surprised that Nailer had refused to accept his resignation. And, in truth, he'd been glad he hadn't. He didn't want to resign from the EMSOU or the force as a whole. He loved his job and desperately wanted to keep doing it. It was his whole life, so if that was taken away, he wasn't sure what he'd do, honestly.

But this weekend had reminded him just what kind of family he'd come from and what they were capable of to get their way. He'd been away from them for so long now he'd kind of forgotten.

He was under no illusions now, though. They were sick and depraved but also utterly ruthless and very dangerous. Seeing Scarlett so upset over her friend had broken him. He couldn't believe what they'd done to get to him through Scarlett. They didn't care one iota for anybody's life other than their own and were more than happy to destroy the lives of countless others to get what they wanted.

Nailer, Scarlett and Nick had all reassured him that he was not responsible for what had happened and insisted that he must not leave now. They needed him now more than ever, or so they said. He wasn't sure that was true and believed they'd get on just fine without him, but the selfish part of him didn't want to leave. He wanted to stay and make his job mean something again. He'd joined the police because he believed he could make a difference and help protect those who could not protect themselves. And if anything, the events of this case only served to reinforce that a thousand times over. He needed to make a difference. In his head, he needed to offset the lives that had been lost.

But that would take time, and he'd need to be patient.

Rob took another sip of his drink, thinking about the wider implications of all this and what it would mean for him going forward. But that was why he was here, wasn't it? That was the reason for tonight.

"Rob, hi."

She was here.

Rob turned to see Matilda standing close by, smiling at him with her head tilted to one side.

"Hi," he replied, smiling as he turned. She was gorgeous, as ever, and it was painfully clear that she'd dressed up to come and meet him, complete with carefully done make-up, an attractive little black dress and strappy heels. He was impressed, but her effort only highlighted how little he'd put in.

He still wore his work clothes, which were as crumpled, stained and creased as ever. A brief look of disappointment passed over her face, but it was gone as quickly as it had appeared.

"Um, sorry, I didn't realise you were…" He waved at her outfit.

"That's okay." She smiled sweetly. "I'll just expect you to look incredible next time."

Rob smiled and stifled a laugh. "Yeah…"

"I heard what happened to Scarlett's friend, and the kid, Ambrose. I'm sorry."

Rob shook his head. "That's okay. Don't worry about it."

"Okay, sure. Shall we get some drinks in?"

Rob grimaced at her assumption that this was a repeat of Saturday night. "Look, before you do that, I think we should talk. I have something I want to say."

"Oh, dear. That bad, is it?" Matilda slipped up onto the stool beside him and got comfortable. "Go on, then. Let's hear it."

Rob sighed. He'd not been looking forward to this, but now the moment had arrived, and he'd need to actually talk to her, his mind went blank.

"Okay, so… I think… Oh, bollocks. I've got no idea how to say this."

"Just say it," she said. "I've got my big girl pants on. I can handle it."

Rob gave her a look. "Okay, fine. This is how it is. I like you. I'm interested in you, and I believe you like me, right?" He felt like he was dying inside, talking so candidly. It sounded almost childish.

"Well, providing we forget about your current outfit, yeah, you're right about that."

"Okay, good." Rob breathed a sigh of relief. "Well, I say good, but maybe it's not so good. I like you, but I don't think I can get involved with you. I'm thrilled and flattered, but now really isn't a good time."

Her face fell, making Rob feel terrible. "Is it work?" she asked. "Because, I've thought about that. We'll just have to agree not to talk about it, and we'll need to make sure we're never on opposite sides of the table."

"Well, there is that too, but no, it's not that. It's my family. Things are complicated with them, and I can't bring you into that. I just... I can't."

He wanted to say more, and explain *why* things were complicated and in all honesty, dangerous, but her just knowing about it could be risky.

"You've never told me about your family," she said.

"I know."

"I've never pried, but you never volunteered anything, either."

"There's a reason for that, but you don't need to know. In fact, it's better if you don't."

"Really?"

"Yeah. I'm sorry. I'm really sorry. I hope this hasn't been a wasted journey."

She pulled a face and looked down into her lap for a moment. Rob watched, wondering what she was thinking about. He waited, expecting her to say goodnight, leaving him to drown his sorrows before going home to his cat.

He seemed destined to live a life of loneliness and isolation brought on by his sick and twisted family. If they were willing to kill Scarlett's friend just to try and get to him, then he dreaded to think what they would do to someone like Matilda if they found out he was in a relationship with her. He didn't want to put her through that. He also didn't want to make her choose between dating him or not because of his family.

It wasn't fair, and as much as he liked her, he did not want to be responsible for something happening to her.

He watched her fidget in thought, her freshly painted nails glinting in the warm light. She was a good-looking woman, and part of him wanted to take it all back and throw caution to the wind. But he knew it was wrong. He couldn't do that.

Moments later, she looked up and smiled, sucking in a deep breath. "I don't know what's going on with you and your family, but it must be serious, and I believe and appreciate you're just trying to protect me. I get that. I can make my own choices, though, and I'm going to make one now. Want to know what it is?"

Rob shrugged. "Sure."

"You asked if this was a wasted journey." Matilda smiled. "No chance. I like a challenge, and this just makes you hard to get."

Rob raised an eyebrow.

"How about that drink?"

THE END

OF ALL FLESH

Detective Loxley Book 4

www.amazon.co.uk/dp/B0BYK1BTCN/

COMING SOON.

Author Note

Thank you so much for reading this third book in the Detective Loxley series. I've had a lot of fun writing this and I really hope you enjoyed it too.

This was a big one for Rob, Scarlett and the others, with some major consequences that came out of it. But we're only just getting started, and there's so much more to come.

Certainly, Scarlett will have a lot to deal with, and I have ideas and plans for her.

Clumber Park, the location of Lee Garrett's murder, is a place I've visited many times over the years, spending lots of time wandering through its grounds. Its iconic Lime Tree Avenue is beautiful at any time of year, but especially during the summer and autumn months when it's green and then yellow and orange.

I would highly recommend a visit, if you've never been.

Thank you

- Andrew

Come and join in the discussion about my books in my Facebook Group:

www.facebook.com/groups/alfraine.readers

Book List

www.alfraineauthor.co.uk/books

Printed in Great Britain
by Amazon